CHASED BY Memories

CHASED BY

Memories

CLAUDIA SHELTON

ALSO BY CLAUDIA SHELTON

ROMANTIC SUSPENSE

The Agent's Legacy Series

Risk of a Lifetime

Chased by Memories

Search for Answers

Shades of Leverage Series

Slater's Revenge

Dangerous Lies

CONTEMPORARY ROMANCE

Nature's Crossing Series

A Week at Most

Time to Grow

PCS Hometown: Awesome

Cocoa for Two

*To my morning author cohorts
—Lisa Wells, Barbara Bettis, Linda Gilman—
Here's to continued motivation and laughter.*

CHAPTER ONE

This had been a really long day. In fact, this had been a really long week. Month. Year...*years*. A lot of people Betsy Peyton had loved were no longer walking the earth, and she was having one of those missing-them periods in her life. Of course, it could have been worse. At least she still had plenty of family and friends to fill her off hours.

Peyton's Automotives, her branded dealership, filled her days with single-car clients and company fleet contracts. The service center handled cars, trucks, SUVs, vans and the occasional emergency RV repair. Motorcycles she referred to the bike shop a couple blocks over.

Sighing, she set the burglar alarm for the night and stepped out the back door of the main dealership structure housing the offices and automotive display area. It was Friday night, and she was headed to Joanie's Pizza, Pub and Pool, one of the places in town she could count on for friendship, laughter and good food.

Sliding into her SUV, parked in her spot next to the door, a couple of trucks parked behind the detached multiuse service center shop, at the far end of the lot, caught her eye as Papa Carrington walked into the service center. Her work ethic wouldn't allow her to leave before her workers were able to go home, especially heading into a weekend. She might be the boss, but others always came first in her way of thinking.

She started the car and coasted down to the service center. Not recognizing the customer's truck or SUV, she shifted into park, then headed inside. She heard indistinct voices from the other side of the closed door, but the moment she opened the back door the instantaneous silence was deafening.

"Hello. Anyone here?" Silly question seeing that she'd just seen at least one person enter less than two minutes ago.

"Betsy. Betsy, is that you?" Papa C stepped out from behind one of the floor posts. "Thought I saw you heading out of the office for the day when I turned into the lot."

"You're right, it's that time. I saw some customer cars sitting down here. Just checking to see if I could help with anything."

Off to the left, a grunt-groan caught her attention. Slowly, Earl Millerton, the service manager, pushed himself up from behind a car, holding his palm to his forehead. A trickle of blood oozed from the side of his mouth.

"Oh my gosh, Earl! What happened to you?" She stepped in his direction, but Papa C waved her off.

"Nothing to worry about, Betsy. He just got startled when I slammed one of the cabinet doors. First, he dropped a power tool. Then he tripped over it. I'm always telling him that you gotta be careful when you're around equipment." Papa C steered her toward the door. "Don't you move, Millerton. As soon as I get Betsy on her way, I'll find the first aid kit and get you all fixed up."

She'd never understood why Papa C insisted on calling employees by their last names. Guess he thought it sounded more professional. More likely, he felt it gave him an edge of control over them. As for her, she wanted her workers to understand she considered them friends. They already knew their jobs, otherwise she'd have spoken to them. Worst case let them go. Either way she'd still call them by their first name.

Movement and a man's mumbled voice caught her attention from the front of the building.

"Customer? I figured the service department was closed for the day." She glanced to the corner where all she could see was the back of a mid-length bomber-style camouflage jacket and red cap on a tall muscular man. He appeared to be talking on his phone.

Papa C cleared his throat. "An emergency repair drove in at the last minute. Some guy heading out to hunt had an oil leak. That's why Millerton called me. I told him I'd come over and help."

"You sure? I don't want you to get all tied up working late tonight."

"We'll be fine. Ain't that right, Millerton?" He raised his voice as he called across the room.

The service manager glanced at the man near the front, then over to her. "Sure thing. You head on out, Betsy. We'll be done and gone in no time flat."

"Hey, can you get a move on back there? I've been waiting a long time for my repairs," the man from the front hollered. "Got places I need to be. Things I need to check on. Or did you forget that part?"

Halfway out the door, she turned to confront the unappreciative customer, but one quick moment of eye-to-eye contact told her the man wasn't one to squabble with. In fact, he sneered right into a threatening laugh as he shoved the red hat in his pocket then unzipped the jacket. She didn't turn away, but a flash of cold raced up her spine as the clean-shaven man raised his sweatshirt's hood and tugged it forward on both sides. He didn't turn away either but did take a couple steps toward Earl.

"Be right there," Papa C answered in return.

"You sure you and Earl will be okay with this guy?" she quietly asked.

He nodded, slowly pulling the door closed between her and him. "Don't worry. We're fine."

"You seen him around before?" Something about the customer seemed vaguely familiar to Betsy.

"Met him a few times. He's just got a chip on his shoulder. Now get on out of here and enjoy your evening."

"Okay, I'm just concerned. Text me once the customer leaves."

Papa C nodded and finished pulling the door closed. She heard the click of the security lock being set from inside.

As she got in the car, she realized just how lucky she was to have Papa C's continued interest in the dealership. Of course, without him she'd have never owned Peyton's in the first place. She used to refer to him as her father-in-law, or Phillip's father. Nowadays she simply called him the previous owner out of respect for all he'd done, and still did, for her and the business.

Her own dad would probably have enjoyed helping around the dealership if he hadn't been killed on the steps of the FBI building in Jefferson City. She'd only been ten, almost eleven years old. He'd been a special agent with the FBI, a man who loved the danger of following clues and solving cases. He also loved to tinker with cars. She must have inherited his penchant for automotives.

The lot's halogen lights kicked up another notch, and she spied one of her perpetual lookie-loo customers strolling through the car lot. Any time she'd talked to him, he always seemed to have an appreciation for cars and trucks running through him, too. She gave a small wave. The man nodded in return as she pulled out of the dealership.

Five minutes later, she turned into Joanie's Pizza, Pub and Pool parking lot. Evidently, she'd beat the Friday night rush and luckily found a spot under a parking light on the second row. Time for food, friends and hopefully a game of pool.

Doubtful any of her family would be there tonight. Her sister Marcy had texted a couple hours ago that she didn't feel like their usual Friday get-together. And her mama, Sadie, and stepdad, Truman Dawson, were spending the weekend in Kansas City. They'd decided to celebrate their anniversary at one of those swanky downtown hotels. How many years had they been married? Enough to make them both happy, and that's all that mattered.

Stepping into Joanie's was like someone had suddenly

lifted all the problems weighing on her shoulders. She felt the smile on her face increase with each person that shouted hello as she made her way to the small counter near the kitchen.

She snapped her fingers and made a detour to the chalkboard by the pool tables area, then printed her name at the bottom of the list of names already ahead of her. Worked for her. Gave her time to sit and chat with her best friend, Joanie Reynolds, as she came and went from the kitchen to the small counter.

"You're just in time to taste my new recipe," Joanie said as she slid a plate of fried ravioli appetizers in front of her. As the owner, her jobs ranged from paying the bills to coming up with new ideas for Friday night specials.

Betsy slipped onto one of the stools at the small counter. "So what's new about this? I've had your fried ravioli lots of times."

Her friend leaned forward and whispered as if this was a world-changing secret. "The ravioli are chicken instead of pork and beef. And you'll notice there are two sauces. The regular marinara one and…"—she set a second small bowl next to the first—"… a special sauteed minced garlic with Italian seasoning in a delightful pool of melted butter."

"Looks good to me." Betsy took a chance on the chicken ravioli and smiled. Not all of Joanie's concoctions turned out well, but this one had potential. "Hey, I need a light beer, wedge salad and a plate of fries to go with this."

For the next hour, Joanie and she carried on a running conversation, in between customers and sharing the fries. Friday nights were always busy. Not much time for chitchat, but that didn't matter. Joanie's was making money, and Betsy was enjoying the noise of the customers. Sure beat sitting at home in front of a television. And once Papa C had texted that Earl and he had locked up and left Peyton's, she felt a lot better.

Cheers from guys shooting a game at one of the pool tables greeted whoever had just walked in the front door. Betsy turned to say hello and made unintentional eye contact with the new arrival—*Cain*. Cain Connery. His blue-eyed nonchalance belied the intensity of his six feet of muscle and masculinity.

Breaking their visual connection, he glanced at the pool table chalkboard. "Could one of you guys put my name on the bottom of that list? I'll be right over after I order a pizza."

"Sure thing," one of the guys said.

"Appreciate it."

Seemingly always at ease in himself, he headed toward the small counter. Stopped to chat with people along the way, shook hands and laughed. Took extra time with some of the townsfolk, moved quick past others.

Knowing her body's heated, heart-thumping reaction every time Cain got within speaking distance, she evaluated her options for avoidance. The sound of his voice, a cross between Sam Elliott and a finely crafted, ultra-smooth bourbon, depending on her mood, became more distinct as he neared the counter.

Quickly, she swallowed the French fry taking up space in her mouth and motioned to Joanie. "Hey, I've decided to head on home. Can I get a box for the rest of this?"

Joanie glanced at her, then Cain, then the counter. "Nope."

"What do you mean nope?" Betsy leaned forward and rounded her eyes, then quickly gave a side-eye between Cain and Joanie. "I'm tired and I'd like to head home."

Her friend smiled, arching her right eyebrow in a "gotcha" moment. "It's about time one of us moves on with their life."

"That goes for you, too," Betsy whispered.

Joanie stared for a long moment at the tri-folded United States flag in the case above the entrance. Batting her eyes, she grabbed the bar towel and started cleaning the counter. "I'm not ready. That means it's your turn tonight."

Cain slid up on the stool at the end of the short counter. "You two look deep in conversation."

"Just talking about life and weather and long past Friday nights," Joanie said. "What can I get you?"

"One of your special Friday night pizzas and a beer. How about you, Betsy? You need another beer?"

"No. I'm...I'm just fine. I...uh, that is..." She shook her head and placed her hand on top of her drink.

And there it was—the quirk of his smile, his questioning glance, the furrow of his brow at her answer, and that smooth-as-metal voice. Add in the scent of his leather jacket and she was done for. She'd felt the blush on her neck as she stumbled over her words. But her emotions would never get the best of her. Any unfulfilled feeling she'd had for Cain in high school had long since been doused with years of life and distance.

Across the room, a groan split the air a second before cheers and hurrahs erupted. Evidently, someone had unexpectedly won. Or lost.

"That's a wrap, guys," one of the players shouted. "Hey, Betsy, your name is next on the chalkboard."

Thank goodness she had a reason to leave the counter. "Okay, who's up for a game?"

No one answered. And the one person who started to stand was pulled back down. What was going on?

She snagged her favorite cue stick from the rack. "Okay then. Is this a joke or something? No one wants to shoot a game of pool with me?"

The guy who had called out her name, glanced at the chalkboard. "Hey, there's only you and Cain's names left on the board. Why don't you two play a game?"

People around the room quieted as if her answer was worth a million dollars.

Cain turned around on his stool. "That's okay. I don't think Betsy has ever shot a game of pool against me. Guess she's afraid I'll beat her."

That did it! Betsy straightened. He'd just stepped over her line.

She picked up the blue chalk from the siderail. Tossed it in the air a couple of times. Took a few steps in his direction. And stared into his eyes. "So, you don't remember the day I wiped you off the table in high school?" She cocked her hip out to the side and tapped her pool cue twice against the floor. "Right over there, at table number four."

"Nope. Can't say that I do." He bit the side of his lower lip and crunched his brow as if deep in thought. Snapped his fingers. "Ooooooh, you mean that day after school when you lucked out and beat me? The day you were wearing those denim blue earrings with tiny gold stars holding them on your ears."

Some of the other customers nodded in agreement. She turned to the crowd and opened her arms in an exaggerated bow. Good to know she wasn't the only one from their high school group that still remembered the fun days of being young and crazy.

She turned back to him and smiled. He'd noticed. Noticed her earrings back then. "You remembered."

"I remember a lot of things from back then." Quick and easy, he shucked out of his jacket, tossed it over the closest chair and grabbed a cue stick from the rack. "We gonna play or not, Betsy?"

CHAPTER TWO

Cain figured a man never knew when his life might hinge on expertise in hand-to-hand combat, weapon usage, or evasive driving. And even though he'd been on leave of absence from the Drug Enforcement Agency for well over six weeks, that didn't mean his skill set would ever change. Even something simple like running a pool table might be enough distraction to throw the opposition off their game.

Or not.

"Well, will you look at that? I've only got one solid left to drop before the eight." Betsy Peyton spun the end of her pool cue on the floor. "Looks like a tricky angle though. Maybe you'll get a chance after all."

"Yeah, I doubt you'll be able to make that shot." Cain cocked his head, pretending to evaluate the placement, then raised his eyebrows as he shrugged. "Of course, *I* could. Easy as anything. I'd just glide..."

With exaggerated emphasis, she tapped the cue on the floor, flashed him one of her sassy squinty-eyed looks, and bent into her stance. Now that was distracting. Hellfire distracting.

He might lose, but nothing compared to watching the way her jeans moved across her bottom and tightened. Or the way her knee-high boots, on three-inch heels, made her legs look like they'd go on forever. Yet, the thing he liked most was the way her long red hair gathered around her face as she leaned in for each shot.

They'd been friends from fifth grade all the way through high school. Of course, something had changed midway through his senior year when their laugh-filled friendship had become awkward. Looking back, he figured that's when he turned into a jock just trying to hold on to his peer status for another day. Whereas Betsy had buckled down even harder on her studies and got accepted to three colleges.

After graduation, he'd left town and never looked back. But she'd always been his best friend in his memories. He'd only been back in Crayton, Missouri, for a couple of months, but every Friday night he'd invite her to a game of pool or dinner. Every Friday night, she turned him down. Except tonight.

She'd won the lag. Dropped a ball on the break. Methodically sunk every one of her solids since. Now, all that stood between her and a win was the black ball.

"Where do you plan to drop that eight?" He knew where, but he wanted to make her call the shot. He knew Betsy's skill at billiards. She was a pool ace. Fifteen years ago in high school, she'd crushed him, and just about everyone else, at eight ball. Since then, though, he'd learned a thing or two about pool. And women.

"Eight ball..." She pointed to the pocket closest to herself. Aimed the cue across her fingers. Pulled the stick back, then firmly tapped it forward.

Standing up after she made the shot, she moved her finger in line with the roll of ball. Across the table. Off the rail. Back across, till it finally dropped into the pocket next to her. She smiled for a speck of a second, then glanced in his direction.

"You didn't even watch." For a moment, her bottom lip almost pouted, but that wasn't something Betsy would ever allow. "That was a darn good shot, and you didn't even—"

"Didn't need to." He hadn't planned on not getting even one shot.

"And that...is how...you run...the table." Betsy's hazel green eyes, along with the tiny upturn at the corner of her lips, spoke volumes.

"I've got to say, you played one heck of a game. How about you give me a chance this time?" He laid the triangle on the felt and reached for the balls to rerack.

She pulled back her shoulders as all signs of fun left her expression. "Uh...maybe another time."

"When?"

"When what?"

Edging slightly into her space, he leaned against the table. "You said another time. How's tomorrow night?"

"No, I'm busy."

Maybe all she needed was a little time. A little space. He could give her that. There were times that's all he needed, too. Most people didn't realize that was just part of life.

"Forget I asked. I don't need to get hit over the head to know you don't want me around," Cain said.

"It's not you. It's just..." Betsy stared off into space for a moment before she looked back at him with an inkling of a smile on her lips. "You're right. You deserve a rematch."

At this point, he figured that was as good as a yes. "How about next Friday night then?"

She nodded. "I'll be here."

"What say we make a little bet on that?" Cain felt the corner of his mouth quirk. "If I win, you have dinner with me next Saturday night."

The pinch of lines across her forehead revealed just how much she was thinking about the offer. "What if I win?"

He'd lived his life based on risking everything if the result was worth a loss. Maybe that's what he needed to do in this situation. Put the risk out there. See what happened. "If you win, I'll never ask you out again, Betsy."

She walked over and held out her hand. "You got a bet, Cain Connery."

He shook, trying to figure out why a night out with Betsy seemed so important to him. He'd never lacked for female company. During the two months since he'd been back in Crayton, he'd had three women hit on him. One wanted to buy him a drink. One wanted to give him a home-cooked meal. And one was just on vacation, looking for fun. He'd turned all three down.

"Hi, Ms. Peyton. You did good." Steven Millerton, the local high school football star, walked up, holding his girlfriend Lisa's hand. Another couple followed them. "Too bad, Mr. Connery. Maybe next time."

Cain couldn't help but like the kid. He'd heard nothing but good things about him and his family. Around Crayton, Missouri, the Millertons were known to be a hardworking, do-anything-for-you kind of people. "I heard you got a full-ride scholarship to college. That's great."

Steven looked at the floor as if he were embarrassed. "Yeah. University of Missouri was my top pick, and I got it. I'll be playing football with the Mizzou Tigers next fall."

"Your dad's mighty proud of you." Betsy patted him on the back.

"Really?" The boy looked up. "He said that?"

"That's all he's talked about the last few days around the service center. He even asked if he'd be able to leave work early some days next fall." She leaned her pool cue in the wall rack. "Wants to make sure he'll have time to get to your games up in Columbia."

Cain saw from the expression on Steven's face that he hadn't heard the words of pride from his father. Too bad. Sometimes that's all that mattered to a kid. At least Steven had heard his dad's words through Betsy. All Cain had heard from his own dad had been something to the effect of don't let the chains of life hold you back from having fun.

"Alright then." Steven grinned and nodded to himself. "Hey, if you all are finished playing, can me and my friends grab the table?"

"Sure. We're headed for a bite to eat." Spying an empty booth, Cain took a few steps in that direction, then turned to let Betsy walk past. Instead, she hadn't moved. "It's just a beer and pizza, Betsy."

When he'd left Crayton years ago, Betsy hadn't been

skittish. Shy maybe, but never afraid of anything, in fact, just the opposite. She'd also been one fiery redheaded hellcat when anyone dared to make a joke at the expense of her sisters or Sadie, her mama. Of course, Sadie never needed anyone to stand up for her. She was also a redhead.

He eased his stance along with his expectation. "Or would you rather sit at the counter?"

She turned in that direction. "I might have time for a soda, but that's all. I have to be up early to open the dealership."

Maybe they could catch up on everything that had happened since high school graduation. He'd joined the Army right after. And left town on the first bus headed for Fort Leonard Wood and basic training.

From off to the side, he saw Steven's girlfriend, Lisa, leave by the front door carrying a take-out bag of food. Then Steven glanced their way. "Hey, Ms. Peyton. Can you do us a favor?"

Betsy walked back to the pool table. "If I can."

"Lisa had to run some sandwiches down to her dad at his office. We'll have to give up the table if we don't keep playing." The young man never made eye contact with Cain, only Betsy. "Could you be my partner till she gets back?"

"Sure. Sounds like fun." Betsy smiled as she grabbed the cue she'd used previously, then glanced at Cain. "Go ahead and eat without me. I'm not really all that hungry."

If Cain didn't know better, he'd think she had paid the kid to get her out of having to spend time alone with him. He walked toward the counter. Grinning, he paused just a moment by Steven. "It's a good thing I like you, kid."

Steven shrugged and played the what-did-I-do look. "Sorry, Mr. Connery. I needed a partner."

Cain opened his mouth to make a smart comeback, but the man coming in the front door caught his attention. Tall, muscular, a slight off-set of his shoulders, the slow, measured swagger of his gait all seemed familiar. A Stetson shielded the man's face as he walked, head down, toward the counter.

As the man passed, Cain eased his hand to the holster of his hideaway gun, then cleared his throat. The man tilted his head just enough to make quick eye contact, then looked back down and continued to the counter.

Shadow. Why the hell was Shadow in Crayton, Missouri? On assignment? Dark ops? Coincidence? Agents never acknowledged each other on a chance meeting until they knew the lay of the land for the other one.

It was almost as if the DEA would be part of his life till the day he died.

CHAPTER THREE

Thankful for the diversion, Betsy figured a game of pool with Steven and his friends would give her time to decide whether she wanted to share a pizza with Cain or not. Would give her time to come up with a good excuse to go home. The need-to-be-at-work-early ploy would only last so long.

Betsy glanced in Cain's direction as he stood at the counter, one leg resting on the footrail. He pushed the sleeves upward on his formfitting black thermal shirt, then leaned forward and braced his forearms on the polished oak top. His jeans were tight around his thighs and backside. She swallowed the flutter in her throat and sighed. Last week she'd seen him working out at Main Street Gym. She had no doubt as to the muscles beneath the clothes tonight.

From behind her she heard someone groan, probably over a missed pool shot. Steven walked up beside her. "Ms. Peyton, are you gonna play or keep staring at Mr. Connery?"

"Shhhhh…" She grimaced as the sound came out of her mouth.

Cain turned to look at her. The tilt of his head along with his raised eyebrows said he'd heard everything. In fact, he might have already known he had her attention.

Her mind scrambled to find a believable response to his "gotcha" moment. "I'll have you know I was watching the game on the television mounted in the corner." There…that sounded believable, didn't it?

Cain glanced up at the monitor, then back at her as he grinned. "You mean that detective show with the cops and robbers running around?"

A slow-moving heat spread across her shoulders and headed south. "Someone must have changed the channel. Or…or maybe it was just a commercial about a game and I assumed that—"

"No disrespect, Ms. Peyton, but you should hush." Steven leaned in her direction. "You're just making it worse."

Music from the jukebox blared forth with a country-rock number revved enough to break the embarrassing tension. She'd lost her composure tonight, but she still didn't intend on letting Cain into her life.

Falling head over heels in love with Phillip Peyton, her almost-ex-husband, now deceased, had been a big enough blunder for one lifetime. Love had blurred the fact of his drug use prior to their marriage. Living with him had blaringly laid everything bare.

Once she'd had an inkling of his drug use, she followed him one night. Saw him meet a guy at the auto dealership. Watched the buy happen. Made it back home, back to bed, before Phillip got back home. She'd stay single forever before she'd chance being in that type of situation again.

Cain raised a finger and pointed at the pool table. "I think it's your play, Betsy. Be careful you don't miss your turn."

Careful? She was always careful when she played a game. Or did business. Or thought about having fun. Or men. Especially a man like Cain Connery. He was temptation in a pair of jeans, never mind his pull-you-in-and-lay-you-down blue eyes.

She'd played that game before. She'd lost. Lost in more ways than one.

WHEN HAD SITTING down to a meal with a pretty lady become so difficult? Cain bit into another slice of the large Friday night special sausage, pepperoni and double cheese pizza he'd ordered. Before long, he'd eaten nearly the entire pizza by himself.

Joanie walked back out and set a large pizza box next to Cain. "Marcy Bradley called and said her husband JB is stopping by to grab dinner for them. She paid over the phone. Can you make sure he gets the right order?"

"Sure thing. Maybe he'll at least have time to talk." Cain glanced across the room in Betsy's direction. For a second, he could have sworn she let her eyes skim his way, then she turned to talk to the people at the next table. "Nobody else seems interested in my company tonight."

"You hang in there." Joanie laughed. "Sooner or later,

she might give you the time of day. That is, if you hang around Crayton for a year or two."

"Won't be around that long. Soon as I finish remodeling the house my dad signed over to me, I'm putting the place on the market to sell. After that, I'm headed to St. Louis." He reached for his flat warm beer, but Joanie poured it out and got him a new cold mug, filling it to the same level as what she'd poured out.

His first night back in town, he'd made a deal with her. Any time he came in he'd have one beer, two at the most, and nurse it all night. But every so often he'd order a cold one and they'd pour him one to his throw-away level, then charge him for a full beer. Worked for him. Worked for the house.

"Say, who was that guy who picked up a pizza right before I came to the counter?" Cain asked. "I haven't seen him around before."

Joanie shook her head. "You're just like JB. In fact, all you lawmen are constantly on the lookout for anything out of the norm."

Cain shrugged. "Old habits…"

"Yeah. Anyhow, I don't know who he is. He calls in a pizza order every so often. Picks it up and leaves. Seems like a nice enough guy."

"You know where he lives?"

She shook her head. "Don't even know his name. He always places the order under the name Running Wild. Always asks for jalapeños on half the pizza." Joanie smiled, then slid the cold mug of beer in front of Cain. "Now, I need your opinion on something."

He nodded a thank you. "Go for it. One thing I've got plenty of is opinions."

She shook her head. "This is a serious question. How do you think folks around here would take it if I changed the name of this place to Joanie's Too?"

The first night Cain had walked into the place, he hadn't needed to be told why she was the one behind the bar instead of his high school friend Larry Reynolds. They'd always called each other by their last names and that would never change. One of the worst days of his life was when he'd received notification on the battlefield that Reynolds had given his life for his country.

To others walking into the restaurant, the tri-folded American flag hanging on the wall above a picture of Joanie's late husband in his uniform, said everything. An engraved plaque gave the specifics that Reynolds had been killed in a roadside bomb in Afghanistan.

After he died, she'd taken over both sides of their businesses—Joanie's Pizza, Pub and Pool Room and the cafe next door known simply as Joanie's. Cain figured since he'd become somewhat of an outsider around Crayton after more than a decade, he might be the closest thing to an unbiased opinion she'd get.

"First of all, I think most people don't care what the name is. They just like being here." He paused for a sip of the cold beer. "Second, if anyone has anything out of line to say, just show them the door."

Joanie smiled, then as the cook shouted from the kitchen that he needed help, she blew out a sigh. "Gotta go. Thanks for the advice."

"Reynolds would be proud of you, Joanie." Cain raised

his mug in a toast to her. "One thing he'd tell you to do, though, is hire more help."

"I think about it every so often. But what else would I do on Friday nights?" Her voice cracked as she swiped the bar towel across the counter, then glanced toward the front. "Looks like JB just walked in. Make sure he gets the right pizza."

Cain watched her walk through the doorway into the food prep area. Most everybody in town liked Joanie, and when the day came she needed help of any kind, they'd be there for her.

Chugging the rest of his beer, he realized his own friends were few and far between. Partly because of his work in the DEA, but mainly because trust and commitment had never come easy for him. But in the past couple months he'd been back in town, Cain had made a couple new friends and reconnected with one from his childhood—JB Bradley.

"You look like someone kidnapped your dog, stole your cycle and wrecked your new truck all in one fell swoop." JB eased onto a stool at the counter. "I thought you and Betsy might—"

"Steven needed a partner." Cain nodded in Betsy's direction, then turned back to his friend. "And I don't have a dog."

"Too bad." JB had been an agent with the FBI before he quit and moved back to Crayton a month before Cain. Once home, JB had got back together with his wife, Marcy, plus joined the Crayton Police Department. He was currently the acting sheriff and would probably be the next sheriff once Marcy's uncle retired.

"Yep. What about you? You're heading home late." Cain pushed the pizza box in JB's direction. "Joanie said Marcy already paid."

JB nodded then lifted the lid, slid one slice out and took a couple of bites. "Been a long day. I just drove back from the DEA in St. Louis. Had a meeting with them about the influx of heroin."

"Problem?" Cain flinched the minute the word left his mouth. He kept telling himself that drugs, cartels and runners were not his concern now. He was on a leave of absence. But damn it, he kept falling back into the old questions.

After sliding another slice of pizza from the box, JB leaned closer. "What do you know about Interstates 44 and 70 being prime routes?"

Cain shook his head. "Last I knew, 44 was busy. Got a straight shot up to Chicago that way. But you and I both know that's been going on a long time. What's changed?"

"Seems to be picking up. There's a rumor of somebody trying to make a move on the region's boss"

"You get the drug captains and lieutenants fighting" — Cain shook his head— "there's no telling where that can lead."

JB grabbed the pizza box and turned to leave, then stopped and glanced back. "Yeah, that's what I'm thinking, too. I've got a feeling the police are going to need all the help they can get on this one. Can I count on you for advice?"

Cain didn't say yes. Didn't say no. Didn't take the bait and offer to help. Or flat out tell his friend to take a flying leap. He didn't even look away from the empty glass on the counter in front of him.

"Good night, JB."

"Night, Cain."

Shadowing bad guys on his last deep cover assignment had almost turned him to the underbelly of crime. This was supposed to be his downtime. His time to recoup his mind, body, emotions and... He just needed some time away. Time to save what was left of his soul. Time to let others take care of the good guys-bad guys fight.

A couple months ago, Cain had turned in his DEA resignation. His boss had tossed it right back at him. Then they'd had an honest heart-to-heart talk. Nothing like baring your soul to someone who regarded you as invincible. The boss had paid attention. Made notes when he told him how the last assignment had pushed him to the limits of honesty and anger and morality.

Then Cain had pulled the notepad to his side of the desk and told the boss how he'd been raised. How he'd learned early on that he had no one to rely on but himself. How, during the last assignment, it had dawned on him that there needed to be more to life than chasing bad guys. That somewhere there was something more for him. He at least deserved a chance at that.

The boss had moved the notepad to his bottom desk drawer and made him an offer. *Take six months' leave of absence. Stay in touch. Go find what you think you're looking for, and then we'll talk again.*

Taking a leave of absence from the DEA hadn't been easy for Cain to accept, made him feel like a quitter. Better than stepping over his drawn-in-the-sand line though. That would take the one thing he'd guard to his dying breath—his reputation as an honest man.

From behind him, the click of a woman's boot heels on the floor caught his attention a second before Betsy walked up beside him.

"That took longer than I planned." She eyed the last piece of pizza. "Looks like you were hungry."

"Good thing you weren't." Cain stood and moved toward the register to pay. "If you're heading out, I'll walk you to your car."

"Out? I thought I'd hang around for a while. Maybe grab one of Joanie's best burgers ever."

Cain raised his eyebrows. "I thought you said you couldn't stay because you needed to be up early in the morning."

Betsy's lips parted before she blinked. "You're right, I do need to get home."

"You know, I can usually figure out what I've done to get the cold shoulder from a woman." He tossed more than enough money on the register along with his bill. "But with you? I have no idea in the world."

Reaching out, her fingertips brushed his sleeve for a moment before she pulled back. "It's not you. It's just..."

The silence hung between them and the background noise faded. He could get used to her touch real fast if he weren't careful. Maybe it was best this night was over.

"Yeah, well...I believe you said that before. You let me know when you decide to tell me what *it* is." He turned to leave, then turned back to her. "There is one thing I'd aimed to ask."

"Okay?" She appeared to stop breathing.

"I've been wanting to do a little work on my truck, and maybe my motorcycle, but the house doesn't have a garage. Would it be possible to rent some time in one of your service bays?"

Her expression relaxed and she blew out her breath. "Sure... I mean... No."

"No?" Cain couldn't believe her answer. All he'd wanted was a place to tinker with his truck and motorcycle. Nothing else. What was wrong with that?

She touched his sleeve again. "I mean no, you don't have to rent the bay. Just stop by and use an empty one whenever you want."

He sighed as loud as she had. "Thanks. I'll get my tools out of storage and—"

"Why? You've probably met Steven's father, Earl Millerton."

"Sure, we've talked over breakfast at Joanie's a few mornings. Why?"

"He's in charge of the Peyton Service Center." She slid onto a counter stool. "I'll tell him to show you around. There's every tool you could possibly need already there. No need to bring your own."

Betsy was all talkative now that anything personal had faded from this evening. The consummate businesswoman. Considering she owned the biggest dealership in mid-Missouri, plus the fact she was known for her honesty in the car business, he wouldn't expect less.

"Sounds good. I'll stop by next week." He walked to the door and held it open for the couple leaving in front of him. "Hey, Betsy."

She glanced across the room. "What?"

"Remember. Next Friday. Seven o'clock."

Her cheeks twitched. "Seven o'clock, what?"

The room seemed to go stark quiet and even Joanie leaned out of the kitchen.

He pointed toward the pool table where they'd played earlier. "Rematch."

"Fine. You'll need to win the break to win the game though." Betsy crossed her arms as she slid from the stool, cocking her hip ever so slightly. "Not. Likely."

Now there was the girl from Friday nights back in high school, when win or lose didn't matter. Hell, winning was just a state of mind anyhow. Slow and easy, he slid into his leather jacket, zipped it part way and raised the collar for a retro James Dean look. Then in a what-have-I-got-to-lose moment, he winked at her.

She winked back in a split-second reaction before her expression turned to disbelief at what she'd done.

"Guess I'll just have to try harder." He winked again and stepped outside. Before the door had completely closed behind him, she'd shoved it open and followed him as he walked across the parking lot.

Her heels popped against the pavement behind him. "Mark my words, Cain Connery. You won't win."

"Are you following me, Betsy?" He stopped and leaned back against the back side panel of his truck.

A few feet away she finished shuffling into her coat, then mirrored his stance, only against the tailgate. Her hair fluttered in the wind, tangling in the air before framing her face again. "Nope. I just needed a breath of fresh air. It got kind of close in there. Kind of stuffy."

She stared up at the clear winter sky as if she'd never

seen so much beauty in one place at one time. He leaned toward her and pointed out the Big Dipper, then Venus. Betsy smiled as she turned and rested her forearms on the top of the taillight, inching closer to him as he drew an outline within the stars. Her brows pinched, forehead slightly wrinkled in question.

He stood away from the truck. Held his left arm shoulder high and straight out to his side. As if zeroing in on the bullseye during an archery competition, he slowly turned his head to face the same direction and touched the fingers of his right hand against his cheekbone.

"The Archer," she said, smiling.

"Absolutely correct." He nodded, turning to stare into her eyes. They were separated by the back edge of the truck bed, but somehow, he felt closer to her than ever before. He sighed. "You know, I've always wanted to kiss you..."

Moments passed. Seconds. A minute. Neither Cain nor Betsy moved.

"You've never tried." Tilting her head, she raised her eyebrows as she straightened. "Why?"

CHAPTER FOUR

How could Cain tell Betsy that he was afraid of what he'd discover? Afraid of what he'd feel? Afraid his whole life might change in an instant? And he wasn't good with change. He had plans. He had dreams. He had past assignments that still lurked with danger.

Tonight, though, there was only Betsy and him. Without thinking, he stepped around the edge of the truck and wrapped her in his arms as she relaxed in his hold.

He lowered his head toward hers as he gently cupped his palm against her cheek. "*Why* doesn't matter anymore. *Now* does."

Her lips parted with the touch of his own. Suddenly, instead of acting their thirty-something age, they were more like teenagers necking in the parking lot. Their embrace tightened, their arms and hands awkwardly groping to find the path to what they felt in the moment. The brush of her fingers against the back of his neck trapped him. Made him afraid. Made him want more.

Then as gently as it had started, she eased away and

stepped back as their hands slid down each other's arms. Their fingers tangled for a moment before pulling apart.

"Yep, that's what I thought." He forced himself to walk to the driver's side door before looking back.

She hadn't moved, just stood there looking lost. Perplexed. "I don't know what you mean."

"You." Hands braced on his waist, he blew out a cheek-puffing sigh and shook his head. Grinned. Then without breaking eye contact, he walked back to her. Slowly, as if he'd done it a million times before, he brushed her hair behind her ear and lowered his mouth to hers.

He kissed her long and slow and smooth before pulling back from her lips. That brief taste was all it took to calm his doubts. "It's always been you."

"No!" She pulled away. "Please stop. Stop before—"

He rapidly moved backwards putting distance between them as he slowly raised his hands, palms outward toward her. "I'm sorry, Betsy. Guess I read the moment wrong. That would be my mistake."

She blew out a soft sigh. Slightly smiled. "I'm sorry, too."

"For what?"

"I didn't mean to lead you on. But there was something..." She paused. Motioned her fingers back and forth between the two of them. "Anyhow, just know it's not you. I just can't do this right now. Maybe never."

"Anything you want to tell me?"

She shook her head and glanced at the front door to Joanie's. "Think I'll just go back inside for a while."

"Do you want some company?"

"No, thanks." She turned and walked away.

Cain had hoped tonight would be the start of something good in his life, instead he'd ended up with Betsy walking away. Something about the way she took each step reminded him of other situations he'd found himself in through the years.

A couple rows over, Betsy paused and turned to face him. "Hey, Cain."

"Yeah?" He leaned back against the tailgate of his truck.

"You haven't been back in town but a couple months."

"So?" He had no idea what that had to do with anything, and he didn't aim to open his mouth on that fact. Might get himself in even more trouble with her tonight.

"A lot has happened since you left Crayton years ago. Mostly good. Some bad."

He noticed she was unconsciously rubbing her wrist again. She seemed to do that a lot. Plus, the tone of her voice had tensed. Wherever this conversation was headed, there was no sign of a smile being included.

"Such as?" he asked.

She pulled her hair back and tightened it with a scrunchie from her pocket. Opened her mouth to speak, then turned and walked away. "Never mind."

"Not good enough, Betsy. You started this conversation." He straightened from the tailgate and stepped further into the glow from a halogen parking lot light overhead. "Now finish it."

She stopped and looked back over her shoulder as the light from the neon Joanie's sign caught her in the splash of its movement. On and off. Shades of green and blue and yellow. Brighter, then darker, then fading into a final burst of color before beginning the neon dance once again.

"Finish it? Okay. I cried the day I realized you'd left town. You see, I was just a naïve high school girl who thought we were friends. You didn't even take time to say good-bye."

"Betsy, I—"

"You say I've *always* been the one. I doubt that." She tilted her head and chastised him with her raised-eyebrow smirk once again. "I really, *really* doubt that."

For the life of him, he couldn't figure out how their kiss had evolved into this. And he sure didn't like the serious tone the whole event was taking. Not many people were allowed to rebuke him, even fewer were allowed to walk away from the confrontation without a fight. But right now, he felt like he was being dressed down by the best of them, so he'd stand and listen. In his opinion, who they'd been in their teens had nothing to do with who they were now. At least, not entirely.

Ripping off the scrunchie, she shook her hair free and let it fall. "Don't worry though, *you* haven't always been the one in my life. Everything hasn't always been sunshine and roses, either. I learned the hard way not to count on anyone but myself."

She turned and walked toward the entrance. Her boot heels were quieter on the pavement now as she crossed the parking lot. Softer than when she'd followed him outside.

"I wish you'd never come back to Crayton, Cain. I'm not the same person you left behind," she said as she opened the restaurant door and disappeared inside.

He had no idea what he'd expected to hear. But

certainly nothing could have prepared him for her words. Caught off guard, he was utterly speechless. His gut told him someone had hurt her badly. Could he have prevented it if he'd chosen a different career? Maybe. Maybe not. But there was nothing he could do to change what had happened.

A bigger question was whether he could do anything to move the past to the side. Would she even give him the chance to show her how the future could be different? That he wasn't like whoever had hurt her. Hell, truth be known, he wasn't even close to being that high school graduate who'd driven away from Crayton and never looked back.

There'd been a lot of times during his DEA career when he'd watched victims or their family walk away from devastating trials or meetings. Whether they reached out to shake his hand or give him a torrent of angry words, he'd always stayed professional. But there had a been a few times when people had walked into his arms and cried. Sobbing in relief. In anger. In fear.

Right now, all he wanted to do was take Betsy in his arms and let her cry. But that wasn't going to happen, so he might as well head home. As he jumped into the cab of his pickup, he caught sight of a white Stetson laying in the passenger's side floor bed.

Shadow!

Cain clicked on the overhead light and set the hat on the dashboard. One of many call signs they'd used when working a case together. Only he wasn't on a case, he was on leave from the DEA. He scanned the perimeter for the response. Maybe the other agent had simply left him a gift as a hello.

Across the street he saw a quick-moving penlight. Cain responded by clicking off the overhead light, then eased out of the pickup and quietly closed the door.

Shadow was here and wanted to talk. That meant trouble for someone. Nothing about this could turn out good. In fact, this whole night had turned into one hell of a snowball rolling downhill.

CHAPTER FIVE

Cain skirted the parking lot in front of Joanie's before walking to the overflow lot across the street. A cold chill crossed his shoulders, and it wasn't the winter wind or the snow in the air causing the sensation.

Gut reaction? Well-honed instincts said he was being watched. From off to his left he heard movement, the kind made deliberately to grab his attention.

"Step from between those cars. And keep your hands where I can see them," Cain said, keeping his eyes trained on the point of sound, he eased toward the gun holstered on his inner calf.

A double knock, then pause, then knock echoed forth. "Wouldn't reach for that hideaway if I were you, Doc. I'd hate to have to shoot you."

Might have been four years, but Cain still recognized the voice of the man he'd named Shadow a few jobs back. Also, recognized the code they'd used back then.

"I doubt you can hit the side of a billboard," Cain said.

"Could if it was shooting at me." The man stepped

forward into the edge of the streetlight's glow. "I heard you were in the area but didn't believe it till I saw you tonight."

"Last time I saw you was in Texas. Looks like you got a new hat." Cain tossed the Stetson to him.

"Yeah. Somebody shot a hole in the other one."

Cain swept his gaze from one end of the lot to the other. For the most part, he trusted Shadow, but Cain was still a careful man. "Enough of the friendly bullshit. You alone?"

"Yep. At the moment." Shadow took a couple steps forward, then jerked back as headlights from a car leaving Joanie's glared in his direction.

Cain ducked behind the hood of the closest truck and pulled his gun. In silhouette, Shadow did the same. The two men stayed still as concrete. Watching each other. Evaluating. Deciding.

Content that the lights had come from a customer's car, Cain holstered his weapon and stepped forward, holding out his hand. Sometimes a man had to take a chance.

Shadow did the same. "So, tell me, Connery. Which side of the law are you working this time?"

"Neither. I'm just here remodeling my dad's house. Need to sell it. What about you? You on assignment?"

"Yeah, trying to get a handle on what and who's making a move here in the Midwest."

Cain couldn't help but notice the man looked tired. Cases could do that to an agent. Working deep cover, like Shadow usually did, could not only grind you down physically, but pushed your emotions to the break point. Especially if you were married.

"How's your wife?" Cain asked.

Shadow sighed long and hard as he centered his Stetson on his head. "Me and her parted ways. Got a divorce a little over a year ago." He walked deeper into the shadows and leaned against the brick building. "She just couldn't take my undercover life anymore."

"Sorry, man."

"Tell you the truth, there's days I can barely stand this way of living anymore myself."

Cain leaned back beside his DEA friend. There weren't a lot of people an agent could talk to personally without wondering if it meant risking his job or his life.

"Besides taking a leave of absence to work on my dad's house, I've kind of been thinking about quitting the DEA, too," Cain said.

"What would you do?"

He shrugged. "Start a security business. Maybe a self-defense or survival school."

"Sounds interesting...or a quick way to lose your shirt if things don't pan out."

"Yeah, that's my thoughts, too." Some days, Cain had the whole setup figured out in his mind. Others day, he wondered if there was even enough call for that kind of training in this area of the country. Deciding always seemed just out of reach.

Shadow stood away from the wall. "I know this was your hometown, but not lately. You haven't been here but a couple of months, but you must have picked up on what makes this place tick over a decade since you left."

"You're the second person tonight to remind me I've only been here a couple months. As for what's happening, you probably know a lot more than I do." Cain grinned. "What kind of case are you working?"

"Drugs. Guns. Captains. Lieutenants. Distribution networks already in place. Routes etched in miles of interstates." Shadow glanced around the area. "Usual stuff."

Cain had always known drug courier routes ran south to north through Missouri. In addition, his last couple of jobs on the East Coast had opened his eyes to some gun running through the Midwest.

"How? Who?" Cain asked.

"That's what the DEA sent me here to find out. So far, I'd say there's the usual drug chains...but...there's something else going on in town. Someone completely different." Shadow grimaced. "In fact, if you ask me, the cartel is just watching and letting the other group weasel in. But mark my words, one of these days the weasel will get too brave and step on the cartel's underbelly. That's the day they'll get squashed like a bug on a windshield."

Cain considered the conversation he'd had with Acting Sheriff JB Bradley earlier. Looked like today's meeting at the St. Louis bureau location meant more than just a routine briefing for local law enforcement. Maybe Cain should keep his eyes and ears open a little bit more, but he'd been trying to do the exact opposite ever since he hit town. He was tired of seeing nice places used for bad people to make a whole lot of money.

"Well, for what it's worth, this is where I grew up. Friendly people. Close to the Lake of the Ozarks." Cain smiled. "Only a two-to-three-hour drive to St. Louis,

Kansas City or Springfield. It's just a nice little town in the middle of Missouri."

"Then? Or now?"

First, Betsy had told him things had changed in Crayton. Now Shadow questioned the status of the town. Maybe he had been out of touch longer than he thought.

"I better head on down the road." Shadow walked over to his black truck and held out his hand. "Good seeing you again."

"Let me know if you're ever in the Jefferson City area. I'll take a run up there and we can find an out-of-the-way place to sit and talk old times." Cain reciprocated the handshake. "Take care of yourself out there."

Shadow nodded and opened his truck door. Paused. Then let the door loosely close, as he stepped closer. "You're the one who needs to watch their back."

Cain laughed. "You always were trying to throw me off my game."

"Not this time." The agent shook his head as a serious expression settled on his face.

Cain tensed as another cold chill crossed his shoulders. "What are you trying to tell me without telling me?"

"For close to two years, I've been ingratiating myself into one of the Midwest cartels. They seem to be using me as a spotter. I get a call to be at a certain place at a certain time and let them know if a certain person is there." Shadow sucked in a deep breath. "No kind of schedule or routine. Just whatever they've got going on. Could be around Crayton, or within fifty to a hundred miles of here. But it always rotates within a few specific places. A few specific people."

What did that have to do with Cain? This was the first time he'd seen his former partner in almost four years. As for himself, he hadn't been around town long enough to have a target on his back. "Why should I be worried?"

Shadow glanced across the street. "When the man on the phone tells me Crayton, I call ahead and order a pizza to go from Joanie's."

Cain's insides tensed.

"In Crayton," Shadow continued, "my job is to make sure a certain person is on the premises. If she's there, I call my contact and say so. If she's not, I pay for the pizza, take it to my truck and watch for an hour. See if she shows up. If the boss don't hear from me within an hour, then the cartel halts whatever was in the works." Shadow shrugged. "Either way I get my pizza."

This wasn't something to make light of in Cain's opinion. "Joanie's a nice lady. I can't believe she'd be involved in anything illegal."

"Not her." Shadow pulled out his phone. Pushed a few buttons. Swiped a few items to the side. Held the phone up to face his friend. "This woman."

Cain couldn't pull his eyes away from the photo. Goosebumps made the hairs on his arms stand on end. His insides jerked as he fought the gag reflex.

"Betsy? Betsy Peyton?" Swiping the back of his hand across his mouth, he didn't even recognize his own voice. "No. No! You're wrong."

A touch of compassion crossed the other agent's eyes, then quickly disappeared. "I saw you and her in the parking lot. For a second, even thought you might be working a

DEA assignment that had led you to her also. Your reaction tells me that's not the case."

"Not hardly."

Raking his hand across his head, Cain stared into the shadows of pickups and cars and old brick buildings. This town had had its secrets even when he lived here. Families had had secrets. Probably still did. But the idea of Betsy having a secret was more than he could fathom. And the depth of the secret might be more than he wanted to imagine.

Just the thought of it all made him wish he hadn't come back to Crayton for even a little while. Like he'd reminded himself through the years, even earlier tonight, in his mind Betsy was always his friend.

"You saved my life back in Texas years ago. As far as I'm concerned, I trust you. But I also know people change sometimes." Shadow jumped in his truck, started the engine, and powered down the window. "If *you've* changed, I doubt there's a chance of me leaving town alive."

Cain figured his counterpart had already pulled his own gun and had it pointed at him from the other side of the door. Probably even had a bullet-size hole drilled in the door panel. One unseen from the outside. One that would easily pop with one shot.

Understanding the trust it had taken on Shadow's part to give him the info, Cain showed his friend that he was still a man to be trusted. He turned his back and walked away. "You got nothing to worry about from me."

With his brain and his heart and his gut fighting amongst themselves, he slowly stopped and continued to stare at the entrance to Joanie's. He needed more info.

"Does the cartel send you to other towns to spot different people, also?"

"Yeah. Targets are as different as night and day. Some young. Some old. Some barely able to walk and others running track at the local gym. For the most part, I get the impression they're just normal people going about their lives with no idea anything illegal might be going on." Shadow shook his head. "*But* there's a few I'm not too sure of."

Cain felt the press of a frown on his forehead. "Occupations? Do they all own a business?"

Shadow didn't answer right away. "Hard to say. Like I said, I've been working on this case for almost two years. Still can't tie a string around anything." The agent's tone had edged a bit higher, a bit tenser. He cleared his throat. "There're times I wonder if the cartel knows I'm DEA and they're just keeping me busy to muddy the waters. If so, one day I'll wake up dead."

That feeling was one all too familiar from the undercover work Cain had done over his career. One hard to explain to people who didn't walk that fine line going to work every day. One an agent didn't talk about often.

"My guess" —Shadow was back to his normal investigative voice— "is that you're going try to find out what's going on here in your hometown. Now you're going to try to see where Betsy fits in to everything. Can't say I blame you. Just don't get yourself killed, Doc. I may need someone to save my life again."

"Yeah. You still haven't got me that Stetson you promised in payment." Cain laughed as he turned toward his truck, feeling himself fall back into the way he'd felt for the past ten years. There were assignments. There were bullets. And best of all, there were friends who always knew what to say to make a situation better. "Stay safe, Shadow. Stay safe."

As Cain walked on toward his silver extended pickup, he heard the black truck pull out of the overflow lot and head down the street. Nice and slow and easy.

He felt like he'd been gut-punched. Hard. Gut-punched and left on the street to find his way home. Pressing the button on his key fob, the lights on his truck flashed once before he reached the door, yanked it open and jumped inside.

Earlier tonight, what had Betsy said about Crayton changing? Nothing specific, just that things were different. But he hadn't noticed anything out of the ordinary since he'd been back in town. Or had he been so busy trying to push thoughts of DEA business out of his mind that he'd overlooked his natural instincts shouting *beware* right in front of him?

Doubting Betsy was not on his radar. There could be a dozen reasons why someone would be watching her...well, at least a few. Yet he had no reason to doubt anything Shadow had told him either. Somewhere in all that was a clue. And he didn't plan to leave town without answers. For now, doubting Betsy was still not on his radar.

Without another thought he pulled out his phone and tapped the number two call button. JB picked up on the first ring.

Cain didn't wait for him to say anything. "We need to talk."

"Where and when?"

Cain raked his hand across his head. He needed some sleep. He needed to think. He needed to decide. "My lake lot, the one where my dad's cabin used to be. Five in the morning."

"Got it."

He checked his gun and laid it on the passenger seat. His friendly hometown trust had been dented tonight. Until he had some answers, the only person he'd trust was JB. "Don't tell *anyone* I called.."

"Okay, but—"

"No buts, JB." Cain's gut feeling made him wish he hadn't come back to Crayton. "Friendship only goes so far when we're talking drugs and crime and your sister-in-law Betsy."

CHAPTER SIX

After re-entering Joanie's, Betsy kept her head down and walked straight to the restroom. Once there she took refuge in one of the empty stalls and slowly slowed the pounding of her heart.

Her strength of self-control had won the struggle between what might be a future of possibility and all her mistakes from the past. Still, she couldn't explain the split-second feeling she'd had from Cain's kiss out in the parking lot. One that seemed to put a crack in the barricade she'd built around events better left locked away.

A few minutes later she made a quick stop at the checkout counter. Chatted a couple minutes with her friend. Just long enough to convince her there was nothing to tell ... Cain was just a friend. Then Betsy grabbed a to-go cup of soda and headed out the front door.

She shivered with the lukewarm air blowing from her car vents. Living at the edge of town had its good points, one being it only took five to ten minutes to get from any place in Crayton to her home. Still, her car should have warmed up by now. She shivered again. Someone in the maintenance shop needed to look at her car's heater system.

Her thoughts turned to what she'd just witnessed in the glare of her car's headlights as she exited Joanie's parking lot. There'd been nothing unusual about Cain and another man shooting the breeze as they stood by their trucks. Always seemed like men would rather carry on a conversation in the dark than the light of day. Maybe it gave them more courage to play out the bragging rights they were sharing.

Something about this scene had grabbed her attention and shouted a warning, though. Like the first night she'd caught Phillip making a drug deal years ago.

The split second her headlights had flashed on the two men in the overflow parking lot, she'd sensed something clandestine. Cain had quickly crouched behind a truck. Meanwhile, the unknown man had stepped back into the shadows. Both defensive moves. What were they afraid of? What were their secrets?

Maybe she should circle the block. Phone-video whatever was taking place. See if her instincts were right.

Then what?

She couldn't call her uncle the sheriff, he was still laid up, recuperating in St. Louis. And if she called Acting Sheriff JB, who also happened to be her brother-in law, or Deputy Evans? They'd probably ask her for more proof than just some dark images in a parking lot. Even her sister Marcy would tell her she was letting her imagination get the better of her. Maybe she was mixing the past with the present and coming up with improbable situations.

Still...why had Cain and the other man dodged the lights?

"Stop it, Betsy," she said to herself and the empty car. "Not every man out there is going to be like Phillip. He was one of a kind."

Besides, Cain had worked for the DEA a lot of years, and she doubted taking a leave from the Agency was all it took to not still have the split-second reactions and instinct for self-preservation agents needed. Since he'd been back in town, the only person she'd seen him talk to very much was JB.

At least, it had been until tonight. Now she wondered just how many friends Cain actually had around Crayton.

Less than an hour ago she'd seriously considered Cain. The kiss had been unexpected, but one she'd longed for back in high school. One she'd never gotten then. Tonight had been enough to let herself think she might have finally found a man she could trust. She didn't have to dwell on that any longer.

Men with secrets weren't allowed in her life ever again. Especially ones involved in drugs. A DEA agent like Cain was more than familiar with where, how and what was available on the drug scene. She'd bet hard-earned cash he'd hooked up with his local supplier only steps from Joanie's front door. Her headlights had been at the right place, at the right time to catch him less than thirty minutes after kissing her.

Phillip used to crawl out of their bed minutes after making love, leave the house for thirty minutes and come back high. She would not live like that again. Not ever.

Cain had been the boy she'd dreamed of back in high

school, but a lot of hard lessons had been learned since then. There'd been nothing between them back then. There'd be nothing between now.

She pulled into her driveway and pressed the door opener on the visor, then drove inside the attached two-car garage. The opener's overhead lights lit the way, and her garage motion lights illuminated the surroundings with their bright halogen glow. Lamps inside the house were always programmed to come on at six o'clock, which had long since passed tonight.

Walking to the door leading into the kitchen, her gaze landed on the snow blower she still hadn't got ready for bad weather. One more thing to add to her to-do list. She unlocked the door, stepped inside. Reset the security panel on the wall. And headed straight to bed, barely taking time to brush her teeth and wash her face.

Bone-tired, she crawled under the covers, ready to get some sleep. The encounter with Cain, the kiss, the shadowy image in the parking lot all merged with her memories, stirring the past few years to life. She could face them down tonight. They were only memories. Memories didn't leave a bruise. At least not physically.

She envisioned her nightly meditation view of the beach, imagined the sound of rolling waves and seagulls flying overhead. Slowly, she drifted off. Four hours later she opened her eyes. Still tired, but at least somewhat rested.

As the owner of Peyton's, the town's premier auto dealership, Betsy made it a point to be in her office, or on the lot, before eight every morning except Sunday. On days like this, when she hadn't fallen back asleep after waking in the middle of the night, she came in earlier. She'd arrived about five fifteen this morning. The lot lights were still glowing.

Like every other Saturday morning, she pulled up the sales numbers for the week on her computer. They looked great. Right on track to make her year-end goal. Of course, a lot could happen in the coming months. If those numbers held, she'd be able to seriously consider opening another dealership. Where to locate was still on the drawing board, but she'd narrowed it down to—

A blast of frigid air shattered the warmth in Betsy's office. Had she forgotten to lock the outside door when she arrived? Missed the jiggle of a door lock being jimmied? Overlooked the muffled sound of breaking glass?

Reactively, she jerked open the bottom right-hand drawer of her desk. Locking her fingers into the notch on the sliding hideaway panel, she felt less alone just knowing an alarm button hid inches away. The ammo and gun, her uncle had trained her to shoot years ago, lying beside the alarm made her even less afraid.

Footsteps approached from the far end of the showroom. Closer and closer. Finally, she heard the easy whistling of her service center manager, Earl. Every morning a different song, a different loudness, a different feel. She eased the drawer closed and glanced at the clock on the wall. Six-thirty. Earl Millerton was always on time. She was the one jittery as hell this morning.

"You're here early, boss," he said, walking into her office and laying the day's work schedule on the corner of her desk.

"Figured I'd get a head start on the day. This time of year, you never know what the weather may be like by afternoon." The statement wasn't entirely a lie. Weather forecasts had been predicting rain and falling temperatures by six tonight, maybe earlier.

"Gonna be a lot of fender benders and ditch calls with the freezing rain. If it changes to snow, the roads'll be slicker than a water slide." Earl zoomed his hand in a downward motion. "I figure the tow trucks'll get their first workout of the new year."

"True. What little snowfall we got in December didn't require any major planning."

"From what I've read in *The Old Farmer's Almanac,* January and February are gonna give us a run for our money."

Betsy smiled. Earl always stayed up on all the new automotive designs and mechanical updates. She could also count on his sage advice according to the latest *Farmer's Almanac* for weather predictions. Some of his garden planting guidance helped her every spring. For now, she'd follow his weather advice...along with the local weatherman.

Ice and snow were heading straight across Missouri in a line from Springfield to the south all the way north of Jefferson City to Interstate 70. The lake area appeared dead center for the worst.

The town of Crayton and three surrounding counties relied on Peyton's and three other dealerships in the extended lake area, plus a couple of road service companies, to help keep the roads clear of fender benders. Never mind all-out crashes. Bracing for the harsh winter weathermen had predicted for this year, local garages had banded together to lease extra wreckers.

She'd volunteered to house them on the back lot of her dealership.

"Are the trucks gassed and ready?" she asked.

"Ready to roll. Me and Bret will be on the two flat rollbacks." Earl shook his head. "What with one of the mechanics out with the flu, we'll be short a driver for the three lightweight wreckers assigned to us."

"I can handle a tow truck." Cain Connery's voice reverberated across the room.

Betsy jerked, knocking her coffee cup hard enough that warm liquid sloshed onto her desk. "You scared the daylights out of me. Where the heck did you come from?"

"Sorry." He picked up a handful of paper towels from the side table holding the coffeepot, then moved to clean up the splatters. "I figured you heard me come in the back door."

She jumped up from her chair and shoved paperwork out of the way of the expanding puddle on her desk. Meanwhile, her racing heart seemed unable to calm itself to a normal beat. She didn't want to question whether that was due to being surprised, or the fact it was Cain.

"I can do that myself." She grabbed the towels from his hand and blotted at the spots.

"And good morning to you, too, Betsy." His sarcastic tone wasn't lost on her.

Pausing in mid cleanup, she tilted her head back to look him in the eyes. She'd taken her shoes off when she arrived early this morning, and her five-six came up short next to his six-foot frame. Still, his gorgeous blue eyes seemed awfully close.

"What are you doing here?" she asked.

Cain walked back to the office doorway and leaned against the frame. "Last night at Joanie's, you said I could use one of the service bays to work on my truck. Did you forget?"

No, she hadn't forgotten. In fact, that's all she'd been able to think about as she lay awake in bed this morning, trying to figure out how to back out on the offer. She'd also tried to figure a way out of the Friday night pool challenge she'd accepted from him for next week. She'd come up empty on both.

"I meant, why are you here so early? In fact, how did you even get in this building?"

He pointed down the hallway outside her office. "Back door was unlocked. Figured it was okay to come in. If not, you ought to keep that locked. Or at least get a buzzer to let you know when it opens."

For once she had to agree with him. Keeping the door locked would make sense, but since she'd lived in Crayton practically all her life, she still thought of it as the place without locks.

She didn't like locks. Opening a deadbolt took time away from a quick escape. She'd had special ones made for her house.

"I've told her that a million times," Earl said. "Maybe you can talk some sense into her."

"I doubt she'll listen to me." Cain straightened away from the doorframe. "By the way, Earl, when Betsy said I could work on my truck here, she said you'd show me around the service center. Maybe get me set up in a bay I can use every so often."

"Sure thing. Whenever you're ready just come on

over." Earl walked out of the office, and from the sound of the click of the outside lock being turned, he'd left the main building.

Cain pulled his wallet from his jacket pocket, then laid his social security card and driver's license on her desk. "If you can use a hand on the tow truck tonight, I'm available."

She smiled. "You sure know how to get a job, don't you?"

"Thought you might could use some help, that's all. If you remember, I'm just in town to rehab a heli. Not looking for a full-time job." He braced his hands on her desk. Stole a quick down and up glance of her.

Her insides heated as she shut down her thoughts. Then she walked to the thermostat and notched the heat down a few degrees. "Guess you'll head back to the DEA after you sell the house?"

"Not sure. Lately, a security business of my own has crossed my radar."

"Where?"

"I've got my eye on some land between Rolla and St. Louis."

"Oh." That at least ruled out his staying in Crayton. And she'd never move from her family. Whether they knew it or not, Sadie and Marcy needed her. She'd always be there to protect them. Her younger sister, Amber, wasn't that open to her help, but there might come a day they bonded.

Taking her chair once again, Betsy stared at his license. The picture didn't do his eyes justice. The weight didn't account for the hard lines of muscles she saw every time he came near her. And the dark, combed-in-place hair in the photo didn't look nearly as good as the tousled look he usually wore.

"Betsy?" Cain pushed his hands in his leather bomber jacket pockets as he stood.

She felt a smile grab the corners of her face. "Sorry. I... uh...I was thinking about something Earl had said earlier."

He raised his eyebrows and grinned. "Sure you were."

There was nothing more irritating than someone who could read her mind. Her sisters were like that, too. So was her mama. She didn't need another mind reader in her realm. Especially him.

"Yeah, I was considering which trucks would be more apt to be used tonight."

"From the weather report, I'd say all of them," Cain said.

Her business side knew tonight's weather might be rough and they could use all the help they could get. "That's my thinking, too. In fact, I'm going to take you up on your offer to work a tow truck tonight. Thanks." She held her hand up for a moment, then dialed the insurance agent. "Yeah, I want to put Cain Connery on our policy. Is that a problem?"

After she hung up with Crestfall's Insurance Agency, the employment paperwork took another ten minutes. Finally, she handed Cain a packet of info plus an employee handbook. "You are now an official employee of Peyton's Automotives."

"Only when I want to be though." Cain headed for the door. "I'll check in with Earl, then head home and get a few things done on my renovation. You'll probably be gone when I get back for the evening."

"Nope. I'll be here as long as my trucks are on the road tonight."

She held out her hand. "Thanks for offering to help. I appreciate it."

"Any time."

He closed his palm around hers and for a moment the feel of his skin against hers felt right. Even the brief back-and-forth caress of his thumb didn't drive her back.

"I'm looking forward to our rematch at pool this Friday night," he said.

"Are you now? You must like losing." She slipped her hand from his. "Besides, I think we may need to cancel because of the weather."

"Seems a might early to cancel something that's almost a week away just because it's going to snow tonight. What say we wait till Friday and see how the forecast is then?"

Shaking her head, she stared at the floor. "I don't know, Cain. I always like to plan ahead. Let's just say it's cancelled for now and I'll get back to you on rescheduling?"

"Nope. Game's still on."

"Then I just won't show up."

Cain walked to the doorway and braced his forearm against the doorframe. "You know, I went through a lot of training as a DEA agent."

"I can only imagine."

"Did you know most people have a 'tell' for one thing or another?"

If she knew where this was going, she'd feel a lot better. "So I've heard."

"You've got one, too. Happens every time you lie to me." He laughed as he walked out of the office.

She followed him into the hallway as he went out the back door. "What? What's my 'tell' you just saw?"

He grinned as he closed the door behind him. "See? I was right."

"Damn." She'd just admitted she lied.

CHAPTER SEVEN

Cain got the lowdown from Earl Millerton as to how the tow truck call-outs were handled, then he headed home. His late-night talk with Shadow coupled with the before-sunrise meeting with JB had put a hole in his sleep. Both had been eye-opening, but neither had given him all the answers. In fact, JB had been blunt about not planning to divulge any of Betsy's personal life, not even when Cain had shared his informant's warning.

At least one good thing had come out of stopping by the auto dealership this morning though. Now, besides working on his truck as a reason to show up around Peyton's, Betsy had hired him as a part-time employee. From the looks of things, he had added a lot to his plate.

Tonight, he'd write his official resignation letter for the DEA, but he wouldn't send it right now. He was still thinking about that decision. But, at least, he'd have the paperwork done and waiting for when—*and if—* he decided to quit the Agency.

After installing one of the two kitchen cabinets he'd

put on his schedule for today, he opted for an early lunch and a few hours of shuteye. Who knew when tonight's shift might end. He made it back to Peyton's just as the freezing rain started to glaze the roads.

The weatherman had been right, rain and falling temps had rolled into the area right as forecast. Trouble was, even though Crayton wasn't big by any means, it still had traffic problems. Plus some people were out on the four-lane divided highway trying to make it home from Jefferson City almost an hour away.

For the past twenty minutes, Betsy and her primary competition in town, Hal "The Hat" Boone, had laid out the towing map for the evening. Teams had been assigned. Thermoses filled. Sack lunches handed out.

Cain learned he was to tag team with Randy something-or-other, a part-timer from the used car lot down the road. They'd concentrate on the north outer limits of the town, including the rural area in that vicinity. Most of the ditch pulls would be from that direction, and sometimes that's all that was needed for the driver to be on their way again. By the time the meeting ended, calls from stranded motorists were already coming in. Everyone scattered outside, headed to their rigs for what would be a long night.

Cain's instincts said that Randy wasn't going to be a high producer for the evening. The mid-twenties guy was fully capable, but maturity seemed to be on hold. He appeared to be in it for some fast money and nothing else.

"Hey, let me grab a coat from my truck." Randy opened the driver's side door and yanked out an orange insulated jacket. "I got another coat if you need one. 'Cause you sure want to have some reflective yellow or orange on you when you're working the side of the road."

"Thanks, but Earl gave me a safety vest earlier today." Besides which, Cain didn't much care for wearing other people's stuff. Especially one that had a skunky body-odor scent. "Hey, man. You smoking weed?"

Randy reached in his coat pocket and eased out the corner of a plastic bag just enough to be seen. "Not today. But I got something even better if you need it."

Cain's first thought was to haul the guy in to the police. His second thought was that there'd been times he'd had to look the other way in his time with the DEA. Tonight might be another. Look the other way and get the bigger fish. "No, I'm good. Just don't be doing that stuff tonight. These roads are gonna get dicey."

"I ain't that crazy. Work and weed don't mix." Randy walked over to the first wrecker in line, jumped inside and sped away.

Cain eased behind the wheel of his assigned truck and tucked his thermos of coffee in the seat beside him. He considered going back inside to let Earl or Betsy know the situation with Randy. Then again, he worked for one of the dealerships, so someone had to know the man and his vices.

Maybe Betsy overlooked things like this too. Deliberately? Unknowingly? He'd sure hate to think she was an enabler. Cain turned the key in the ignition. Maybe he was going a little over the top on being the good guy.

Distress calls started hitting his scanner within minutes of being on the road. His first call went fast and easy—out of the ditch and on their way. So did the second. Same with the third. He glanced at the clock on the dashboard and figured he'd been out close to two hours. The actual work didn't amount to that much, it was the drive between locations that ate up the time.

During the past hour, the roads had gotten worse. Snow had started falling, which meant icy patches would be hard to read for a driver.

His cell phone rang with Betsy's ID. "Yeah, this is Cain."

"How's it going?"

"Good."

"Have you heard from Randy lately?"

"I haven't been in contact with him since we left Peyton's. I just keep getting calls transferred to me," Cain said. "Something wrong?"

Betsy sighed loud and heavy. "He's one of Hal's men and, well…"

Her pause lasted long enough to let him read her hesitation to put her thoughts into words.

"You're not sure you can trust him?" Cain asked.

"Something like that," she sighed. "Since he's not one of my employees, I don't see him very often."

"I had that same thought on the way out. You want me to try to find him?" Cain wished he'd followed his first instincts about the guy.

"I'm probably just overreacting. A couple months ago I tried to talk him into rehab. Even offered to pay for it. Maybe this—"

A phone rang in the background on her end.

"Let me get this other call," Betsy said.

Cain kept driving. Since you never knew where the

next call might come from, the wreckers just kept moving, slow and steady. Besides, there were still people without cell phones, and you might spot someone alongside the road who needed help.

Off to his right, headlights blazed upward from a deep ravine-type ditch. He pulled onto the shoulder and pushed the flasher button. Grabbing his phone and flashlight as he left the truck, he followed the tire marks over the embankment.

Scanning the light down the hill, he caught a glimpse of a tire crashed into thick brush. He jabbed the speaker phone button. "Betsy? Betsy."

Nothing. He was still on hold. He slid down the incline on his back which did nothing to keep him dry and warm, but was a hell of a lot safer than trying to walk the slick snow. At the bottom, he jumped to his feet. From where he stood, he could see the outline of what looked like an overturned tow truck.

"Damn it." He swept the surroundings with the beam as he started forward. "Randy? Randy, can you hear me?"

"Cain, are you still there?" Betsy's voice came through the phone. "Why are you calling for Randy?"

A loud moan came from the edge of the tree line and Cain ran to the sound. He zeroed in on the moan as he ran, and then knelt next to the body lying in the snow. Turning him over, Cain saw the blood on the shirt before he shined the flashlight in Randy's face. Looking back at him were the eyes and expression of a man high as hell.

"Betsy, call an ambulance to my GPS location stat. Randy's crashed down the side of a ravine." Cain shucked out of his coat, spreading it to cover the man. He quickly strapped the yellow safety vest back over his shirt. "Man, you said you were clean tonight. Said work and weed didn't mix, and I trusted you."

Randy grabbed into the air, chasing something in the vacant sky. "That's right...don't do weed and work..." His words were slurred.

"I think you're lying to me." Cain tried to locate the source of the blood, hard to do without moving him. His priority was to keep the man talking and warm till the paramedics arrived.

"Swear to Old Crow...I wouldn't lie to you." Randy tried to push himself up on his elbow but slid back down, half laughing as his shoulder hit the ground. "Nooooo weed... Had me a little junk."

"Heroin? You're pumped on heroin?"

"Yeah, man. Got me some good dope tonight." Randy's eyes rolled backward.

CHAPTER EIGHT

Slick snow had stacked up earlier in the week, so had the wrecks. Two days later the sun, along with a light drizzle, had melted everything. Even the usual small piles of dirty snow in the gutters had washed away. Now, the January-February cold had set in.

In case he ended up working the wrecker again, Cain had resorted to buying a set of insulated coveralls, plus an extra pair of ski gloves and a couple of face masks. Not for everyday use, but just in case...although just in case *what*, he wasn't sure. Lately he felt as if he wasn't sure about anything.

He'd thought Randy would have been a lead headline on the local radio station. Instead, he'd been a short two-paragraph blurb in the local twice-weekly newspaper. No thanks to the local community, Randy had made a recovery and even entered rehab. Time would tell on that front.

Shooting pool for the second Friday night in a row, he was losing his game of eight ball against Betsy once again. Once she'd beat him on the lag for the break, the game had been like a replay of last week, with her running the table. All she had left to sink was the black eight ball.

He tossed the chalk on the side rail, then stood his cue against the wall. Maybe tonight she'd at least let him buy her a beer.

After accidentally-on-purpose running into her every time he was at Peyton's to work on his truck for the past week, she'd crept into his bones. Not enough to change his plans for leaving Crayton and opening his own security business in St. Louis, but enough that he wanted to spend time with this woman any way he could. For as long as he was in town...and later. After all, St. Louis was less than three hours away.

Betsy tapped the eight ball, sliding it across the green felt along an invisible straight line with precision. Slower... and slower...until it stopped.

A collective throat clearing went up from the usual Friday night crowd gathered around. The win-or-lose eight ball rested tight at the point of the pocket. Hugging the rail like a kiss, while blocking the pocket like a concrete traffic barrier.

"Oh, I hate to see that. Looks like you get to play after all." Betsy stepped back from the table, picking up the chalk he'd just laid down.

Not an ounce of humor graced her expression. As usual, she was all business where he was concerned, but he'd caught a hint of sass in her tone. And the worst player in the world could have made her shot. She was a million times better than that.

"Why, thank you, Betsy," Cain said.

He knew she thought she had him beat. Trouble was,

he never gave up even when the odds were against him. Seeing as how she'd given him grief ever since he'd pulled her from a wreck up on the mountain over two months ago. Tonight, he planned to beat her at her own game.

She moved off to the side, then leaned against the small high-top table before sliding her bottom onto one of the stools. "Now don't mess up. You only get one chance."

Who did she think she was fooling? Certainly not him. She'd laid the ball up on purpose. The one woman in town he knew better than to push had given him a pity shot, one he'd take for all it meant. The game on the table. The game going on between them. One, he knew he could win. The other seemed completely out of his control.

Seated at one of the hi-top tables surrounding the game area, Marcy smiled as she raised her mug of root beer to toast her sister Betsy. "Good shot."

JB got up from beside his wife and walked over to stand by Cain. "You know Betsy set you up? Right?"

"Oh, yeah."

"Need any advice?" JB walked to the end of the pool table and gave a look at the lay of the game.

Shaking his head, Cain chalked the tip of his cue. "Nope. I got this one."

Raised voices from across the room caused the two men to turn and look at the same time. Seated at a table in the shadowed corner of the pool room were Earl Millerton and a couple of other men from town. No sign of Steven and his friends tonight. Earl and another man seemed to be having a disagreement.

"Wonder what's up with them?" Cain asked.

"Probably just blowing off some steam." JB braced his

arm against the wall. "I'd bet their wives have gone on a shopping weekend in KC or St. Louis. That's usually when the guys hang out around the lake."

Cain glanced back at the table where the other two men from the group looked anything but happy. He figured whatever was going on was more serious than steam because the tone of voices had changed to belligerence on Earl's side.

Betsy tapped the bottom of her cue stick against the floor. "Are you guys gonna stand there and talk all night?"

"We're not talking. We're strategizing." Shaking his head as if he wasn't already dead-on sure of his next shot, Cain pointed to the far pocket. "You've left me in a world of hurt with that eight ball blocking the pocket."

JB pointed and angled and leaned, all the time trying to give the impression he was laying out shots. "Cain, with my expert guidance I do believe you've got this game won."

"I can't believe you're taking his side, JB." Marcy pretend-complained. "You better remember how cold it is outside, because the way you're going, you're gonna find yourself walking home."

"Don't you worry. I'll give him a ride home," Cain said.

Marcy turned to her sister. "I still wish you'd reconsider going to New York with us. Mom and Amber want you to come along, too."

For a fleeting moment, Betsy let the idea of having fun with her two sisters and their mom grab her emotions. As the girls had grown up, the grown-ups had always referred to them as Sadie's Girls. The sisters' own peers had called them Sadie's Trio of Sass, among other things.

"Maybe I'll go with you all next time."

"That's what you said when the rest of us went to Chicago," Marcy said, rolling her eyes.

Betsy walked back over to the pool table and deliberately bumped her hip against the side. "Hey, are we shooting pool, or what?"

JB laughed as he went back to his seat by Marcy. She turned a cool shoulder toward her husband before he slid his arm around her waist, pulled her close and whispered in her ear. She whispered back, ending their standoff with a kiss.

Cain figured it must be nice to have that kind of invite waiting for you at home every night. JB might have only been back in town for a few months, but no one could even remember when JB and Marcy hadn't been together and in love.

Cain glanced at Betsy. "Now what was our bet?"

"If you win, I have dinner with you." Betsy glanced at the eight ball, then back at him. "And if I win, you—"

"If you win." Cain quirked the side of his mouth. "I'll have dinner with you."

"No way. I already took that bet from you years ago." Her tone had chilled. "You stood me up."

"I never—"

"Yes...you did." Betsy chalked the tip of her cue till the dust fluttered to the floor. "I believe you were distracted by a better-built model back in high school."

Truth be told, Betsy hadn't been the type he liked fifteen years ago. She'd been scrawny and smart and so into sports he'd thought she could probably beat him at a lot of games. Still, he sure didn't remember making a bet with her. Or standing her up. As he recalled, he was always unsure how to approach Betsy.

Besides her uncle, Cal Davis, being sheriff of Crayton, her dad had been an FBI agent—gunned down when she was still in grade school. The shooter had been taken down within a minute, but there'd been no saving her dad. That's when Betsy's family—mama Sadie, sisters Marcy and Amber, and her—had moved to Crayton from Jefferson City.

"I'm sorry if that happened, Betsy. But we were both young." Cain crouched into his stance and lined up his shot. He'd have paid closer attention if he'd known what Betsy at thirty-two would be like.

"Well, we're not young anymore. In fact, I'm getting older by the minute waiting for you to finish this game." Betsy blew out a sigh. "For the record, I don't need your apology. And if you let me win without a fight, I'll—"

Cain shot the first ball without even thinking. Hard, fast and to the pocket, it dropped like iron drawn to a magnet. Then six more, one after the other, found their mark in the pockets. Down the line. Off the rail. Two for one.

Betsy never changed her expression. Never moved except for her clear green eyes that tracked every shot he took.

With only the eight and one of his solids left on the table, he decided the fun was about to begin. She'd set him up to lose. Turnabout was fair play.

He played his solid just enough to sneak the ball between the eight and the cup. Had been a gutsy play on his part. A half a dime's length less of felt and he'd have lost for sure, but it had been worth the chance just to see her expression.

"You did that on purpose." Betsy walked the perimeter of the table, pausing only once by a side pocket.

Suddenly, the voices from the far side of the room got louder. Earl scraped his chair across the floor as he stood, then half stumbled on his way across the room. A little wobbly on his feet, he stopped next to Betsy. "Hey, Ms. Peyton. Looks like you're up against the rail there."

She reached out and steadied the man. "Sure am. You okay tonight?"

"Why does everybody keep asking me that?" His words slurred together as he shoved her hand off his arm. "Can't a guy go to the men's room in peace?"

"Sorry. I was just—"

"I'm tired of people trying to take care of me. My wife...my son...you..." Earl pushed to get past Betsy.

She jerked back, grabbing her right forearm as if she'd been nicked by fire.

"What do any of you know about my life anyhow?" He swept his arm around as if including all the restaurant, then focused his look on her. "Least of all you, boss lady. Not that you even know what goes on right in front of your eyes. Now get out of my way. What I do in my free time is none of your business."

"You don't talk to her like that." Cain dropped his cue as he stepped between her and the usually even-tempered Peyton's service manager. "And keep your hands to yourself. Got that?"

As if a switch had been thrown the crowd quieted. What had been laughter, singing and friendly chatter throughout the large two-story brick building dimmed to a whisper. JB moved to get up, but Cain motioned him to stay where he was. No need to bring the police into the outburst at this point.

"You okay, Betsy?" Cain asked.

From behind him, she touched his back. "Yeah. I'm fine. Don't make a big deal out of it."

"What's wrong with you tonight, Earl? Have a bad day?" Cain inhaled deep before exhaling his anger in one breath.

Earl's expression flashed from sad to mad to wobbly and back again in less than five seconds. "A bad day?" he said as he sneered. "Try twenty years of bad days."

Earl started to turn away as the crowd noise once again elevated to fun.

"I think you owe the lady an apology before you go," Cain said.

"Sure, man. Sure. I'm sorry, Ms. Peyton. I was...I mean..." Earl pointed back across the room to the men at his table. "But those weenies"—his voice grew louder with each word—"better stop telling me what to do."

Stepping in the line of sight between the man and his friends, Cain tried to diffuse whatever had set Earl off. "You might want to tone it down a bit. This is a family place." Cain nodded toward Joanie as she stared across the room from behind the counter. "I'd sure hate to see you kicked out."

For a few seconds, the man stared at Cain, then he broke eye contact and walked on toward the men's room without another word.

Cain braced his hands on the table and nodded in the

direction Earl had gone. "You were close to him. Do you think he's been drinking? Smoking pot?"

Betsy sighed. "I know Crayton's got its share of drug problems, but not everybody's walking the wrong side of the street, Mr. DEA Man. Besides, you don't have to worry about Earl. He's a good guy. Works hard." She narrowed her eyes into a questioning gaze as she rubbed her forearm once again. "But you're right, he seems…"

"Amped?"

"Yeah, kind of hyped up tonight. That's not like him. But thinking back, anytime his wife is out of town he's easier to rile. That might explain it." Betsy chalked her cue and turned back to the game. "I believe it's my shot."

Eyeing the table, she started to walk around Cain, and when he stepped to move out of her way, she bumped into his arm. His gut reaction was to reach out for her, but he didn't.

"Do you mind giving me some room?" Betsy said. "Or are you trying to make me miss my shot?"

He raised his palms in surrender mode. No need to answer. He had no one to blame but himself if, by some stroke of luck, she dropped the eight ball and not his. Of course, that would be hard to do, seeing that Joanie's had a sign on the wall that read "All eights must drop clean."

Betsy glanced up at the sign. Then at the table. Then at her sister. Marcy shrugged in response while JB covered his mouth to keep from grinning. Betsy shifted her eyes back to the sign one more time and shrugged.

"What say we call it a draw?" Cain didn't need to win, he'd already got what he wanted when she'd agreed to the challenge. He walked over and stood his cue in the corner. "After all it's just a game."

"Don't give me that crock, Cain Connery." Finally looking him in the eye, she stepped around the table and into his space. She tilted her head to the side and lifted her eyebrows, wrinkling her forehead in the process. "A game? Really?"

His core stirred with the heat she'd added to his personal space. Never mind that the way she said his name stoked his insides. Something he didn't need fueled in the middle of a crowded pool room.

Cain met her head tilt with one of his own. "Why? You got a problem with playing games?"

"Nothing in life is just a game." She turned away, lined up her shot and let it fly. "Didn't you get the message?"

As if a professional hustler on the prowl had taken the money shot, the eight ball dropped into the side pocket.

Betsy pumped her arm in the air, then leaned into his personal space. Her smile sassy, as if flirting, before she thought better. "You're in shock, aren't you? Go ahead. You can admit it. I left you in the dirt."

He'd never seen her so happy. If this was all it took for her to smile and go crazy, he'd lose to her twenty-four seven for the rest of his life. For a moment he thought she might actually kiss him. Or he'd kiss her. Or they'd kiss each other and let everyone else in the room fade away. But she didn't. They didn't. And the moment passed.

She pulled back, and turned toward her sister and JB, who were still watching the table. Everyone else standing around that corner stared in the same direction.

Plop.

Cain and Betsy turned toward the sound. After a long slow roll down the felt to the other end of the table, the cue ball had dropped. She'd lost.

"I should have known not to give you a chance." She shoved her cue stick in Cain's hand and walked away.

The crowd dispersed as she headed to the counter. JB covered his mouth, while Marcy hurried to her sister's side, and Cain just stood there in disbelief. He had to do something. Had to make Betsy smile or sass or even flip him off. He didn't care what he had to do, but this evening couldn't end on this note.

"Thanks for letting me win, Betsy," he shouted after her. "Let me know when to make the reservation for dinner."

She stopped and turned, fluffed her hair as if she *had* let him win. "You're welcome, Cain. But don't—"

Coming back from the men's room, Earl bumped into Betsy and Marcy hard enough to knock them against the wall. Cain heard more than saw JB get to his feet and head toward them.

Staggering, Earl spun around, reaching out to help the women. Instead, he stumbled backward. Barely standing, his body circled from his waist up. Knees buckled.

"Call 911." Cain caught the service manager before he hit the floor. "Tell them they'll need the Narcan."

Eyes wide in panic. Pinpoint pupils. Pale. Earl grabbed Cain's hand and squeezed. "Hel...help." His hold tightened. "Help me. Tell them I'm sorry."

"Hang on, Earl. I've got you." Cain lowered him down, never letting go of Earl's hand. The man's body went limp.

"Stay with me, Earl." Cain had seen this too many

times not to know what would happen next. Just like every other overdose he'd ever witnessed, he hoped like hell this time he was wrong. "Stay with me."

Breathing stopped. Heart stopped.

Cain jumped into compression mode on Earl's chest, pumping again and again and again. He knew the rhythm. Knew the pace. Knew the procedure. "Come on back, Earl. You can do it. Think of your family. Your wife. Think of Steven. Fight, man. Fight."

In the background he heard JB make the paramedic call. Heard Marcy and Joanie clearing people to the other side of the room. Heard half the voices in his own head shouting defeat, the other half shouting you can save him if you don't quit.

Cain didn't quit.

The man's eyelids popped open as he inhaled a breath on his own. Within another minute, the EMTs arrived. Cain stepped back to let the professionals handle the situation as JB walked over to the group of Earl's friends all huddled together in the corner.

"Betsy!" he shouted. "Call Earl's wife and son. Have them meet the ambulance at the hospital."

Without a second thought delay, she pulled out her phone and followed his instructions.

Cain had wondered about Crayton's drug problems the other night with Randy. That incident had been a buried news story. Now a good, hardworking, respected family man had OD'ed. Meant front page news. Lead radio news for the day. That would scare the local community. No ignoring the situation now, Crayton's drug problems had just made an appearance, loud and clear.

Citizens would rise up in arms. Form a committee. Make a plan. Demand action before it was too late. Someone needed to get the word out that it was already too late, because whether the drug was heroin or fentanyl, for some lives it was already too late.

Right on time, beads of sweat peppered the back of Cain's neck. He hated that sensation. No, hate wasn't even close to what he felt. He rubbed the dampness away, but it peppered again.

There'd been other towns he'd been assigned to for DEA surveillance. People he'd saved. People he couldn't. Maybe he should have stayed undercover. Kept walking that line between right and wrong until a bullet made the choice for him. He swiped his palm down his face, struggling to push the thoughts aside. He'd given a lot of years to saving others.

Hopefully, Shadow would have more leads to share the next time they made contact.

Part of the reason Cain had taken the leave of absence from the DEA was to find some kind of peace. From what he'd just seen, peace and moving on wouldn't be coming any time soon.

He glanced at the paramedic. "Will Earl make it?"

CHAPTER NINE

For the past hour, Betsy had stood off to the side, staying out of the way as police did a quick questioning of everybody in Joanie's. A déjà vu moment spiraled her back to Phillip. On drugs. Belligerent. Paranoid. Was Earl using? She'd never seen him like tonight. Nothing unusual at work.

A line of customers had formed at the checkout counter to pay their bills and leave. All thoughts of fun for the evening had ended, and Joanie had decided to close early.

Betsy moved to the pool table she and Cain had played on earlier in the evening. Trying to get the vision of Earl's collapse out of her mind, she pulled the balls from the pockets and racked them in the center of the felt. Gently she tapped her fingers against the cue ball and watched it skim the length till lightly bouncing off the far rail. For a moment the heaviness of the evening lifted.

"Let me pay and I'll be right there." Walking toward

the checkout, Cain shouted across the room to Deputy Evans and JB leaving out the front door.

"What's going on?" Betsy asked. "I mean, I know drugs seem to be everywhere now, that's why I'm so determined to keep my workers out of harm's way. Peyton's is a drug-free zone, and everyone there knows my rules. Maybe it's not drugs. Earl's a good family man."

Cain found it odd that she'd made such a point of telling him no drugs were allowed at Peyton's. That she was naïve enough to believe drugs hadn't been the culprit in what everyone had just seen. Stressing that Earl was a good family man, as if drugs didn't happen to good people and their families. She was right about one thing though. Drugs were everywhere. In fact, if this were any other time, any other place, any other case, he'd be putting her name on a Persons of Interest list, right alongside her company.

"JB said you hadn't been able to reach Earl's wife, Wanda, so the police have called Steven to meet them at the hospital. They want me to be there. See if I can pick up on anything that might point to where Earl got the dope."

"Since you don't work for Crayton Police, how can you be part of the questioning?"

"Can't. But I can provide the police with a list of what to ask. Maybe I'll even pick up on something in Steven's answers. Something I've encountered before." Cain tossed two fifties on the counter. "Does that cover it?"

Joanie waved him aside as she took the next customer in line. "Keep your money. You stepped up and took care of Earl tonight, that's payment enough."

"Thanks." Cain sighed heavily as he pocketed his

money. "I wish I could say Earl will be okay, but he's not out of the woods yet."

He moved in Betsy's direction. She'd hoped he'd pay and leave. So much for hoping. Easing around to the side of the table, she spun the cue ball on the felt. He stepped up behind her, reached around and scooped up the ball.

"Hey!" She grabbed it out of his hand, then leaned away from his heat. Being that close had its effects on her, some of which she couldn't control. Like the fact she found herself holding her breath.

She felt a hint of warmth rush to her cheeks and tilted her head forward, letting her long hair ease to the front to shield her emotions. Their silence carved its way into their space. A space so small, she couldn't help but feel the change in the air as he slowly moved his hand in her direction. She didn't flinch.

"Hey, yourself." He gently brushed her hair behind her ear. "For a second there, I thought you were hiding from me."

When she looked up, his lay-you-down look focused on her, and before she could stop herself, she felt the unconscious parting of her lips. She reached up and kissed him on the cheek.

"What's that for?" This time he was the one who stepped back.

She shrugged. "A thank you for what you did for Earl."

"All in a day's work." His gaze skimmed across her face, finally resting on her lips. "I don't know how long I'll be helping the police tonight. Guess we'll need to change my game winning dinner to another time."

"That's too bad." Why the hell had she said that? She

wasn't a fool. Like it or not, the two of them had chemistry. Didn't mean they had to act on the attraction. "I mean... Uh... That is..."

Cain grinned. "How about tomorrow night? I can pick you up about—"

"I don't think I feel like having fun after what happened here tonight." At least she got that out without stuttering like a teenager on her first date. The idea of sitting across from him tomorrow night, or any night, for that matter, scared her senseless. Right now, she was feeling a little vulnerable.

"You're right. How about sometime next week?"

For more than a moment, she let that idea float within her. Let the warmth and thoughts of what could be fill her with longing.

This past week had been hard enough, what with trying to keep herself from learning to like having him around. He'd showed up in her office at least once every day, usually two...three times. Made her smile. Made her laugh. Made her forget she had any qualms about being alone in the same room as him.

Then he'd cut himself on a piece of metal and she'd plunged into downright female panic mode. Got him ice. Got him antiseptic and a bandage and told him he needed stitches. She'd made a fool of herself. Never mind the fact Cain had let her take care of him like she'd been doing it for years.

That's when she'd realized how much he affected her reasoning and reactions. "You know, it's hard running a business on your own. And—"

"Stop right there." He popped the cue ball into the

table's side pocket, then stepped away from her. "Let me get this straight. First, you gave me a chance to win at pool tonight. Which I connect to our bet of me not asking you out again if I lost. Next, you kiss me. Now when I ask you out, you slam the door in my face."

"I only gave you a little kiss on the cheek."

"Coming from you, that was like a full-blown lip lock."

Footsteps on the wood floor broke into their discussion, then Marcy stepped up next to her sister. "Good, you're still here. I'm going to need a ride home since JB had to go the police station." She glanced from Betsy to Cain and back again. "I'm sorry, did I interrupt something?"

"Nope. Not a thing. Your sister was just telling me how busy she is at Peyton's." Cain pulled his keys from his pocket. "Don't worry, Betsy. I won't ask again." He turned to leave. "Good night, Marcy...Joanie."

Marcy didn't say a word, but the sideways tilt of her head said there'd be questions later.

After locking the door behind Cain, Joanie turned off all the lights except the ones near the counter. "What just happened here? I thought you and Cain were going to turn out to be the hottest item in town."

Betsy pulled her hair back into a loose ponytail with her hands as she pinched her brows together. She had to be in control. Had to be on guard. Had to take care of herself. Wasn't that what she'd done? Kept a safe distance between her and any feelings she might still harbor for the opposite sex. Especially Cain.

And ever since Earl had collapsed, visions of her Phillip kept flashing in her mind. She recalled seeing him stumble and fall when he was on a binge, but she'd never seen him stop breathing. Never had to call for Narcan.

She bit her bottom lip to keep the tremble in her chin at bay, then gave Joanie a hug. "I know you mean well, but I can't do this right now. Not after what happened here tonight." Squeezing her friend one more time, she stepped away. "Understand?"

Joanie nodded and unlocked the door. "Go on. It's been a long night for all of us."

Betsy followed Marcy out the door and heard it lock behind them. Fog from their breath formed in front of the two sisters as they walked side by side toward the car.

"You want me to drive?" Marcy asked as she pulled her jacket tight around her.

"No. I'm fine." Betsy beeped the unlock on the car, then stopped. Shivering, she quickly realized she was more than a basket case right now. She tossed her keys to her sister. "You know, I think you're right. I'll let you drive."

Marcy gave her sister a tiny hug, then pushed her toward the passenger side of the car. "It's cold out here. Get in and let me start the heat."

Once inside the car, it didn't take long for the seat warmers to beat the dashboard vents in heating up the car.

"What's this about being too busy to go out with Cain?" Marcy's tone sounded like the one their mom used when they were growing up. In fact, the same tone she still used with them even now, if the time was right. "Don't you like him?"

Betsy knew that she might as well answer the question, because once her sister started on a subject, the thread seemed to never end. Marcy had always been tenacious, not just since she'd gotten her counseling degree. In fact, that stubbornness ran in the family.

"I like Cain. I like him a lot. That's why I can't afford to let him get too close." Betsy rubbed her lips together and felt the chapped roughness. Didn't matter. "And before you ask, I do realize that you and Joanie are right that I need to move forward."

"So why not with Cain?"

Betsy pulled on her gloves, then reclined the seat a few inches. Closing her eyes, she let herself feel the emotions building inside. The ones so ready to overflow, she could hardly breathe. "Don't you understand? Cain makes me feel like I want to jump his bones."

"Nothing wrong with that."

"Oh, yeah, there is." Betsy turned off her seat warmer. "He's like a cookie sheet full of fresh-baked cookies. Once you've had one, you just can't stop."

Marcy stared straight ahead as she drove down the road. "You do realize you sound like a crazy woman, right?"

"I am not a crazy woman. A crazy woman would have said..." She threw back her head and laughed. "...Cain makes me want to wrap my legs around him and not let go till we're both sweaty and exhausted and I'm screaming his name at the top of my lungs."

"Whoa, baby. What are you waiting for, Betsy?" Marcy fanned herself with her gloved hands. "I think you need to open that big sexy gift called Cain as soon as possible. It's about time you had some happiness."

Betsy fidgeted her hands while she put a lid on the steamy emotions churning deep inside. Wouldn't take much for her to speed-dial the man and ask him over.

"What if he turns out to be different than everyone thinks he is? What if when he has a few drinks he turns into a monster?"

"You're reaching, big time. Can you really tell me you believe for one minute that Cain Connery would ever be like that? Can you?" Marcy pulled out onto the main highway and headed home.

"No." Betsy focused on the headlight path beaming down the road. "I also never thought Phillip would either. But once he got all jacked up on drugs and booze, he became someone else."

It had only taken one time, and she'd walked out the door. If she hadn't paused to grab her coat, he wouldn't have had time to stumble out behind her and grab her arm. Only took a second and a kick to his knee to put him on the ground. In her mind, she still couldn't say for sure if her jerking her arm away or his body twisting as he fell was what pushed her down the front porch steps.

She rubbed her thumb across her forearm, feeling the imprint of the pins holding the bones in her wrist together nowadays. The ones she'd broken as she braced for a fall on the concrete sidewalk that summer night. "I won't ever let that happen again."

CHAPTER TEN

Cain walked into the police station and headed straight to the sheriff's office, which for the time being had been transferred over to JB. Had it only been a week since JB had asked him to consult? He'd passed on the request, but lots had happened since that night. Too much for one small town.

"Glad you could get over here so fast." JB braced his arm on the doorframe. "From the looks of you and Betsy, I figured you might be awhile."

"Nope. She gave me my walking orders."

"What do you mean?"

"I said I'd like to see her again. She said she was busy at Peyton's." Cain shook his head. He'd been turned down before, but this time it had felt like a gut punch that buckled your knees.

"Don't give up yet. Betsy's just a complex woman."

"Complex or not, I don't need to be told again." Cain shook his head.

He grabbed a chair from the corner as Deputy Evans and Officer Kennett walked into the room.

"Okay, let's get down to why we're here." JB turned to Cain. "From your experience, what do you think?"

"From the few answers I heard as your policemen questioned Earl's friends back at Joanie's, my gut tells me they're as much in the dark as the rest of us. They don't know where Earl got the dope. Par for that age. But I'd lay odds that way over half of the students in Crayton High School know who to contact for a hit."

A shadow seemed to cross the deputy's face as his eyebrows pinched together. "My son's a freshman in high school. One of my daughters will be there next year. If there's a problem with drugs in our schools, I want it stopped now."

Cain couldn't blame Evans for putting everything in perspective from a personal level. Being a parent meant your first thought was to protect your children. Being a cop made the danger on the streets that much clearer.

JB tapped his fingers on his desk. "We all know that drugs aren't just something that comes into play the first day a kid steps through the front door of high school."

"That's right," Cain said. "Middle school and junior high are the breeding grounds for future business as far as dealers are concerned. If you dig deep enough, substance abuse falls all the way into grade school sometimes."

"Yeah, I know. Still, I hate the idea that even as a policeman I can't protect my kids from all the crap on the streets," Deputy Evans mumbled. He was a reliable, hardworking man, and when he clocked out, his family came first. So much so, he'd refused to even consider taking on the position of acting sheriff. He'd more than endorsed JB for that position. And, true to his word, he'd brought JB up to speed on Crayton.

"Kennett, check with the hospital and see when they think we'll be able to talk to Earl," JB said. "Our job right now is to get a handle on what happened tonight."

"And don't forget the incident last Saturday with Randy," Cain voiced.

"Right. In fact, let's pull all reports pertaining to drug involvement for the past six months. Break them down into two categories. Over and under eighteen."

Kennett nodded and left the room.

JB turned back. "Maybe we should embed an undercover cop from St. Louis in the high school as a student. Maybe another one as a substitute teacher."

"Might be worth talking to the school district. Get their opinion," Evans said.

The idea of a couple undercover cops for the high school might help, but Cain doubted one teacher would get much. Besides, the kids were smart. Too many new people in the mix could send up red flags to lay low and keep their mouths shut.

Kennett stepped back into the room, closing the door behind him. "Earl's been moved to ICU. From what the doctor said, he won't be talking to anyone for a while."

Cain didn't like the sound of that prognosis for Earl. Or for the police. That meant all they had to go on would be the quick lab test the hospital was running. Maybe they'd find something in Earl's car. Maybe in the bathroom at Joanie's.

"Where should we go from here?" Evans asked.

JB glanced in Cain's direction. "Any suggestions?"

"Think I'll go back to the hospital. Talk to Steven if he's still there with his dad." Cain figured the boy could use all the support he could get right now. Seeing his dad like that would be bad enough, but if he had any inkling that this was not the first time, that might be a clue to what happened tonight.

"Hard to know." Evans said. "Don't get me wrong, they're a good family. But Mr. Millerton's kind of obsessive. A little uptight. And he's a very private person. *Very* private."

"You know, first Randy, the tow truck driver OD'ed. Now Earl. Both, within a week. I think there's another question we should consider." Cain got to his feet and stretched. He'd always been a man who thought better moving around. "Have we got some bad dope out on the street?"

A short rap on the door and a quick opening caused them all to turn as Officer Hastings entered. "Call just came in from a house party over on Willow Street."

"Kids? Adults?" JB asked.

"Adults. Two throwing up on the kitchen floor. One in the bathroom passed out. Others at the party okay."

"Drugs?"

"Yes, sir." Hastings nodded. "The woman on the phone was crying. Trying to talk. Hard to understand. Someone in the background told her to shut up."

Cain's gut instinct kicked in. "That's not weed. They got some hard-core stuff going on there."

Kennett pushed past Hastings before she finished her report. Deputy Evans followed close behind. And JB followed Hastings to the front office, motioning her to take the additional squad car and head out also. Then he instructed the dispatcher to have a couple of off-duty cops meet him at Willow Street. Plus, check to see if the EMTs would need additional alarms called out.

"Come on, Cain. We need you in on this, too." JB ran out the front doors, headed to his police SUV.

"You do remember I'm just a sideline advisor, don't you?" Cain jogged alongside.

He'd heard other agents talk about how hard getting out of the business could be. How they'd been lured back in with the thrill of the chase. The adrenaline rush of tracking the dealers all the way up the ladder. Taking down a drug lieutenant or captain. Not him. He would not let that happen. He'd been too close to the edge to risk going back in.

"I know. May need to make that more permanent." JB opened the driver's side door, motioning Cain to the passenger side. "But can you honestly say you're not chomping at the bit to see where the hell this leads? Besides you owe me one."

"Owe you one? Like hell." Cain slid inside and buckled up. "More like you owe me big time, buddy."

"Maybe one."

"Two. Or have you forgot about the cabin."

JB laughed. "What's one little cabin among friends?"

"Friends like you can get a man killed." Cain pulled back inside himself to think. The banter felt good, and he rolled his shoulders to release the tension even more. Nothing wrong with helping the police. He'd just stay to the side and observe.

After a quick drive over to Willow Street, Cain walked into the house already knowing what he'd find. This might be an considered an upper-middle-class neighborhood, but drugs didn't differentiate. Money bought the same everywhere. The flashing lights of two EMT vans had only been a preamble to the stretchers waiting by the front and back doorways.

From the shocked expressions on the faces of the men and women gathered in the living room, it looked to have been a friendly get-together. Looked to be some mid-to-late thirty-somethings. Looked to be your everyday group of parents and coworkers just glad to have a night out.

This part of the group had evidently not been into the serious partying happening upstairs. A few of them looked angry. A few were crying. Some eyed the front door as if given half a chance they'd escape into the night. One problem with that idea, the patrolman stationed on the front porch. Plus, Officer Hastings didn't look like she'd allow one person to slip out the back.

He leaned in her direction. "Do we know who brought the drugs?"

"The man we found passed out upstairs. This is his house."

Paramedics were wheeling two people from the kitchen out the back door to the waiting ambulances.

"These two going to make it?" Cain asked.

The EMT nodded. "Due to some quick thinking on the part of the others, they will. But the man we found upstairs was in critical condition. We did a Level 1 triage on him first thing. Transported him straight to ER."

Officer Hastings nodded in agreement then turned in

Cain's direction once again. "We allowed his wife to ride in the front of the ambulance. Paperwork has been initiated on the initial report. And, as far as we can tell, no one has moved anything upstairs."

Cain felt the twitch at the corner of his eye, the hitch in the breath he'd just inhaled. He braced his hands against the counter and stared out the window over the sink.

JB walked up beside him and leaned back, surveying the room. "We could sure use your help on this problem."

"Not my problem this time." Cain had stayed with the DEA years longer than he should have for this very reason. He'd walked a thin line between right and wrong. He needed to pull himself out once and for all. "I'm sorry, but I can't help you."

"I know you and I talked about why you want to get out of the DEA. Believe me, I do understand. Can you at least point me in the right direction?"

"Call the DEA Division Headquarters in St. Louis. Or even the Post of Duty in Jefferson City. They'll get somebody down here fast." Cain felt like a brick building was about to fall on him. He pulled out his phone. "I'll even get you the numbers if you need them."

"I've got the damn numbers." The acting sheriff scanned the room, then focused back in Cain's direction. "You know that's not what I'm getting at. I don't have time for any bullshit right now either. Bottom line. Yes or no. Can I count on you to help us out?"

Just like clockwork. There it was. The question that would follow Cain the rest of his life. "Man, I know you need help on this. But—"

Across the room a man and woman walked in the front door, disbelief written in their expression.

"What the hell's going on here?" the man asked.

"I'm Officer Hastings. May I ask your name, sir?"

"No, you may not ask my name. This is my brother's house. Where is he?" Fear and agitation worked his tone and volume and words. "Where is he?"

"Calm down, honey. Calm down." The woman beside him pressed her palm against his shoulder as she turned to the policewoman. "My husband and the owner are brothers. Has there been an accident?"

Clearly, they had walked into this cold.

JB, Evans and an EMT gathered around them and started speaking in low tones. Cain saw the moment their worlds changed. The brother's face blanked as JB reached out to support him.

The woman began to pace, fidget with her hands, gasp for a breath. "Hospital...we need to get to the hospital, honey. Your brother...and his family...will need our support. I'm sure the police can take care of what needs to be done here."

"Yes, ma'am. We'll lock everything up when we leave," JB said.

Hastings stepped up to guide the couple out to a police cruiser. "Come with me. We'll get you to the hospital right away."

"Thank you," the man said. "I'm...I'm sorry for being... I was out of line."

"Don't you worry about that one bit. Let's get you two to your family now."

Cain had hoped to never be in the middle of that type of scene again. But here he was. *Here he was.*

JB stepped up beside him as the couple left. "I know what I'm asking of you, but—"

"I'll go back to the station. Make a few phone calls," Cain said. "See if I can come up with a plan for you. See if my boss will give permission for me to consult with the Crayton Police while I'm here in town."

"Thanks. I owe you one."

"You got that right." If things kept going the way they had since Cain got back to Crayton, he'd have a mile-high stack of IOUs from JB. Trouble was, he'd pay hell ever cashing them in. "How about you start with answering my questions from our Sunday morning conversation at the lake?"

"I don't know what you mean," JB replied.

"Give me the lowdown on Betsy? And don't look through rose-colored glasses this time."

CHAPTER ELEVEN

Eight o'clock the next morning, and once again Cain sat in the chair next to Evans and Kennett while JB sat behind his desk. All of them looked like sleep had been non-existent last night. Cain knew it had been for him. Plus, he still didn't have answers about Betsy from JB.

His DEA boss had called JB to get details on the case Crayton wanted help on at the moment. After a lengthy question and answer conversation between the three of them on a conference call, his boss agreed to Cain consulting with them.

At this point all the men sitting around him could do was brainstorm. Take the info on everything from the two events last night and see how they matched up in any way. Turn it upside-down. Shake the tree. See what, if anything, fell out.

Cain wrote down a few more details in his notes. Peyton's Automotives. Earl worked there. Kennett reached over and added that Steven sometimes picked up odd jobs around the lot.

"Are you two geniuses going to share with the rest of us?" Deputy Evans glared at Kennett and Cain, making sure his tone hit the point that there'd be no secrets.

The deputy was known for his to-the-point attitude when it came to business, but if you met him on the street during downtime, he was carefree as a kite in an uplifting lazy breeze.

"Might not be anything, but Earl works at Peyton's, and evidently his son makes spending money there, too." Cain bit the inside of his cheek as he tried to remember what all was in a report he'd recently read on drug deal targets in the Midwest.

"So?"

Cain tossed his pen on the table. "A few months ago, I read a report on drug runners using auto dealerships as drop points because it was so easy to blend in as a customer. So that scenario jumped out in my mind. You know...Peyton's, Steven, his dad, the report. I thought maybe—"

"Betsy would never tolerate anyone using her lot for drug deals. Never." The look JB shot him across the table would have leveled him if it had been a fist.

Deputy Evans pointed his pen at Cain. "You need to mark that idea right off your list."

Obviously the two men had jumped to the wrong conclusion. They seemed to think Cain was accusing Peyton's, and Betsy in particular, of being part of the whole corrupt arrangement. Nothing had been further from his mind. Innocent people unknowingly ended up in a bind all the time because of crooks surreptitiously using them to hawk their own crimes.

"That's not what I said." Cain didn't like having his words twisted. Especially where other law enforcement was concerned.

The deputy wadded up a piece of paper and made a three-point shot at the trash can in the corner. "Well, that's what it sounded like."

JB hadn't said anything further, but the clench of his jaw spoke loud and clear. What was Cain missing? What had he missed in the years he'd been gone from Crayton? But he for sure wasn't marking the idea off his list.

Kennett mumbled to himself, then folded his hands on the table. "Let me give it a try. First, as Evans and JB already know, I worked undercover up in Illinois before I moved here. At one point I was assigned to an auto dealership because we'd tracked the runners to their lot." He paused, walked over and poured himself more coffee, before taking his seat again. "I think Cain's trying to say we might be able to use Peyton's to set a trap."

The tension in JB's face eased as he glanced at Cain, then turned his attention to Kennett. "Is that where—"

"Yeah." Swallowing hard with his coffee, Kennett's hand had a slight tremble as he set his cup down.

"The same place the report talked about in Illinois?" Cain asked.

"Yeah." The patrolman straightened his collar, then stared at the wall. He intertwined his fingers in front of him, clenching them so tight they appeared to lose all blood flow.

Cain prided himself on reading people and situations. The idea that dynamics could turn on a dime or a word made sense in the world of law enforcement. This conversation was filled with enough innuendos and loopholes to sink a boat. "That went down hard, if I remember correctly. Weren't there some hostages taken at one point?"

"Yeah. The whole assignment crashed and burned. Before it was over, there were three dead."

"You closed down a drug lieutenant as I recall. At least that was something." Cain realized Evans and JB were looking down, studying the papers in front of them as if their lives depended on it. "How long ago was that?"

Kennett rubbed his thumb across the empty ring finger on his left hand. "Two years. Five months. One week. And six days."

In that moment, Cain wished he hadn't asked, because something told him Kennett could have even given a count up to the exact minute. Anyone who worked law enforcement was still a person, and sooner or later there would be an assignment that grabbed your gut and didn't let go.

He could tell Kennett had a story. Cain had stories, too. Some he never shared. Others turned his memories to scalding thoughts that never burned out.

JB smoothed the papers in front of him as if pressing wrinkles on a shirt, except there were no wrinkles. "We'll keep this open as an option, but let's see what else we've got on the table."

By the end of the next hour, the men came to a consensus that the Peyton's Automotives idea was the best plan. Even Sheriff Davis had agreed when they talked to him by speaker phone. None of them were all that happy with going the Peyton's route, but figured they'd be able to protect the lot with surveillance after hours.

Cain hadn't shared his contact with Shadow with anyone but JB. Even then, he hadn't mentioned his contact's name or any other info. Not even the exact specifics on Betsy. In fact, there really weren't many specifics to share.

"Before we go any further, we need to ask Betsy if she'll even consider the stakeout," JB said. "I'll arrange a meeting for this afternoon with Betsy at Peyton's. Evans, you don't have to do the asking, but I'd like you to be there to discuss police protection for the dealership."

The deputy nodded.

JB turned his attention toward Cain. "Since your DEA boss gave permission on you consulting with the Crayton Police Department, can you be there at three o'clock?"

"Me? I don't know about that." Cain had hoped not to be involved with the actual stakeout. Making calls had been one thing, but being part of the setup was totally different. "I've given you everything you need to carry out the job. Besides, I don't think Betsy would take kindly to me being in on an official meeting about her business."

JB braced his hands on his desk and leaned forward, glaring at Cain. "Oh, get over it. What the hell? She turned you down. Now suck it up and get on board with the plan. Or did you lose your nerve?"

Cain shot to his feet. "You better watch where you're leaning, man. 'Cause I'm not your lap dog." He walked to the door, had his hand on the knob. "We're done talking."

"Fine. I thought you were volunteering when you said there needed to be eyes on Betsy and the dealership during the work hours." JB straightened, sarcasm lacing his tone. "Guess I was wrong."

Cain slammed the door open. Stopped in the doorway. He and JB had sparred all their life. One jab after the other—football, girls, words, actions, fists. He felt the roll of his fingers inward, but he didn't tighten them. They were both grown men, each fighting to get what they wanted out of the situation. Of course, the only way JB got what he needed was if Cain agreed to work at Peyton's.

He blew out a cheek-puffing breath, then turned and walked back into the office.

"You know, you and me are this close to going a few rounds at the gym." Cain held up his thumb and index finger less than an inch apart.

"Any time." JB clenched his jaw and stared his stare. "Cut to the chase, what's it gonna be? You in on this all the way?"

A million reasons to ignore the taunt rushed through Cain's mind. Not one of them could replace the image of Betsy's smile when she thought she'd won the pool game. The way she'd kissed his cheek. Even if she didn't want to be with him, he still couldn't bring himself to desert her in what could be a dangerous situation.

"Might as well. I've already been working on my truck there. I'll keep an eye on Betsy. And I'll make sure none of the customers as much as stub their toe. The rest of this play is on the police." Cain walked out the door of the office already knowing that his last statement wouldn't hold water. He was in on everything about this case. *Everything.*

"Thanks. By the way...I owe you another one," JB shouted from the doorway.

Cain didn't even acknowledge the comment. He was too hellfire mad. At JB. At himself. And at ever coming back to Crayton.

Kicking himself for agreeing to help, he jumped into his truck and sat. He should go back in and quit right now. Tell them to get another consultant. Then again, they did need help. This time he knew the boundaries he'd set for himself. He'd known them last time too.

He turned the key in the ignition. One thing for sure, he might help the police with this stakeout, but no way in hell would he ever walk into a family drug cartel again. Never again stand in front of the head man, knowing he had slim to no chance of leaving alive. Knowing the two choices he had. Turn. Or die.

The only thing that had saved him that day had been the quick thinking of another agent so deeply embedded he'd already kissed any chance of a normal life goodbye.

Cain figured a man only had so many free passes in life, and he doubted he had any left after that night. Still, he sometimes wondered what his answer would have been if the cavalry hadn't come charging in at the last minute. Would he have traded his ethics for his life? Or his life for his reputation?

He'd never know that answer. He'd never put himself in that position again. He'd made himself a promise to *never again* risk everything.

His cell phone rang, and he answered before the first ringtone ended. "This is Cain."

"This is Joanie. I'm over at the pool and pub side of the

restaurant. I've got a special-order pizza waiting here for you."

"For me? I didn't order a pizza." Cain glanced at the clock. It was barely 9:30 on a cloudy Saturday morning. "Especially this early in the day."

"You're telling me." Joanie sighed. "Less than an hour ago, I was greeting all the breakfast customers at my café next door. Next thing I know, this guy sitting at the end of the counter slips me an envelope with your name on it and a hundred-dollar bill. Said you were a little busy last night, and he didn't get to say hello. Thought you might like a pizza first thing this morning."

Cain appreciated the gesture. "Listen it's a little early for pizza. Why don't you give that to the first customer at the bar today?"

"Don't think I can do that," Joanie said, almost as quiet as a whisper. "The man told me to double box the pizza and put the envelope between them. Said he trusted me."

Cain didn't need to ask, but he did. "Who was it?"

"Don't know his name. I just think of him as the guy in the white Stetson who orders jalapeño pizza."

"I'll be there in a couple minutes. And Joanie, I trust you, too."

CHAPTER TWELVE

Saturday, 3:00 p.m., and Betsy breathed a sigh of relief as she watched the last customer of the day drive out of Peyton's lot. Today had been especially long and stressful.

What with Earl in the hospital, they'd been short-staffed in the service center. Appointment times had backed up from the get-go. There'd been the usual roadside emergencies. Lots of people upset with the inconvenient situation. To top everything off, there were the usual just plain cranky people.

Thank goodness a few customers had rescheduled for next week when she'd offered a twenty percent discount. Saturdays were usually short days, and everyone was out by 1:00, but the employees had taken the overtime in stride.

Steven had called early that morning to let her know his dad had had a severe reaction to whatever the drugs had been laced with. The doc thought he'd pull through, but for now Earl was hooked up to a breathing machine. Steven planned to stay with his mom at the hospital.

Betsy told him family was his number one priority right now. And not to worry about his dad's lost wages, she'd make good on every cent, whether Earl worked or not. The job would be waiting for him when he recuperated. No one deserved the phone call that family had received last night.

Finished for the day, she set the alarms for the main showroom, then headed down the hall to the conference room and the police. JB had called a few hours ago asking if they could get together for a talk after Peyton's closed. She'd said sure, but still asked why. All he'd say was that there'd been a number of drug calls last night. By that time, she'd already heard five versions of the past eight hours from five different customers.

Walking into the conference room, she was surprised to see not only her brother-in-law, Acting Sheriff JB, dressed in all his spit-and-polish police uniform, and Deputy Evans, but also Cain Connery. Upon seeing her, he leaned back in his chair, crossing his arms over his chest. Guess he wasn't happy about being there either.

"Why is he here?" She stared in Cain's direction as she made eye contact with him, then moved to the chair at the end of the table. "I didn't realize there'd be anyone except the police."

"He's working on the drug case with us, so we wanted him to be here," Evans said.

"Is that a problem?" Cain braced his hands on the armrests of the chair and started to rise. "Because I can leave."

She wouldn't let him get to her, but if it weren't for the fact he might be of help to the police she'd ask him to leave.

Her business was her priority at any meeting. "No problem. If JB wants you here, there must be a reason."

One of Joanie's pizza boxes sat on the table in front of him.

He paused, lowered back down into the chair, and crossed his arms again. A bristling vibe floated between them, one she had no one to blame for but herself. Her rejection of dinner last night must have done the trick because she had the distinct impression there'd be nothing between them today but business. Probably every day for the rest of the time he was in town, too.

She'd tossed and turned most of the night, so any good news would be a bright spot in her day. Now she turned toward JB. "You said you needed to talk to me about Earl. Has there been a change this afternoon?"

"None that we've heard of," Evans said.

"Maybe no news is good news." Her statement didn't even make sense to herself. "Anyhow, you said you had a proposition for me. What's up?"

JB leaned forward. "As it stands right now, we have no idea where Earl got his dope. But one of the people at the house party last night said the owner got the goods from a salesman passing through town early that morning."

"How's the man from the party doing?" Betsy asked.

"He and the other two at that party ended up lucky. They got them to the ER in time," JB said. "Thankfully, no one else at the house party had used."

Closing her eyes, she let the implication wash over her. A feeling of déjà vu of words spoken over four years ago came rushing in. Difference was the bearer of the news. Today JB. Back then the news had come from her uncle,

Sheriff Cal Davis. She noticed JB had paused as if giving her time to process what he'd said and come to grips. Much as she grumbled at him, JB was a good man.

She glanced at Cain and was met by his noncommittal expression. What had he seen in her expression? If he thought he saw weakness, he'd be badly mistaken. That flaw of hers had been crushed years ago. She'd never be a moth drawn to an inferno ever again.

Kennett walked in and took a chair. "Sorry I'm late. It's been busy on those streets. Don't think I've eaten all day."

The patrolman reached toward the pizza box.

"Not yet." Cain double tapped his fingers on the lid, then leaned back once again.

"Well, since you said you had a proposition for me," Betsy said, "I take it you want something. And since we're meeting at Peyton's, I take it this has something to do with my dealership."

JB nodded.

"Then get to it. You know I'll do whatever's needed. What is it this time?"

Evans cleared his throat. "We'd like to—"

"Stop right there. What haven't I been told?" Cain uncrossed his arms and swiveled the chair in her direction. It wasn't as if he looked angry, but he sure as hell didn't look happy. "If one of you doesn't tell me what the elephant in the room is all about, then I want no part of this plan."

JB leaned forward in his chair. Rested his elbows on the table in front of him. "Let it be."

Cain stood, bent just enough to brace the palms of his hands on the conference table. "Not this time."

In a split second, both men were standing straight and strong. The look that passed between them held a challenge, and Betsy got the feeling neither was going to back down. Even the deputy and patrolman didn't appear to be ready to step between them.

She could swear the room had become smaller... shorter...hotter. Felt like they were all under a magnifying glass. A group of five people in a still-shot photo with only one of them in charge. Question was, who? Might be her conference room in her dealership, but she sure wasn't in charge.

"You can leave now, Cain," JB ordered.

"I could. But I'd rather talk about my pizza." He pointed toward the box sitting on the table. "The one Joanie made bright and early this morning as a special request from someone I know. Someone I trust. Someone who saved my life once, and I've saved his a time or two."

Cain flipped open the lid to reveal a large half sausage and pepperoni/half jalapeño pizza. "You may notice that it's double boxed. I've passed many a message using this technique in my career. So has my friend."

He paused, looking at JB. "Now, should I stay or go?"

"I'm listening." The acting sheriff sat. Settled back in his chair.

Carefully, Cain lifted the carton containing the pizza from the one below. Set it in front of Kennett, who immediately grabbed a slice and took his first bite. Meanwhile everyone else at the table stared at the bottom box. Nothing there but an envelope with "Cain" written on it.

Slow and easy, he looked each person in the room

straight in the eye. Seemed to be snapping each one's expression into his mind. Evaluating. Deciding. He gave Betsy an extra-long appraisal, then glanced at JB.

Cain picked up the envelope and showed them that he'd already opened it, then pulled out a folded piece of paper. "There's only one word written on here. And I'm the only one besides my friend who knows what that is."

Unfolding the note, he flipped it upward and watched it land print side up on the table. "Now I want some answers. *Who is Phillip?*"

Betsy tilted her chin up, then focused on the picture hanging on the wall at the end of the table. The one of a beach and clear blue water and colorful cabanas. Key West? St. Thomas? Barbados? Didn't matter as long as she felt the sun's warmth through the painting and heard the crash of the waves in her mind. Because she for sure didn't like the direction this conversation had headed.

"I figured you'd kept up to date on Crayton while you were gone," Betsy said.

"Nope. I've been a little busy working deep cover for years at a time." Cain quirked the side of his mouth. "What with staying alive and everything, Crayton was the furthest thing from my mind. "Who's Phillip?"

JB leaned back in his chair. "The short version is that about four, five years ago, a kid OD'd at a party here in town."

"Maybe it's the same dealer."

"Can't be. Sheriff Davis caught the guy and sent him to prison." JB spoke like a man proud of the outcome. "I was part of that sting before I left town and joined the FBI. Got a lot of bad stuff off the streets that night."

"He could have got parole by now. Old haunts are hard to leave if he's dealing again." Cain pulled a small notebook from his back pocket. "If you give me his name, I'll check him out."

"That won't be necessary." JB glanced at Betsy.

"Why?" Cain asked.

Breathing in deep, she realized he really didn't know her past. Of course, not everyone knew, but she figured he'd have pulled up her profile on the Internet. Evidently not. For some reason that made her feel good. He'd given her privacy and asked her out no matter what.

The past hadn't been easy, but she'd survived. And she wasn't ashamed of what she'd done. Not one bit. Now she needed to be the one strong enough to tell him her secrets... or at least one of them.

Betsy cleared her throat. "The man died."

Cain turned to face her. "How do you know?"

"His name was Phillip Carrington. Papa Carrington's son." She sat up straighter in her chair. "He was also my husband."

THE ELEPHANT in the room landed on Cain like a two-ton brick. He didn't know what he'd expected, but certainly not that Phillip had been her husband. "I'm sorry, Betsy. I didn't know."

"Nothing to be sorry about." Betsy pushed an escaped curl back behind her ear. "Life is what it is. Now tell me about this plan you and the police have devised."

"We may need to rethink this, since your informant has

mentioned Phillip," JB said. "Especially when you couple it with the info you got dropped on you the other night."

Cain nodded.

Kennett reached for another slice of pizza. "I would not make light of this clue. In the drug arena, names, dates, places, everything means something."

"I agree." Cain grabbed the last slice. "I'll try to get more info, but sometimes passing info is risking your life. How long has Phillip been dead?"

"Almost two years." Betsy sighed. "In fact, after his death, Papa Carrington started stopping by the Peyton's more and more. Guess it finally sank in that he didn't have much left in life, so he turned back to the business he'd previously owned."

A light went off in Cain's head. All along there'd been something throwing him off when he thought of Peyton's Automotives. The place had opened when he was still in grade school, just two or three years before Sadie, Marcy and Betsy moved to Crayton permanently, after her own dad had been killed.

Used to be called Carrington & Son New and Used Cars. He'd always found the original name strange since there'd been three partners in the beginning. Started small. Stayed small. And then suddenly expanded into an overnight success.

"What do you mean?" Playing one of his who-do-I-trust questions, Cain just wanted to make sure everyone was on the same page of information. He noticed she'd returned to staring at the beach picture, just as she had been a few minutes ago.

"He still owns a tiny percentage of Peyton's, but not

enough to make business decisions" She turned her attention back to him. "And he still has keys to the service center and this building. That way he can come and go whenever he wants. I think it gives him something to do. Of course, when he does stop by, he spends most of the time in his old office or tinkering in the service center. He's big on walking around the lot and inspecting the car trunks, also."

"Anything else?"

She shook her head slightly in aggravation. "Always carries a trash bag with him because, and I quote, 'Never know what you'll find in the crevices of the trunk. Just consider me your *double-check* cleaning valet'."

Cain got the impression she didn't appreciate the intrusion. "So how—"

The three cops' pagers vibrated at the same time. Within seconds they were all on their feet and headed to the door.

"There's been a major accident out on Highway 54. We'll have to do this another time." JB shook his head. "A hell of a lot going on around here for it being winter and no tourists."

Cain motioned to get the man's attention before he left, then stepped into the hallway with him. "Why don't I fill Betsy in on the plan? I'll give her the layout. See if she's still willing to help after she knows all the details. If so, you can call her later to finalize the arrangements."

"That'd be great. I appreciate all the help you can give us on this." JB cocked his head to the side. "And yeah, I know I should have told you about her and Phillip. But..."

"Anything else you're not telling me about Betsy?"

CHAPTER THIRTEEN

The silence said everything Cain needed to know. In hindsight, he should have kept up on Crayton. Might be too late for what had just transpired in the conference room, but tomorrow he'd spend some time on the Internet catching up on the past twelve years. He doubted Betsy would be the only one whose life had felt the ups and down of living.

JB headed down the hallway. "When she's ready she'll tell you anything else she wants you to know. Don't give up on her."

"You told me that last night."

"Well, I'm telling you again." JB let the door close behind him as he headed to the parking lot, then he suddenly popped his hand out to stop it. "And since you're all about knowing the particulars about the people you work with, me and you will talk about Kennett when I get some time."

"Way ahead of you on that one. I Googled his name and that assignment. Damn shame," Cain said.

"You got that right," JB mumbled as he let the door completely close this time.

Heading back into the conference room, Cain ran into Betsy as she was headed out. Suddenly the doorway seemed too small for the two of them. She reached out to steady herself against his chest, and he could swear he felt her heat all the way from the top of his jacket to his skin. She'd rejected his offer of dinner last night, didn't mean his body got the message.

She stepped back. "What's a shame?"

Should he tell her what he'd found out about Kennett? Part of him said follow his age-old belief to keep his mouth shut unless absolutely necessary. Another part told him she needed to know, especially if she decided to help the police with their plan for staking out her dealership.

"Why don't we talk about what the police have in mind for you and Peyton's." He swooped his hand in the direction of the conference room.

"Okay." She grabbed a bottled water from the mini fridge in the conference room and offered it to him. Plus, a small orange juice for herself. "What's the plan?"

Over the next ten minutes Cain explained the police theory on places Earl and the man at the house party might have picked up the dope. That led to the DEA report Cain had read on Midwest auto dealerships being prime targets for major drug deals.

"Long story short, JB called Sheriff Davis with an idea. Ends up, before the attempt on his life, the sheriff had already been talking to one of the DEA agents assigned to this region. They'd figured out a drug runner was marking a trail across the state. Directly through this county.

"Your uncle and the agent talked about using Peyton's to lure the guy to this area and set a trap but decided against the idea." Cain paused long enough to down his bottle of water. "At the time the DEA agent didn't think Crayton had enough of a drug problem to make it plausible the guy would even pay attention to the small town. Last night put a whole different spin on things."

Sipping on her orange juice, she seemed perfectly fine with everything being said, while he almost hoped she wouldn't agree to the stakeout. This wasn't about some small-town dealer who sold a few bags now and then. They were talking about someone big trying to move in. Someone who reported to a drug captain, or might even be the one reporting to the lieutenant in the region.

"What would I have to do?" she asked.

"You wouldn't do anything. The police, along with the help of the DEA, would handle everything. Really, half the work is done. Peyton's already has a big reputation in mid-Missouri, plus Crayton sits pretty much center of Interstate 70 and I-44."

She wandered around the room. "You know if it were just a question of my own safety, I'd say yes in a heartbeat. But I've got a lot of customers to think about."

The police had taken that into consideration when they laid out the plan back at headquarters, but for the moment he needed to let her think this through herself. Putting yourself on the line was one thing. Putting others in danger was a whole other thing. Right now, he was mad at himself for agreeing to this idea in the first place.

"Peyton's gets a lot of families who stop by to see what's new. People who've got nothing better to do on

Sunday afternoon than walk around looking at cars they'll never have the money to buy." At least she hadn't just blurted out yes without thinking about repercussions. "I need your assurance I won't be doing anything that might get them hurt."

He certainly agreed with her concerns, but didn't see them as insurmountable. At least not for the moment. "The DEA agent who'd been working with Sheriff Davis said the drug runner liked to make his deals at car lots after closing. Makes sense. Their cars would blend in with the inventory, and anyone going by would think they were customers looking at cars after hours."

"That's the problem. A lot of my customers and lookie-loos come around in the evening on the way home from work."

Cain wouldn't keep anything from her, nor would he mislead her. There were other places they could station their stakeout. Maybe not as good a spot as Peyton's, but still, other places. He didn't want her to end up in the middle of a sting gone bad. Of course, this wasn't his call. She was the one on the line.

"Sit down, Betsy. Let's talk off the record," Cain said.

"Okay." She took the chair across from him.

Cain wished he could reach out and put his hand on hers, but the table was too wide. And they were too far apart on a personal level for him to move beside her. She'd made her feelings known, and any moving forward for them would have to come from her. He didn't see that happening any time soon.

"Here's the thing," Cain said. "You know Officer Kennett."

She nodded.

"Before he moved here, he lived on the outskirts of Chicago. Worked undercover in a nearby major city. The police had a sting set up at an auto dealership to catch gun runners. Everything worked just as planned, until one of the undercovers got recognized. Things went south fast." He sucked in a breath and blew it out. "Hostages were grabbed. SWAT had to go in. Things got messy."

Cain had been in those situations. Knew the chaos hostages felt as the final moments unfolded. More than once, he'd shielded someone's body with his own and taken a bullet as payment. He swallowed down the thoughts.

"What happened?"

"The owner of the dealership was wounded. Two suspects were killed trying to escape. And two hostages were rescued." Cain paused. Sucked in a deep breath. "A woman waiting in the television lounge, after her car had been towed to the service center, was hit by a stray bullet coming through the wall behind her. She was the third fatality."

Betsy leaned her head back and stared at the ceiling before closing her eyes. "Tell me they got the rest of the gang."

"For the most part."

She glanced back across the table. "I always wondered what Kennett's story was. Figured sooner or later he'd tell people. Must have been hard being part of that. Maybe that's why he moved here and took on cruiser duty."

Cain rubbed his palm down his face. *Tell her your story. Your day. Your assignment that crashed and burned.* No. Now was not the time. Maybe never. Depending on how this case all washed out in the end. Betsy's cooperation felt genuine. But many's the time the lawbreaker thought to cover their back by working with the police or DEA or whoever was closing in on their operation.

Besides, how would telling her change his aftereffects. Dreams. Nightmares. Regrets. Losses. Self-blame. The telling would change absolutely nothing. Maybe it could help him explain his reason for the line he'll never cross? Maybe. Maybe not. That day had not been a mistake, but the memory's heavy load was hard to carry.

When had life become so difficult? That day. That second. That...

"Some takedowns go off like clockwork. Others shatter into a million pieces." His insides burned like the touch of dry ice. "They both stay with you. But one of them leaves a vise-grip on your brain."

He struggled not to divulge his worst day. Struggled and won.

Betsy eased up from her chair and reached across the table, stretching to rest her hand on top of his clinched fist. The warmth of the touch lasted only a moment, and then she leaned back in her chair.

His mind fuzzed with the thought they'd just shared a moment. What was that about? Nothing. Absolutely nothing. Friends shared moments all the time. She turned her head trying not to let him see her wipe the corners of her eyes. Friends did that too. Or maybe she knew exactly how those emotional vise-grips linger.

"Okay. I'll do it. Set up your stakeout. Pull in whatever you need." She braced her hands on the table. "Let's get the dealer who sold this dope off the street."

"Works for me." He got to his feet, shoving his hands in the pockets of his leather jacket. This was about more than the dealer. This was about the region's organization. "One more thing. Somebody needs to be in the service center to see what's going on during the day. Pick up on what's being said. See if you've got a bad apple working for you."

She stood up and met his stare. "Sounds good. I'll just tell the workers that I need someone to fill in for Earl while he's in the hospital. Who are you sending?"

"Me."

"No. You may know a little car repair, but we do big stuff around here and..." A tinge of pink brushed her cheeks. "And I'm sure you've got a lot of other things you'd rather be doing than babysitting my cars."

What would she do when she realized he'd already been hanging around the service center to protect her? He'd face that when it came.

"Can one of your other workers run the service center for a while?" Cain asked. "Then you can hire me to help out."

"Yes. In fact, I've been trying to get Earl to promote Derek Johnson. Take some of the work off himself. He just keeps saying the man's not ready." Her tone said she wasn't happy with that evaluation. "You've met him. What do you think?"

"From what I've seen, Johnson's competent, confident and careful. Exactly what a businessperson needs to be. No matter the line of work."

"I agree. So, it's settled." Betsy nodded as she picked up

the empty pizza boxes. "I'll call him tomorrow. Tell him as of Monday, he's in charge of the service center."

Cain liked the way Betsy made decisions. "Be sure to tell him I'll be around to help out on a part-time basis, too. Whatever he thinks I can handle, I'll be glad to do."

Shooting him a side-eye, she tossed the empty boxes in the trash. "You, JB and the police department are set on this plan, right down to you being around every so often. Right?"

"Yep." He grabbed the note with Phillip's name on it from the table and crumpled it into his pocket.

"Just remember, I'll pull the plug if I think my customers are in danger."

"Yep."

He'd expect nothing else. That's exactly what JB had made top priority for the police department's plan. As for himself, he planned to make Betsy's safety his top priority.

"Or my employees," she said.

"Understood."

Waiting at the conference room doorway, he leaned against the doorjamb while she finished straightening chairs. Closing blinds. Refilling the coffee tray with sugar and cream and stirs, cups and lids and assorted coffee pods. When she finally walked in his direction, a flame of heat hit his core.

Suddenly she looked at him with a touch of fear in her eyes. "Or my family. Me I risk. Family never." She bit her bottom lip to stop the quiver in her chin. "Promise me. Promise..."

Everything inside him crumbled. Why had he ever left Crayton? Left Betsy? She'd always been too honest and upright for her own good. Standing here in front of him, begging for her family, only reaffirmed nothing had changed on that front.

Shadow hadn't lied about the cartel giving him assignments to watch her at Joanie's, but he *had to be* wrong about her being a willing part of whatever was going on. Now it was Cain's job to keep her from stumbling into something she knew nothing about.

"I promise, Betsy. I'll do everything within my power to keep everyone safe." He pushed an errant strand of hair back behind her ear, then cupped her chin in his hand. "Especially you."

She didn't pull away, just looked up into his eyes as her lips slipped a sliver-of-hope apart. Slowly, he lowered his head and lightly kissed her lips. She barely returned the offer before she broke contact and clicked off the conference room lights as she walked into the main area of the dealership.

"What's the matter, Betsy? Afraid you might learn to like me?"

Following her as she locked up for the day, he made sure to watch her ritual. Noticed a few things he'd have done differently. Maybe he'd gradually mention some security improvements. Not today though.

Walking beside her across the parking lot gave him a chance to ask her some business questions. Most were easy and relaxed things about the business. Some had her making a detour to show him something specific.

Finally, as they headed back across the lot to where she always parked by the back door, she clicked the start button on her key fob. "Heat should at least take the chill off before we get there."

"That's one thing I regret not having." He glanced at his seven-year-old truck. Might not be new, but it was paid-in-full. Had a lot of miles on it though. He'd used it a few times on assignments besides a couple road trips to Alaska to visit his dad. "Might have to think about an upgrade soon."

Betsy smiled. "I know someone who can get you a good deal on a brand new, top of the line RAM or F-150." Betsy smiled as she swept her arm around the dealership as if she were a car-show model pointing out the features on the newest line.

He laughed. "I bet *you* can."

"Extended cab. Upgraded rims. Any color you want. I'll even throw in the price of the remote start."

"I'll take a raincheck on that. Once I sell the house, I may just take you up on a new one." Raising his hands in surrender, he realized just how much he'd missed the joking way he and Betsy used to banter with each other. His gut tightened... Or was this a bribe cleverly mingled in with the conversation?

"By the way, if I have any more questions about this plan, who should I contact? You? JB? Deputy Evans? Officer Kennett?"

"I'll get back for sure with you on that," he said. "For now, just make sure you've got all our numbers on speed dial. If you can't reach one of us, then push the next button until you do."

"Sounds good. See you next week." She clicked the unlock button on the driver's side door.

Resting his hand on the handle, he paused instead of opening the door. "I just wanted to say how proud I am of you. You've got a nice business here, Betsy."

"Thank you. I work hard to give the community what they need." She raised her eyebrows. "Keeping the bills paid isn't always easy, but I've been able to expand every year."

"That's a feat unto itself. Before I left town after high school, I remember this being maybe a third of this size. One of my last memories, as I was on my way out of town, was watching them bulldoze down the car lot's sign. They'd already flattened the building on the lot next door."

"A week later the new sign was installed. Lots bigger. Huge spotlights on it and" —she rolled her eyes— "the dealership's name had changed to Big Papa Carrington's Dealership. BPC for short. The next month he held a massive used car sale. You should have seen it."

"Wouldn't have mattered to me. I wasn't in the market for a new car. I was in the market for getting the heck out of Crayton."

"Oh, but there's more. A few weeks after that, BPC announced they'd signed a franchise agreement with one automotive company. And that the modernized, cutting-edge service center would be opening soon."

Cain's interest was peaking. How had that small car lot become such a thriving business so fast? The franchises weren't cheap.

"Interesting. Did he have a backer?"

"Not that anyone has ever been able to prove."

"The Carringtons never struck me as wealthy. Of course, you never know what's in a person's bank account."

"True, but he seemed to be working hard to grow the business," she said.

"Such as?"

Betsy raised her eyebrow once more. "The next month he held the first annual picnic, with free food and drinks and statewide advertising. Early October, he started his annual fall chili festival, complete with campaigning politicians to work the crowd and speak."

Cain would bet money Big Papa hadn't paid a dime for any of the food or drink. Probably made a deal with one of the political parties. "Let me guess. Only politicians he agreed with were invited to attend."

She nodded. "Representative Shorestone led the way each and every year."

"He and Carrington have always been friends, as I recall."

"Business partners for a long time, too. Even after Joanie's dad, Mr. Dash, their other partner, was killed."

Cain only vaguely remembered the crime. "That was just a few years after the three of them had pooled their money to open the car lot, right?"

"Yeah. Happened in broad daylight, right there at the original lot's location across town." She sucked in a deep breath and blew out a long sigh. "Papa C and Representative Shorestone decided to relocate after that. I heard the whole story from Joanie."

"Did they ever catch the killer?"

"No. In fact, a few years later it was declared a cold case."

"Really?"

"Yeah. It was hard on Joanie and her mom when he was

killed. A little over a year later my own dad was killed. So when we moved here permanently, Joanie and I naturally bonded as friends." Betsy voice softened into sad, and her chin briefly quivered.

Cain gauged how much to ask, how hard to push for answers. "Did they ever look into why it went cold?"

"Sounded like there weren't many clues. No security cameras. No witnesses. No fingerprints. Big Papa had been out of town on vacation, and Shorestone worked a full-time job eight-to-five Monday thru Friday. That left Mr. Dash alone to watch the lot that day."

Still standing by the car, Cain felt the wind pick up and the chill deepen. He opened the car door so she could get into the heat from the idling car.

"When did you buy the dealership?" he asked.

Her expression morphed into a serious mode as she glanced at the Peyton's Automotives sign at the entrance. Then she slid into the driver's seat and clicked her seatbelt in place.

"I didn't *buy* the business." Tossing her hat and gloves next to her purse on the passenger side, she sighed. "It was a wedding gift from Big Papa Carrington to me. Not to Phillip. Not to both of us. Can you believe that? Ninety-five percent of the dealership signed over to only me."

To say Cain was stunned was far from strong enough for what he felt in his gut. "That's a *really* nice gift."

"Yeah. I've always wondered why." She questioningly stared at him, then she turned and for a long, long moment she stared at the Peyton's sign. "Maybe we'll talk about that sometime."

She pulled the door closed. Clicked the lock. Drove away.

The glow from the illuminated Peyton's sign lit the area where he'd parked. And as he walked toward his truck, he felt himself staring at the sign, also. Peyton was Betsy's maiden name.

Ever since he'd returned to town, he'd wondered at the name on the sign. Now he knew...except he still didn't really know. Sometimes women took back their maiden names after their marriage ended. But to change the name of a well-established auto dealership was confusing. *Stunned* was definitely not a strong enough word.

What if Shadow's warning was right? Even partially right? What if Betsy was more than what she seemed? Damn, there was that nagging doubt again. Peyton's... *Peyton's*. Why Peyton's?

CHAPTER FOURTEEN

The past two weeks had gone better than Betsy expected after she agreed to let Cain work in Peyton's service center as part of the police stakeout. Never mind their kiss the night she'd first agreed.

Plus, Earl had been released from the hospital. His family had convinced him to take time off from work to get his mind and body healed, and they'd been able to get him into drug rehab. Thankfully, the company insurance would pay a good portion of the cost, and Betsy planned to pay the remainder of his medical bills. He still hadn't said where he got the drug or who gave it to him.

On top of that, she'd been at a management seminar in Anaheim, California, for the past five days. She was more than glad to be heading back home.

Today had been long, what with the flight from Los Angeles into St. Louis. Marcy, Amber and Sadie were also in St. Louis, en route to New York. They had tried to convince Betsy to stay with them until they boarded their flight tomorrow. As usual, she'd claimed she had lots of work to do back at Peyton's. Now, since she'd been up since 5:00 a.m., the over two-hour drive home to Crayton, near the Lake of the Ozarks area in the middle of Missouri, had turned into a long ordeal.

Last weekend, before she left town, she and Cain had agreed there was no reason for him to report to her daily unless a direct link had been found between the police investigation and Peyton's.

Evidently there'd been nothing new, because he had only called twice, and she'd let those go to voicemail. Then when she listened to the messages, she saw no correlation to anything she needed to be involved in, so she hadn't returned his calls.

Instead, she had talked to Derek, her newly promoted service manager. He seemed to be on top of everything. Any problems with business had been resolved or would be waiting on her desk.

The seminar was informative. The weather in California had been warm. Crayton and her past had been out of sight. Just that distance had given her time to evaluate her life for what it had become, not what had followed her for so long.

She'd even played hooky from the seminar one day. On a whim she'd made a short trip to downtown Los Angeles and strolled down the Hollywood Walk of Fame. In a crazy whim of a moment, she'd texted a picture of herself and the Chewbacca character standing on the sidewalk to Sadie, Marcy, Amber and best-friend-forever Joanie. Even to Cain.

After lunch at the Grand Central Market, she'd taken an Uber to Venice Beach with all its skateboarders and inline skaters. The younger beach vibe had turned back the clock for a brief time, so later, when she took an Uber to Santa Monica Pier to enjoy the sunset and lights, she'd ridden the Ferris wheel—twice.

That California day she felt free from all the responsibilities. Sun on face. Wind in her hair. Music and sand and waves of the ocean, all bursting with life. She'd been relaxed for the first time since Phillip's death. She'd felt alive again.

And she'd thought about Cain. About the kiss. About what it would be like to give herself to him.

Tomorrow, she planned to call him. See when he'd like that dinner she owed him. Maybe she'd even cook for him... at her house...in the evening... After dinner they could sit by the fireplace...enjoy a bottle of wine...laugh...share a few more kisses.

That was tomorrow. Right now, she was tired.

Pulling into the outskirts of Crayton, she debated whether to head directly home or stop by Peyton's. Even though her body was exhausted and all she'd eaten today was an egg sandwich and a bowl of fresh fruit for breakfast, she still opted to make a quick stop at the dealership. She'd been away long enough.

Besides it was already way past closing time, and everyone was always ready to clock out promptly at 6:00 on Saturday night. She couldn't say she blamed them though. Some days she wanted to clock out an hour after she arrived.

She pulled up to the back entrance of the showroom and grabbed the keys from her ignition. After quickly unlocking the door and deactivating the burglar alarm, she headed into her office. Maybe this had been a bad idea. Cain would not be happy that she'd been here alone. After all, there was nothing she could do this late in the day, so why not head home. Better yet, she'd take the mail and deal with it first thing in the morning when she woke up.

As she shoved the mail into one of the dealership's marketing totes, she noticed a large manila envelope propped against the back of her desk chair. Scrawled in black marker across the front were the words: BETSY PEYTON - CONFIDENTIAL - URGENT.

"Okay. Let's see what's so important." She hung her jacket on the coat rack, mumbling to no one as she sat down in the chair and opened the envelope. Surely the service manager would have called her if there'd been an emergency. Or maybe Cain had got a break and was filling her in on the findings.

She ripped open the envelope and a folded piece of paper dropped to her desk. Straightening the page, she stared at the few words written in black marker:

Dear Ms. Peyton—
Is this really the man you want working at PEYTON'S?
Have a nice day—

Reaching back inside the envelope, she pulled out a stack of photos and papers. Top picture—cocaine. Next picture—Texas mug shot of Cain Connery.

"Oh my God." She dropped the stack on her desk and gasped.

Slowly she moved the photo aside. Next was one of Cain selling dope on the street, then one of him with a suitcase full of money, and the last one, a photo of a woman who looked higher than high hanging onto Cain as he wrapped his arm around her. She had her hand wrapped around the back of his head as if she were pulling him in for a kiss. The rest of the paperwork was newspaper clippings on his arrest and the police report.

For a moment Betsy couldn't catch her breath. Cain had turned out to be just like Phillip after all. What was wrong with her? Where was her judgment when it came to men?

"Heaven help me. I nearly messed up again." She swiped her cheek, then stared at the wetness on her fingertips. Tears? Why was she crying? She never cried. Never let herself be that vulnerable. Never. But this...this was too much.

She shoved everything back in the manila envelope and headed outside. Numb to the world, she enabled the security system as she locked up and walked to her car. What should she do? Any other time she'd call JB, but he was with Marcy in St. Louis waiting to fly to New York tomorrow. Even her uncle was still receiving physical therapy rehab in St. Louis.

What were her other options? Go to Cain's house? Call the police? Both?

Unable to decide, she started the car and steered her way across the lot, headed to the other entrance/exit. A car parked next to the service center, its engine running, caught her eye and she threw on her brakes. If one of the employees had forgotten to turn off the ignition on a customer's car, there'd be heck to pay.

Quickly, she recognized it as the car that belonged to one of her lookie-loo customers. He'd been stopping by a couple times a month for well over a year now, always dreaming of the day he'd buy a brand-spanking-new car. He knew his way around the lot, and she was in no mood to chat right now, so she just waved at him as she drove past his car. He stared in return.

That wasn't the top priority on her mind now. The envelope and its contents were. She headed straight to Cain's house. There was no way she would go home without an explanation, although she doubted he'd be able to deny any of what was in the envelope.

Parking on the street in front of his house, Betsy placed a call to the police as she stepped out of her car. Her feet hit a cluster of sweet gum balls littered across the damp pavement from a nearby tree. A second later, they flipped out from under her, and she hit the ground flat on her back and hard. She should have known better than to think her day would get any better. "Dang it!"

"Crayton Police, how may I help you?" Deputy Evans answered the call. "Betsy?"

Luckily, she hadn't dropped her phone, and quickly shoved it against her ear. "Don't worry, I'm okay."

Deputy Evans at least had the courtesy not to ask what happened. "You need something?"

"I'm sitting in front of Cain's house because I've got proof that he's not who we think."

"What do you mean, proof? What kind of proof?"

She must have bumped her head because right now she wished she hadn't called the police before talking to Cain. That didn't make sense, she knew. Of course she'd needed to call the police. "Someone left me a manila envelope filled with incriminating photos and news clippings." She paused. "And a copy of an arrest report."

Evans cleared his throat. "Are you sure you know what you're looking at?"

"Of course, I'm sure. I want you to send an officer over here and arrest Cain."

"On what grounds?"

"On...uh..." She couldn't think that far ahead at the moment.

Still on her back, she stared up at the clear, star-filled January sky as wet coldness seeped through her clothes. She could now officially say she couldn't walk and talk at the same time.

"Now, Betsy, I want you to talk to Cain. Show him what you've got. Let him explain," Evans said.

"You're not going to send a cruiser, are you?"

"Not until you listen to the man. And I do mean listen." The deputy's patient tone sounded like he thought he was talking to one of his kids. Also sounded like an order.

"Fine. I'll listen. I won't like it, but I will."

"That's good. If you still want him arrested after he explains, then call me. I'll come over personally." Evans ended the call before she said good-bye.

Maybe she could just close her eyes and forget everything that had happened so far tonight. She tried...for a whole five seconds she tried. Ultimately, the contents of the manila envelope in her hand kept flashing though her mind. Then the spiky, barbed sweet gum balls poked through her blouse, prickling her flesh with stings of pain.

Where was her coat? In the car? No. The coat along with her purse and hat and gloves and sanity were back across town at Peyton's. If only she'd headed on home and waited till tomorrow to get the mail, things would have been different. No, things would still be the same, except it would be daylight.

She didn't like the dark. The dark could hide a million things. And people.

Staring at the sidewalk leading to Cain's front porch, she slowly pushed to her feet. He might have most of the people in town believing his return was the best thing to happen to Crayton, Missouri, in years, but she would not be fooled.

Rubbing her bruised backside, she limped to the front door and punched what appeared to be a new doorbell. No doubt part of his remodeling. She listened to the rolling chime from inside. No footsteps. She punched again. Still no footsteps. She glanced at the time on her phone—7:14. He wouldn't be in bed yet. Of course, technically it was the weekend, maybe he'd gone out for the evening.

She pressed long and hard on the doorbell. Then punched and punched and punched with every ounce of mad she could muster.

What if he wasn't home? What if he'd got wind that someone had made him and already left town? She'd hunt him down. Make him pay for using her place as a cover to deal.

"Cain Connery. You better answer this door. You hear me?" She punched the button one more time.

"If you want to keep that finger, you better ease off the buzzer." Heavy, to-the-point footsteps echoed through the door along with the words. The lock jiggled. Handle turned. "This better be damn important."

The door jerked open along with a jerk to her senses.

She blinked at the scowl on Cain's face, the flash of his blue eyes and the rigid line of his lips. Jeans riding low on his hips and shirtless. She struggled against the ease of her shoulders, the stretch of her neck, the part of her lips. She knew her body's reactions to mind-crashing need all too well. She clamped her lips back together.

Still her gaze scanned down from the width of his shoulders to the narrow of his waist to, heaven help her, even further. It was as if she were still seventeen and had no control over herself, not the levelheaded woman she knew herself to be.

Rivulets of water trailed from his espresso-colored hair downward, hugging the contours of the pulsing veins in his neck, spreading across his chest, tracing the swell of his abs and... The streams finally merged with the hair trailing beneath his waistband. Her imagination filled in the rest, and she struggled not to reach out and let her fingertips trace the path of one of those little drops of water.

Guess she'd interrupted his shower.

She sucked in a stutter of air and felt the heat rise in her cheeks. Returning her eyes to his face, she tried to focus enough to remember why she was standing on his porch in the first place. At this point she didn't care.

He braced his hand against the doorframe as the corners of his mouth quirked. "What's up, Betsy? Glad to see you got back okay."

With his I-take-care-of-business attitude, he impressed her. With his pure, rock-hard-and-knowing-it masculinity, he flustered the hell out of her. Plus, his expression floated somewhere between glad to see you and mad as hell. Good. She was mad, too.

She shook the manila envelope in his face. "Who do you think you are? I've worked long and hard to turn Peyton's into a place known for honesty and good deals."

He stared at her like she wasn't making sense.

Lightheaded, she wobbled, then reached out to steady herself on the side of the house. She should have grabbed a sandwich after she got off the plane back in St. Louis. "What made you think you could..."

If the world would just come back into the spotlight from its double-shadowed nauseating haze, she could continue her tirade. Maybe if she lowered her head, she'd be okay. Confused over why she was having such an intense hypoglycemic reaction, she stepped toward the swing on the porch to sit down, but her legs folded like pudding. Cain grabbed her around the waist, holding her up.

Where had she seen him do that before? Photo...the photo of him and the woman. Now, he lowered her to her knees on his front porch.

"What's the matter, Betsy?" Kneeling beside her, his voice was soft, like an echo.

Desperate to stay alert, she pushed to get away from the scent of sandalwood and testosterone his closeness held. Her stomach grumbled. Her mind fuzzed again. Giving up the fight, clammy wooziness permeated her skin with a chilly tingle as she leaned against him. Her body screamed its need for food like squealing tires firing against the go-line at the racetrack.

Cain smoothed her hair, held her close. "Are you okay?"

"It's...it's nothing. I just haven't eaten since this morning." She hated the loss of control over her body. Her emotions. But most of all, she hated being in a position where she needed to depend on someone else.

"What's got you so riled up?" His hold eased.

"You will not use my dealership to sell drugs. Got that? Take your operations elsewhere." Her voice resonated as if in a haze deep inside her head.

Two little frown lines scrunched between his eyebrows. "What are you talking about, Betsy?"

She shoved the manila envelope at his chest, and for a split second her fingers touched his skin. Her skin tingled with the feel of him while he didn't even seem to notice her touch, instead he undid the flap and let the papers and photos slide out into his hand.

His nostrils flared while he fanned the papers out like playing cards. When he got to the last page, his eyes narrowed. "Where'd you get this?"

CHAPTER FIFTEEN

Cain flexed to his feet and tried to help Betsy up, but she pushed him away and stood on her on. He glanced at the papers in his hand. How the hell had this happened? This had to be someone who'd been following him or at least keeping a dossier on him for future use. The question was who. Might have been one of the dealers he took down the day these photos were taken. Maybe their boss. Whoever it was had gotten hold of the damaging information within twenty-four hours of the takedown because after that it had all been washed by the DEA and local authorities.

Now here it was out in the open little more than six months later. Crayton must be a bigger operation than he or the police figured. Criminals usually held blackmail-worthy stuff back until a big operation called for it.

"Don't play innocent with me, Cain Connery. Or did you think no one would recognize you in this little town." She poked his bicep. "There's a lot of people spend their days on the Internet just searching for gossip. The people in Crayton aren't any different."

She poked his shoulder, swift and to the point, as if putting a period on her tirade.

His shoulder flinched and his abs jerked in reaction, then his muscles relaxed along with a clearing throat growl. Part of him hated people who thought they could get their point across by poking at him. Another part had been surprised she'd even touched him again after her reaction to the brush of her fingers on his chest. The way her lips had parted had almost done him in.

"This isn't what it seems," Cain said.

"You might as well know that I called Deputy Evans. He said I should let you explain." She held up her phone. "But he's on standby if I need to call him back."

Cain's mind raced to what might have happened with his personnel file. He'd been a DEA agent for over ten years. Stuff like this didn't just happen on a dime.

She stood on her own for a moment, then wobbled and reached for the side of the house again. He steadied her with his arm as he pushed her through the doorway and walked her to the sofa. Even this late in the day she still smelled like orange blossoms. Suddenly, what little color had returned to her face took a nosedive.

"I'm going to be sick," she moaned.

"No you're not. Not in my living room." He picked her up and headed down the hallway.

She squirmed in his arms, her long legs kicking against his side. "I can walk."

He blew out a cheek-puffing sigh and stopped. "Are you sure?"

"No." Her shoulders slumped as she leaned her head against his chest. "I need some orange juice."

"Are you diabetic?"

"No. Hypoglycemic...which means..."

"I know, I know." The usually in charge Betsy melted like ice cream in his arms. Under other circumstances good. This circumstance, bad. "Means you're supposed to eat small meals throughout the day. Keep your blood sugar up. Why didn't you stop to eat on the way back from St. Louis?"

He retraced his footsteps and detoured to the refrigerator, stood her on her feet and grabbed the bottle of juice. "Here. Drink this."

"Glass?"

Why did women always need a glass? "Open the lid and drink some juice. Do you want me to make you a sandwich?"

"No. I'll be fine." Slowly, she shook her head while intermittently gulping down some of the orange juice.

Next stop would be his bedroom since most everything else in the house was torn apart with remodeling. He pointed her in that direction and steadied her as they went. He led her to the king-sized bed and sat her down. Backing away far and fast.

She rolled to her side, tucked his pillow under her head, and curled into a fetal position right in the middle of his slept-and-left rumpled sheets. "Tell me why I shouldn't believe my eyes. And don't give me any cock-and-bull story that they aren't real."

This sure wasn't how he had imagined having Betsy in his bed. Not that he'd imagined it. Much.

In his dreams, she was soft and willing. Her sheer hazel-green eyes sparkling with laughter and desire. Her red hair spread across the pillow, free of the always-in-place band that loosely pulled it back every day. He liked the way escaped curls teased her face by mid-morning at the car lot, but the thought of letting his fingers tangle through the free silkiness ranked higher than winning a triathlon.

Another slight moan preceded Betsy opening her eyes. "I'm listening."

"The photos are real."

"See? Where's my phone?" She tried to sit up, but plopped back down, covering her eyes with her arm. "I need to call Deputy Evans back and tell him I was right. You're a drug dealer using Peyton's for your operation."

"Are you crazy?" What would possibly have given her that idea? "I am not a drug runner. Got that? Never have been. Never will be."

"How can you tell me those pictures are real one second and that you're innocent the next?"

"Because there's real. And pretend real. Understand?"

She waved her hand wildly above her head as if to include the entire universe. "Well, whatever you're into, my uncle will have your hide."

That much was true. Sheriff Davis would have at least part of his hide if anything happened to his niece on his watch. Only one thing would save Cain from a good toss under the bus. Her uncle had come up with the idea to use Peyton's, and he already knew all of Cain's background with the DEA.

"Look, Betsy, I worked deep cover for the DEA. Deep means exactly what it sounds like." He brushed his hands down the sides of his jeans. "Suffice it to say, what you see in the photos happened, but only as I worked the case. Trust me, if you went looking for that mug shot right now...it's not out there. The very next day it was cleaned from the files by the DEA."

He grabbed his cell phone from the nightstand, punched in the direct number to the police department and waited. Within seconds dispatch answered, and he didn't let them get through their spiel. "This is Cain Connery. Give me Deputy Evans, ASAP."

"What's going on, Cain?" The always serious tone of Deputy Evans filled the phone.

"You need to get over to Peyton's. We need to brush for fingerprints in Betsy's office and at all the doors." Cain paced. "And we'll need to view all the security video inside and outside."

"I'll make sure the lab guys get on it right away. Why?"

"Someone snuck in and left Betsy a manila envelope filled with info from the last DEA job I worked. The one where I was arrested so my cover wouldn't get blown."

"I figured it was something like that when she called all hyped about arresting you. She okay?"

Cain glanced at Betsy, and felt his jaw tighten. At least she was sitting on the side of the bed now, although her cat-green eyes didn't hold the sassy spark they usually flashed.

"Yeah, she's okay. Anything else you want to tell Deputy Evans, Betsy?" Cain pushed the speaker button. If he really wanted to push her buttons, he'd flat out ask if she needed the deputy to come and arrest him.

"No." Betsy headed to the adjoining bathroom, then looked back out. "Oh, I forgot to mention that one of my lookie-loo customers was at the dealership when I left. The guy who creeps me out."

"You talk to him?"

"No. I just waved as I drove by his car. He just sat there staring at me from behind the driver's side window."

Cain tensed. "What kind of car?"

"A powder blue 1995 sedan that can't remember the last time it was washed." She entered the bathroom, and a moment later he heard running water in the sink.

A sigh of relief eased from his mouth, followed by one from the deputy. If she'd mentioned a gold SUV, they'd have known their plan was working. The trouble was, drug buyers and sellers didn't like being interrupted. They liked a witness even less.

Right now, he didn't like anything about this whole stakeout scenario. Or the fact Betsy was involved. He took the call off the speaker and turned his back toward her. "Doesn't sound like the drug runner's MO that we've been able to piece together. Definitely not the car model and color."

He pulled a Glock from behind the headboard and checked the magazine before slipping it back into the quick access panel he'd built. Never hurt to have an extra hideaway gun. If the drop guy he was zeroed in on was brazen enough to show up when people were still at the car lot, then the man had no qualms about taking someone out if necessary.

Keeping one of his weapons hidden but close was a lesson Cain had learned from his first partner. Home. Truck. Job location. Wherever he planned to be for any length of time, he planted a gun. Had saved him more than once.

"Evans, it might be a good idea to get a look at what's on those cameras we installed, too."

"Already top of my list. Plus, we'll pull recordings from Betsy's own security at Peyton's. In fact, I'll have some patrolmen meet me there to take a look around the entire dealership."

Still on the phone, CAIN walked into the hall and lowered his voice as he talked to Evans. "You know, Betsy's gonna blow a gasket when we tell her we moved some cars into her lot with surveillance cameras attached."

"Yeah. But then again maybe we picked up the man in charge coming or going. All we need is one break."

At what price though? Cain had told the sheriff, the deputy and every other lawman involved in this setup that this was a case riding on top of a grenade. They all disagreed. Said he was being overprotective.

"Maybe so, but she's still not gonna be happy when you tell her."

"Don't you mean when *you* tell her." Deputy Evans chuckled.

"Don't *you* forget this is a team effort. Technically, I can end my consulting contract with the Crayton Police any time I want." Not that he would, but that was going to be his story if ever needed.

The familiar scrape of Evan's chair on the floor echoed through the receiver. "I assume you're headed back to Peyton's, so don't go off half-cocked if you get there first. We're on our way."

Cain rummaged in the clean laundry basket sitting on

the chair in the corner of his bedroom. Grabbed a pair of socks. "Don't worry, you'll be there first. I've still got to get dressed."

"What?"

"Long story." Cain shuffled into his boots. "We'll be there soon." He disconnected the call and bent down to lace them up.

The conversation had definitely not been one of his better reports. Cain grabbed a black T-shirt from the chest of drawers. He pulled it down over his head and tucked it into his jeans, then finished by raking his fingers through his still damp hair. He was ready to go. "You ready, Betsy? We need to meet the police at the lot."

"I hope you don't mind, but I used some of your mouthwash." She walked back in the bedroom with a clean scrubbed look to her face. Her hair neatly pulled back in her signature long, loose ponytail once again. "You don't happen to have any Chapstick around, do you?"

"Not hardly." He opened the closet and tossed her a sweatshirt.

"What's this for?"

He pointed at her blouse. "There's mud on the back of your top. You might want to change before we head out."

"Where are we going?"

"Like I said, we're going to meet the police at Peyton's."

She nodded and scurried back into the bathroom. "Why aren't there any doors on these rooms?"

"Stored in the spare bedroom for now." He knew he should turn away, but when she slid the blouse off, he continued to stare at her reflection in the mirror. The skin on her back flowed beneath the straps of a deep purple bra, smooth and supple with each move.

"Makes it kind of awkward for a guest." She skimmed his way-too-big shirt over her head, then turned around and caught him looking. Planting her hands on her hips, she shot him a look to cool his gut. "Or did you plan it that way?"

"Didn't plan to have an uninvited guest drop in." He grinned and knelt next to his bed, then pulled a metal box from underneath.

"What are you doing?"

He glanced over his shoulder. Standing right behind him, she stared at the now exposed ammo and pistol box as he pushed in his code. Instantly, the lid popped open, and he paused to pull and check the magazine in the Glock nestled inside, then shoved it into the black holster and strapped it on.

Good thing he had kept all his concealed carry permits, those had been one of the first things he'd showed the sheriff and JB when he got to town. They'd both told him to keep them. Maybe somewhere in the back of his mind, he'd known he'd be back in the business one way or another. So had they.

"You sure you know what to do with that?" She clutched her arms across her chest and watched every move he made.

He grinned. "Just a little bit."

"Ever had to fire one of those?"

"Yep. What about you? You ever fired a gun?"

"Uncle Cal taught all his children plus me and my sisters how to fire a gun when we were old enough to take the safety courses. Of course, my dad had already taught my mom how to shoot."

Cain nodded. He'd figured as much, but had to ask. Knowing what the person you're working with can and can't do came in handy during an emergency.

"Ever shot anyone?" Her tone was soft. Not defensive. Not antagonistic. Not hostile.

Now it was his time to ask a question and watch her reaction. "I've done a lot of things in my life. You sure you want me to answer that one?"

From the fading tension lines in her forehead, he could tell she was taking everything in. Processing. Putting two and three and four together. Coming up with more questions. Also probably coming up with some of the answers on her own.

"Sorry. I was out of line on that last question," she said.

He nodded and untucked his shirt, shoving an extra magazine into the back waistband of his jeans, then he threaded a belt through the loops and tightened it. He locked the lid before he kicked the box back under the bed.

"Excuse me." Cain brushed past her. "You ready?"

Her fingers did a slow pitter-pat on her left forearm. Impatient? No. Analyzing? Yes.

Tilting her head just a tad to the right, she released her arms, shrugged her shoulders in one impatient sigh, and wet her lips. "Okay, let's say I don't believe you're a drug runner. But somebody thinks you are. Otherwise, why would they go to such lengths to get you kicked out of Peyton's?"

"That's what I want to know. The sooner the better."

He tossed her a pair of his gloves from the hall closet as he steered her to the back door. "In case you get cold."

"Thanks." She looked confused on a lot of levels, but the Betsy he knew was back in control. The orange juice had done its job.

Whoever was jacking around with him this time didn't want him dead. At least not yet. But whatever they were up to included him. He had no idea why.

A pumped-up adrenalin rush charged through his body just like it used to every morning of his life with the DEA. For a moment, the familiar feeling of being in the zone felt good. Felt powerful. Felt like he could step over the line and disappear. He hadn't, and he wouldn't. Still, old habits were hard to break.

"We'll take my truck," he said as they exited the back door of his house.

"Good. I'm all driven out for the day." She hoisted herself into the passenger seat and snapped her seatbelt. "Cain?"

He reached across to the glove box and retrieved a couple of chocolate power bars. She followed them with her eyes, until he ripped them both open and handed one to her. Could be a long night.

"Cain?"

Ignoring her might be best right now. Sure, he had answers to probably every question she had, but they might take longer than a ten-minute ride across town. He started the truck and eased out of the driveway.

"Cain Connery?" With each syllable she poked her finger into his bicep.

"Like I said earlier, if you want to keep that finger, you

better ease it back." He shot her his best mean-guy, I'm-in-charge look. She didn't flinch. Guess ignoring her would not be easy after all.

He quirked the side of his mouth and chuckled. Might as well pull the pin and let her rip. "What do you want to know?"

"I want to know exactly what all you've done that may show up on my" —her serious expression accompanied a tone laced with a steel-edge of controlled anger— "I mean Peyton's doorstep. Who's the woman in the photo?"

"*Now* is not the time or place for that conversation. Just remember—if you're ever in a bind, do whatever you have to do to protect yourself. *Without the danger, there'd be no way to stay alive.*"

That might have sounded harsh, but there were other more important things right now. Like catching the person able to get so close to Betsy.

CHAPTER SIXTEEN

Having an uncle, brother-in-law, and stepfather all in law enforcement gave Betsy good insights on when what you saw wasn't exactly all there was to see. She was beginning to wonder what all she hadn't picked up on when all three of them had vouched for Cain. Even Officer Kennett.

"I get the feeling there are things about this stakeout that I don't know." She tensed as they turned into Peyton's lot. Police cruisers with silent flashing lights guarded the entrances. A couple more were parked among the vehicle inventory. Even a reporter from the local newspaper had taken up a spot at the edge of the lot.

"We gave you the overview of the setup. But some of the specific details are confidential." Cain scowled. "You see, part of my job is to watch out for you. Especially while you are anywhere in the vicinity of Peyton's."

She blew out a slow sigh through her rounded lips. Maybe she should have just stayed in California...or St. Louis. "I've seen you leave before me."

Cain pulled to a stop in front of the display room and office center, then shifted in his seat. "I may leave, but I stay within sight of the back door. And I follow your car all the way home, or to wherever you stop and go in."

Suddenly she realized her mouth had dropped open and her brain was sparking on nervous disbelief. As if on automatic, she pointed her finger in his direction. "No. I've never seen you anywhere behind me. *Never.*"

The corner of his mouth quirked upward in a more than cocky smirk. "What can I say? I'm good."

"That's going to stop right now."

His expression snapped into a hard set of his jaw. A narrowing of his eyes. And as the angles hardened even more, he leaned ever so slightly in her direction as he shook his head. "No, Betsy, it's not." The tone of his voice was edged with concern and determination. "Even if you decide to pull out of this operation, I'm still going to keep you on my radar."

Nothing about any of this sat right with her. She's worked hard to become a trustworthy, professional and knowledgeable automotive dealer. She's worked hard to keep the promise she'd made her dad to always take care of her mama and sisters. She'd worked hard to protect herself including defensive skills to surveillance training, plus security systems guarded her home and Peyton's.

Her shell of invincibility had taken hold in her world. She liked it that way. Yet in less than a minute, that confidence of being indestructible had shattered. Shattered in more ways than she'd ever imagined possible. Being vulnerable didn't feel right.

"Cain, I don't want to be anybody's responsibility. Not now. Not ever."

"I understand, but somebody was able to get awfully close to you. Might have even sat in your chair. Means the ante has increased. That's not something any of us wants to happen."

"Anything else?"

"First, let's see how tonight's investigation turns out." He shot her a glance that flashed somewhere between *hope that satisfies you* and *damn it, I'm screwed*. "We've known one of the higher-ups usually drives a gold Honda Accord. Thankfully that's not who you saw today."

A chill whispered through her body. A cold that wasn't the January weather. "Not today. But I've seen it before."

Cain opened the driver's side door and jumped out, then stomped toward Deputy Evans at the corner of the building. "We've got a bigger problem."

"You look like a man escaping the hell hath no fury," Evans mumbled.

Shaking his head, Cain stared into the night.

Betsy walked up beside them. "I heard that remark."

"Nice to see you, too." Deputy Evans looked like he always did—meticulous, tired, and serious. "Now what all have we got?"

She shook her head. Why didn't anyone see the problem with this scenario? Was she the only one thinking? Betsy hated when people tried to put one over on her. "Am I or am I not the owner of this car lot?"

"Yes, you are," Evans said.

"So wouldn't it have been wise to let me in on all the

particulars of the stakeout?" She paced a five-foot line back and forth, back and forth in front of the deputy. Wait till she called JB. He might be in St. Louis with Marcy and the others right now, but that didn't mean he wouldn't get an earful just the same. "Did it ever occur to you that I've had self-defense classes? That I know how to spot what doesn't belong?"

Her insides jumbled with all the times watching, hiding, running had saved her. Half the town knew what had happened to her.

"I could have been on the lookout. Told you anything out of the ordinary." Her voice hitched, even with control. "Left work when everyone else left."

"All that might sound good on the surface, but it can also make you react differently." Cain leaned against the front fender of his truck. "Right now, we can't even be sure who's on the right side of the law. I always keep that in mind when I start a case."

"Like surveilling me?"

"Like surveilling you."

"Are you implying I can't be trusted?" She stopped, turned to face him head on.

"As you so eloquently said the other night, I haven't been back in town for very long. So I'm still getting my footing on who's who now." He stared without flinching. "But understand, part of my job is keeping you safe. That's one of the reasons I'm there."

All those nights she thought he'd been working up his nerve to ask her out for dinner or a drink or a ride on his bike, he'd only been doing his job. Her lips dried with the jerk of her stomach and the grab of her heart. Only his job.

Her shoulders slumped. Immediately, a don't-let-him-see reaction caused her to straighten.

Regaining her composure, she lifted her chin. "Well, you weren't there tonight, now, were you?"

"No, I wasn't." Cain's tone narrowed to almost a growl. "But *you* weren't due back in town till tomorrow."

"Admit it." She poked her finger in his chest. "You didn't do your job. You messed up and I could have been—"

He folded his hand around her finger and held it. He leaned toward her as he stared into her eyes. "Calm down, Betsy. I've got you."

The two of them glared at each other, and when he gave an exaggerated sigh, she shot him one right back. Time he got a bit of his own medicine tossed right back at him.

She leaned into Cain's space. "That doesn't alter the fact you messed up and I could have been—"

Evans stepped between the pair. "Let's get on with this. I just pulled in a few seconds before you arrived. Give me a minute to check my people's status."

So much for grumbling. This fiasco would scare customers away or make for a boom in nosy lookers. She didn't care either way. She just wanted to go home. First thing tomorrow morning she planned to fire Cain Connery.

No need to fight the inevitable. They were the law, and she was the niece of the sheriff. As such, she should make her uncle proud. Be compliant. Make a good, clear report. And stay out of the way.

Officer Kennett walked up. Whispered in Evans' ear. Deputy Evans swiftly headed around the side of the building with Kennett close behind. Guns drawn. Cain and she followed, but the deputy paused and looked back.

"Betsy, you and Cain stay here for the time being." Evans raised his eyebrows at her. "In fact, Cain, you make sure she stays here. And find some cover just in case there are any problems. Understood?"

Cain nodded, then motioned her behind him at the side of his truck as the other two disappeared further into the dealership's property, heading toward the service center. After tossing his jacket on the seat of his truck, he unsnapped his holster and slid the gun out. She watched as he crouched into the flat-footed shooter's stance, double handing the gun. The veins on his forearms pulsed with each heartbeat as he steeled to a wall of concentration.

She stooped behind him, suddenly wishing she were any place besides here. Any place besides in the middle of a possible shoot-out. Whether she liked the idea or not, Cain was her guard and defender for the moment. Didn't mean she couldn't fire him from working at her dealership. Of course, her uncle would have the final say on whether Cain stayed in play undercover or not.

"Mr. Connery, you are no longer an employee of Peyton's." That made her feel better. "Please leave your forwarding address at the front desk tomorrow, so your final check can be mailed to you."

"Fine with me." He didn't move. "Now hush. This isn't a game, Betsy. The man who drives the gold Honda Accord has killed five people. Two of them women. Now stay down and be quiet. Just because you didn't see his car today, doesn't mean he isn't here."

Okay, she might not have been scared before, but that

information ramped her adrenalin up a few more notches. She inched closer to his side, leaning just enough to make contact with him. The muscle in his leg flinched but reset and pressed against her as if he knew she needed assurance.

"Betsy." Patrolman Kennett rounded the corner of the building. "Deputy Evans needs you at the service center."

She pushed past Cain as he holstered his gun, and the two of them crossed the lot in a few fast strides. Kennett went to join the huddle of policemen congregated around the same car she'd driven past on her way out earlier. One of the cops pointed at the line of cars parked on the pavement behind the car, then further down the service center customer pull-in lane.

On the other side of the service center entrance, Deputy Evans stood beneath one of the bright overhead lights, his face a map of concentration.

"What's wrong?" Betsy asked as she neared Evans and realized the deputy had on his clenched jaw, narrowed eyes expression. The one that meant business. All business. Seemed to be a lot of that happening tonight.

"Earlier, you said you waved at a customer..." —Evans flipped a couple pages in his small spiral notebook — "...you referred to him as a lookie-loo— sitting in a blue sedan."

"Yes. I called him that because he was here so often looking at cars. Months ago, he told me he couldn't afford one, but just enjoyed stopping on his way home from work to look around."

Evans scribbled on the page. "Did you happen to notice if the passenger side window was shattered?"

"No. I wasn't on that side of the car when I drove pass."

"Anything else seem out of line with him? With the car?"

"No. Just the fact he didn't acknowledge me at all when I waved." Betsy tried to remember anything that might help. "Why?"

"What time would that have been?" he asked.

Time? She had no idea what time it was even now. "Maybe—"

"Evans!" Kennett shouted as he straight-arm waved from the other end of the lot, then pointed at a dumpster.

"Wait here." The deputy hurriedly walked in that direction, pausing only long enough to point other patrolmen toward the customer's car.

She scanned the inventory again, then looked at Cain's questioning profile. "I wonder what's going on down there?" she asked.

"Don't know. Probably just need to piece together what happened to that car."

He hadn't blinked. Hadn't thought about it. Hadn't faltered one bit. Yet she noticed something about his stance had tensed. A second later his phone rang. "Yeah?"

Another second later, he jerked his head up as he turned in the direction of Deputy Evans and Kennett. Shoving the phone in his pocket, he ran in the same direction. "Stay where you are, Betsy."

"What's wrong? Did they find something?" She ran behind him.

"Go back. I told you to stay there."

She kept pace with him. "Why?"

"We've got a dead body in the dumpster."

Never flinching. Never slowing. She processed the information like a true lawman's relative. Faced the statement and its implications head on. Her car lot had just become a crime scene, yet she'd kept her emotions intact.

Cain reached the container and hoisted himself to a straight-arm brace on the rim. Too short to see anything but the top part of the trash bin, Betsy dragged a ready-for-recycle tire over next to Cain. She stepped on top and peered into the dumpster.

A chill ravaged her body, and this time she gagged. Could this night get any worse? Hell no. Well maybe. Oh, hell yes. Nighttime could always get worse. Bad things happened to people at night. She knew that for a fact.

Shaking her head, she steadied herself against the metal of the dumpster. "That...that's him."

"Who?" Cain asked.

"The customer. Someone's killed my creepy lookie-loo customer."

CHAPTER SEVENTEEN

Betsy flung her hand out to push the snooze button. How could it be time to get up already? With all the police questions and the coroner's removal of the body, she hadn't made it home till after midnight. Hadn't crawled into bed till almost two. She pounded the snooze button again. Why the heck wouldn't the noise stop?

The noise stopped and was immediately replaced with the distant sound of her outgoing message on her answering machine. *Guess the noise had been her phone.* She glanced at the dial on her clock. Who the heck would be calling at five in the morning on a Sunday? The phone on the nightstand rang anew just as the cell phone which she kept next to her pillow at night vibrated.

Without looking for caller ID, she flicked the cell phone on to speaker phone. "Leave me alone. I need some sleep."

"So do I. Not gonna happen any time soon."

"Cain?"

Betsy rolled to her back and stared at the ceiling. He

sounded wide awake and agitated. As he'd said yesterday when she'd hung on his doorbell, this better be good. She wasn't in the mood for any more of his questions. "What do you want?"

The phone on the nightstand stopped ringing.

"Throw some clothes on and meet me at your front door in five minutes." A phone in Cain's background rang and he answered. "I've got her on the cell. We're on our way."

She closed her eyes, tugging the blanket over her shoulders. On their way? She wasn't going anywhere right now except back to sleep. "This will have to wait till later. Bye."

Click.

She snuggled deeper into the covers. Her cell phone rang again...once more, she pushed the speaker phone button. "What? What do you want?"

"Don't you dare hang up on me again, Betsy." Cain barked the order loud and clear. "Every burglar alarm at your car lot is going off full blast. The police called me when you didn't answer."

Her feet hit the floor a second after her eyes popped open. Every nerve in her body was awake now. "Why would—"

"No time for questions. Just get dressed. I'll pick you up in five minutes." A door slammed behind Cain's voice. "I'm heading out now. Wait inside. By the way, Crayton Police has already checked your security camera footage from yesterday. A gold Honda Accord had pulled out of Peyton's lot about a minute before you arrived."

Quick and to the point, she dressed, gargled, and

zipped her jacket into place. Grabbing a couple small bottles of orange juice from the fridge, she headed to the front door and stepped outside. She set the alarm and pulled the door closed behind her. This way she'd be ready to run to the end of the driveway as soon as she saw Cain's truck lights round the corner.

She wrapped her coat tighter and shivered with the morning cold. The crisp air flared through her nose as the memory of another night flashed in her mind. Another time she'd stood on her front porch waiting.

Waiting for the police. Waiting for protection. Waiting to survive.

A cold tremble overtook her as she rubbed her gloved hand back and forth on her coat-covered forearm. Her breaths barrel-rolled out through her parted lips and into the cold, fogging the air around her face. At least she wasn't in pain tonight.

The pine tree at the corner of the house creaked as a hunk of leftover snow from last week's storm tumbled to the ground. Where was Cain? He'd said five minutes. Her watch showed that was six minutes ago. Of course, he'd also told her to stay inside, but she figured the sooner she ran to the truck, the sooner they'd get to Peyton's.

She jumped at the sound of a thud against the side of the house. Then another thud closer to the front of the house. A footstep-like crunch shivered through the night along with more falling snow from the pine.

"Who's there?" What a thing to ask. If someone was there, which they weren't, would they have answered? Not likely.

She should have done what Cain said. Stayed inside.

Kept the doors locked. But just like years ago, she'd run outside. That time she'd had no other option than to leave the house and hide in the dark.

A scrape of pine branches sounded against the siding. Strange. There wasn't any wind. Why had it moved this time? Maybe someone was there after all. Did she stand a chance at unlocking the door? Getting back inside?

She glanced at her keys. At the lock. Where are you, Cain? Where are you?

A crisp, closer, crunchy step pulled her back to stay-alive mode. She clutched her keys in her palm, one key pointing outward between her fingers. Where was the mace? Where was the canister she always carried in her purse?

Her warm insides shivered. "I said, who's there?"

Another crunch. And another. And...

The roar of a truck's motor barreled down the street, coming in her direction. Cain? Please be Cain. She stumbled down the steps and ran to the curb, waving her arms in the glare of the headlights.

Reaching for the door handle before the truck even stopped, the jolt of her panic attack reached the crest and began a fast free fall back down. She sucked in a breath as she climbed into the truck cab before glancing back at her front porch. Counting to ten, she slowed each breath, then closed her eyes and focused on the dashboard.

Strange to think that even after being panic free for over a year, the stress of darkness and the danger happening at her car lot had triggered an attack. Should she tell Cain what she'd heard? No, make that what she *thought* she'd heard. Panic had got the best of her, but no one had been there. She was sure. *Absolutely sure.*

Nothing but memories of a night years ago. Memories she refused to let take hold of her life.

CAIN FELT his brow bunch as he spotted Betsy running to the curb. She looked like a woman scared for her life. He slammed on the brakes, but before he could jump from the truck cab, she flung the passenger door open and climbed inside. Glancing back over her shoulder, she slammed the door closed, then popped the seatbelt in place.

"What's wrong?" He braced his arm across the back of the seat, narrowing his focus to try and see whatever had her spooked.

"Nothing. Nothing's wrong. I'm just cold." She shook her head. "Let's go."

"I told you to stay inside." Cain flicked the heat to high. Something told him she had been scared. Scared as hell. Of what? "You're trembling."

Shucking her gloves, she rubbed her palms back and forth in front of the vent. "You're late."

He pulled away from the curb with one final look over his shoulder.

She scrounged in her oversized purse and produced the two bottles of orange juice, opening his before handing it to him. "Why would all the alarms at Peyton's be going off at once?"

Evading another explanation about information he'd

withheld, he chugged the small bottle dry. He'd kept her in the dark this long, what was two more minutes.

"You're ignoring me." Swallowing the last drop of juice, Betsy stretched her neck, straining to catch the glow of Peyton's lights above the Main Street business district.

Her place sat across the street from Davis Hardware, at the opposite end of town from Joanie's Pizza, Pub and Pool Room.

Cain took the last turn on a dime, and the dealership lights came into full view along with an armada of local police and highway patrol cars. He doubted this was normal procedure for an alarm call in Crayton, Missouri. Something must have happened between the last time he talked to Deputy Evans and the time it took him to get here.

A cop waved them through the roadblock. Another stopped them at the lot's perimeter.

"Why are there so many police cars?" Betsy unbuckled her seatbelt before the truck even stopped.

He didn't answer because he didn't know. And he didn't plan to lie to her again.

She slid from the truck and ran toward Deputy Evans and Patrolman Kennett. Cain stayed right beside her, his gaze scanning the lot. The sight of flashing ambulance lights behind the service center didn't bode well for everything still being status quo. Betsy started in that direction, but the deputy grabbed her by the shoulder as he ended his call.

"Let me go. This is my business. I'll go where I please." She jerked to pull away.

Evans released his hold but stepped in front of her as

Kennett angled to one side. Cain stepped up enough to pin her in on his side. He didn't like the feel of the situation. Didn't like putting Betsy in a box either.

"What's up?" Cain cringed inside.

Betsy peered over the shoulders of the men. "Why the ambulance? Has someone been hurt?"

Deputy Evans clenched his jaw as he nodded. "Papa Carrington."

Cain had spent the last few weeks getting to know the previous owner better on the few occasions the man came into the service center. One day he'd said he liked having a place to go when he woke up early or couldn't sleep. The older man mentioned he liked to come in and piddle around, as he'd called it. Could be Carrington might have stumbled and fell. Injured himself on equipment. But from the lit-up version of the dealership's lot, Cain figured that wasn't the case.

"Let me see him. How bad is he hurt?" Betsy begged. "You know he's not as steady on his feet as he used to be. Not as young. Now he's gone and got hurt." She sniffled, blinking back her emotions. "At least he had sense to pull the alarm."

"There's more to it than that. Evidently, Mr. Carrington walked in on someone who hadn't counted on anyone else being there," Evans said.

"Didn't he know better than to walk through a cordoned-off crime scene?" Cain wondered aloud.

He hadn't liked Deputy Evans telling him to stay behind earlier in the evening to protect Betsy, but in that case Cain had understood. He wasn't part of the Crayton Police Department. He was just a consultant, he'd reminded himself. Not the lead agent, investigator or whatever was needed. He grumbled under his breath. Not being the lead would take getting used to. Or not.

But things had evidently been overlooked earlier. Carrington got hurt because Cain hadn't spoken up. Well, his silence had ended. He would keep living his life the same way he always had. Up front and in your face when need be. "Well? Wasn't there a patrol car watching the crime scene tonight?"

The deputy winced in a half nod, half shrug. "We only taped off the back half of the car lot. Once we narrowed the trail of blood from the dumpster to the point of the attack, the patrol car parked around back, too. Besides, everybody in town knows Papa C doesn't stop until after church on the Sundays." Evans glanced at Betsy. "And no one..."

"And no one called to tell him about last night because I said not to worry him." Looking upward, Betsy puffed her cheeks in a self-blaming sigh. "Told you I'd talk to him this morning before church."

Cain didn't buy this one bit. "Still doesn't explain why he wouldn't have seen the yellow tape when he pulled around back to park his car. Why wouldn't he have called you? Asked what's going on?"

She sighed again, clearly frustrated with herself and his questions. "Because, Papa C doesn't drive much in the dark any more. So most times when he has trouble sleeping, he calls an Uber to drop him off. Then one of us take him home later in the day."

The howl of whooshing winter wind blew through the pathway of the cars and trucks and motorhomes lined up for sale. Mid-Missouri in January and February could mean everything from freezing rain and snow to shorts weather and a warm breeze. From the looks of this morning, the weather forecast for a light wintery mix might be right.

Betsy scrunched her shoulders against the cold as she pushed to get past the group, but the deputy stood his ground. "Let's go inside where it's warmer."

Like a barricade against the enemy's charge, Cain and the police didn't give an inch to her demand. This might be her property, but his priority number one was keeping her safe.

"So, what have we got? A robbery?" Cain hoped for a simple explanation more than he hoped for a profit on the sale of his house. He doubted he'd get either any time soon.

Deputy Evans pulled his notepad from his pocket. "From what we've seen so far, robbery wasn't the mission."

The paramedics emerged from the service center building, pushing the stretcher toward the back of the ambulance. Betsy slipped around the men and took off running in the direction of her injured father-in-law. Cain figured there was no stopping her, so he followed in her footsteps to the other end of the lot, Deputy Evans close behind. The paramedics slammed the ambulance door closed a moment before she got there.

"Open that door." Betsy reached for the handle. "I need to talk to Papa C."

"Ms. Peyton, we need to get him to the hospital." The ambulance driver gently pushed her away from the vehicle, then jumped behind the wheel. "Besides, he's not even conscious. Lucky to be alive from the hit he took to the side of his head." The driver shifted into gear and sped away, sirens blaring.

Betsy pulled her cell from her pocket, then stared at it as if not knowing what to do.

"I'll have the office call Uber to see if we can get a better idea of timeframes." Evans stepped up beside her, blocking her path to the service center. "Now, there's just a few questions I need to ask about the lot."

Kennett walked in front of Cain, motioning toward the service center door. He followed the patrolman while the deputy kept Betsy busy with his unnecessary questions. Going to be a long day.

CHAPTER EIGHTEEN

Cain followed Kennett through the back door to the service center door and stopped. The place had been ransacked. No. Ransacked wasn't a strong enough word for what panned out in front of him. "What the hell?"

"Good question." The patrolman narrowed his focus to a blood-covered crowbar on the concrete floor.

Tires sprawled like obstacles on a football training field, blocking pathways, as Cain made his way further inside the shop. Wrenches and ratchets and gauges lay in heaps next to overturned tool chests. Cut air gun hoses dangled like vines in a jungle, their apparatus smashed through windshields of cars pulled inside to be to be ready for early morning service. Even the cars had been ransacked.

This wasn't a robbery gone bad. Someone had been looking for something. Something they figured was hidden in this building. Not a random act of a quick grab-and-run with enough to trade for a bag on the street either. This was a big money hit.

A gasp caught his attention. Knowing it had to be

Betsy coming into the building, he turned to gauge her reaction. He wanted to be sure she understood the danger lurking around this hit. From the look on her face, she understood.

"Don't touch anything, Betsy," Cain shouted.

She nodded. "I understand."

With a look of shell-shock and bewilderment, she made her way through the maze of catastrophe littering the building. She scanned the space from floor to ceiling, side to side, stepping around the police busily tagging and photographing the scene.

At the sight of the bloody crowbar being bagged for evidence, her expression changed. Now she was mad. Mad as hell. That could be dangerous for her. Could be dangerous for him protecting her. Because like it or not, they were going to be a pair until this was solved.

He met her in the middle of the building. "You okay?"

She raised her eyes to his. "Why didn't they just take what they wanted and leave? Why tear everything apart? The most expensive tool or car on the lot isn't worth Papa C getting hurt."

"Anger. Greed." Cain swallowed the thought of what would have happened if Betsy had been there. "Fear."

"I don't understand."

He steered her behind Deputy Evans as he led the way back outside and headed toward the main building. She wrapped her coat tight against the cold for the half-block walk.

Evans' steps were firm and all business. "Whoever did this was searching for something."

"And they're mad as hell they didn't find it." Cain was mad, too.

Kennett followed close behind. "Mad enough to make a point with a man's life."

"Or..." Cain's gut tensed with a warning. "...did Carrington recognize someone in the bunch. I'm not telling you your job, Deputy Evans, but you might want to put a guard outside his hospital door."

"Agreed." Evans motioned to Kennett to get that in place. "Check to see when the doctors think we'll be able to talk to Papa C."

"Got it." Kennett stopped as he made phone calls.

"But what could they possibly think I have worth this much destruction?" Betsy asked.

"I'm just speculating here, but last night could have been about a drug deal gone bad. And if the thugs didn't get what they wanted, they may think you've got the money or goods that were in play with the lookie-loo's death," Cain answered. He ran through the DEA checklist in his mind as they walked across the lot.

He had to make sure he didn't miss anything. Not being in the Agency or on the police force, he wouldn't have as much access to evidence, so he needed to stay alert right now.

"I don't have whatever they want." She hadn't missed a beat with her answer. "Besides, why would they think it's hidden at the dealership?"

"That's what we've got to figure out. And that's why it's important that I'm in place at the dealership. Makes it easier to spot someone working on the inside.

Entering the main dealership building, they were met

with the same destructive search scene. Cain and Betsy made their own pathway through the display room as Deputy Evans and Kennett disappeared down the hall leading to her office. Every vehicle had been vandalized. Seats sliced. Door panels ripped open. Trunks ravaged. She shook her head as they kept walking toward the business area.

The two lawmen stood in the center of the hallway.

"We haven't moved anything in your office yet, so don't go all the way in," Kennett cautioned, shooting a quick shake of his head at Cain. "In fact, why don't you wait out here, ma'am. I'll catalog and bring you anything you absolutely have to have right now."

This time there was no smart remark about being called ma'am, Betsy just pushed past the officer. "Don't be silly. I won't touch anything. I'd just like to see for myself what the—"

She stumbled backward and spun around, crashing into Cain's chest. On reflex he folded her against him. Held tighter when she clutched his shirt, then leaned enough to see inside her office.

Every muscle in his body tensed. The bastard had left calling cards of spray paint. First wall—*Where's my money?* Second wall—*I want my goods!* Third wall—*Don't make me ask again!*

Guiding her back outside into the cold night air, Cain kept a grip on her, and on his emotions. He'd seen this over-the-edge anger search plenty of times during his career. Didn't have to be the same man to have the same personality. Evidently, something of value had gone missing. From Cain's experience, if the item or items—

money, drugs, information, blackmail list, etc.—didn't show up soon, then things would only get worse.

"Breathe, Betsy. Just breathe." Cain rubbed his palm in circles between her shoulder blades. "I've got you. No one's going to hurt you."

"But...but..." Her jerky little not-gonna-happen sobs tapped against his chest.

He held tighter. "Not now. Not ever, I promise."

Yeah, she was one tough cookie. But even a strong person had a pressure valve. Last night and now were enough to raise anybody's emotions to the boiling point. She'd be okay. Give her a little time and she'd be tough as titanium once again.

No one said a word as she calmed down, easing her breathing back to normal. The dealership's lights deactivated with the first rays of sunrise. Distant bells from All Souls Catholic Church tolled the hour. Another day of chaos loomed on the horizon.

She stepped back from his hold.

Cain felt partly responsible. He should have made her take the time to go to the police station last night to look at photos. To see if she'd had other not-so-nice visitors at the lot posing as customers. They should have viewed the security video. Although, he'd bet money that this guy knew the placement of every camera view of the lot.

Evans cleared his throat. "Are you thinking what I'm thinking?"

"That whatever drug deal was happening last night, didn't get finished. And somebody thinks the stash is still here."

The deputy nodded. "By the way, I've already called JB and the sheriff."

Cain braced his hand against the side of the building. Thinking. Analyzing. Step by step, he worked through the last few hours. What was he missing?

"What time did the first alarm come in?" Evans asked Kennett.

"About—"

Cain snapped his fingers. "That's it. That's the missing cog."

He motioned Betsy to his truck as he took off running for the driver's side. "Why would the jerk set off all the alarms when he'd just worked for hours ripping everything apart without setting off the system?"

"One reason. He wanted us here!" Kennett shouted as he raced toward his patrol car.

"Right. He made the alarms go off on purpose. I'll lay you odds we find him at Betsy's house." Cain pulled his Glock from the holster and laid it on the console as he jumped into the cab of his truck. In the background, he heard Evans calling for backup.

Betsy jumped in the passenger seat of Cain's truck and buckled up. Any shock and fear she'd felt five minutes ago had disappeared. In its place was the cold determination of a woman analyzing everything that was happening.

Years back, Cain had worked an undercover job where everyone talked about a man who used alarms to get people where he wanted them to go. That was his routine. His tag. His MO. If he was still around, he would likely still have the same routine. And every agent, lawman and private investigator worth their money knew one thing for sure: Routines got people caught.

Follow the routine. Catch the perp.

Only one problem. He'd worked for the same high level "importers" Cain had been sent undercover to infiltrate back then. At that time, the drug runner had been small potatoes. Now? By now, he'd have worked his way up the ladder. Might even be the ace. That meant he'd be more than dangerous. The man had too much to lose to fail.

Cain glanced in Betsy's direction. "When we get to your house, I want you to stay in the truck. Got it?"

Betsy nodded.

"I'm serious." Racing across town, he stayed on the bumper of the siren-off, lights-flashing deputy's car. "I can't be worried about you when I go inside. Understand?"

"I understand. I'll stay in the truck, but—"

"No buts."

Cain considered stopping long enough to drop her beside the road. That might be the only way to keep her out of range of flying bullets. Then again, he couldn't leave her alone either. She was the target right now.

Betsy sucked in a breath and exhaled long. "He was there."

"What do you mean? Who? Where?"

"Before you picked me up. While I was waiting on the porch." Her fingers trembled as she warmed them in front of the heat vent on the dashboard. "I thought I heard footsteps in the snow. By the side of the house."

Cain clenched his jaw. "Why didn't you tell me that when you got in the truck?"

"I thought I imagined the sound. Thought I was remembering..." She stared out the side window.

"Remembering what?"

She rotated back to face him. "Nothing. I just thought it was my imagination. Besides, why wouldn't he have grabbed me while he had the chance?"

Because the jerk liked to play games. Taunt his prey with his power. Play God with their lives.

Cain pulled to a stop in front of her house. "Which end of the house were the sounds?"

She pointed toward the right. "By the big pine tree."

Grabbing his gun, he jumped from the truck. "Lock the doors and stay in here."

She nodded.

"And if you need it, there's a gun hidden in a compartment at the back of the glove box."

She nodded again. "Don't worry. I won't get out."

Crouching, Deputy Evans, Officer Hastings and Cain started across the front yard as Kennett led other cops in through the back. Likely the thugs had already come and gone. Cain angled toward the pine at the corner of the house and glanced beneath the boughs.

Footprints in the fallen snow. The jerk had scared her. Then let her go. Why?

Because no one knew for sure who he was, what he looked like. At least, not yet. Basically, all the drug runner wanted was his money, his drugs and his hidden identify. That way he could hide in plain view and never be caught. Could be anybody, on any street, in any town.

Cain knew she didn't have whatever the man was looking for. But the guy wouldn't give up. The biggest problem was that she didn't have his money or his goods. In fact, she had nothing to save herself. Cain had nothing to save her either. Nothing except himself and his gun.

What could have possibly made him think leaving the DEA would mean a nice, peaceful life. He still hadn't officially resigned, but he had options at least. Good news, he'd bought a swing for the front porch. Bad news, he just wasn't built to sit on a porch. He chambered a bullet as he started into Betsy's house.

Maybe he should consider this as the first day of his new private security firm. Should be interesting—if he didn't end up dead.

CHAPTER NINETEEN

Close to twenty minutes later, Betsy ached to get out of Cain's truck. To race across her front yard. To see for herself why every cop who walked out the front door didn't have the nerve to look in her direction. But she wouldn't. She'd keep her word to stay put.

Rummaging in her pocket, she realized she hadn't bothered to check her phone messages after setting it to vibrate back at the car lot. She scrolled down her list of missed phone calls—Sheriff Davis, JB, Marcy, Marcy, Marcy, Sadie, Marcy, Marcy, Sadie, Marcy. Her family didn't know the meaning of "give up." Never had. Never would. Betsy clicked the volume back to ring just as Marcy called again.

"You know you are being one persistent pain," Marcy said. "And don't try to tell me nothing's wrong. JB got a call from Deputy Evans earlier. Went straight into the bathroom, locked the door and turned on the shower to keep me from hearing. I hate it when he does that. Hate it."

Betsy knew there was no need to expect anything less

from her sister. Heck, if the situation were reversed, she'd be just as determined to get through, too.

"Well, if you ask me, your husband always takes everything way too serious." Betsy wouldn't tell her that for once he had a right to be worried. And for once she wished he were in town instead of in St. Louis, waiting to take her sisters and mama to the airport to catch a plane for New York. "Are you all at the airport yet?"

"Don't you pull that with me, sister of mine. You are not going to change the subject." Marcy paused. Blew out a sigh. "Betsy, JB took off back to Crayton well over two hours ago. Told us to get a shuttle to the airport. Now why did the deputy call?"

If JB hadn't wanted to ruin the women's trip, then far be it from her to say anything that might make them grab a rental car and head straight back home. "How would I know what all goes on in the Crayton Police Department? Heck, did you know Cain Connery hired on at my business just so he could stake out the car lot to catch a drug runner?"

"So did he capture the guy?"

Cain stepped out the front door of her house and started toward the truck. At least he looked her in the eye.

She unlocked the truck door and slid out. "Marcy, I've got to go. Enjoy your trip and say hello to Broadway for me. Tell Sadie and Amber, I miss them already. Miss you, too, sister of mine. Love you all forever."

Ending the call before there were any more questions, she headed to the front door of her house. Halfway there, she stopped in front of Cain.

"It's not pretty in there." He stared into her eyes with a warning look. And warmth. "You ready to go in?"

"I'm always ready." *Except when I'm not.* "Let's go."

"Remember. Don't touch anything inside or out," Officer Hastings said, wearing gloves as she held the front storm door open for them. "Forensics will be here most of the day."

"Got it. How's my car in the garage?"

He shook his head. "Let's just say, it's not pretty."

Betsy tightened her hair back in the scrunchie, straightened her stance and sighed heavily. Ready to face whatever came, she stepped into her home, the one that had been nice and neat when she'd arrived home late last night from California and the crime scene at Peyton's.

The home had promised a welcoming respite as she raced out the door a little over an hour ago. Now all it offered was a view of what was left of her living room furniture and wine stains running down the far wall. Broken bottles littered the carpet below.

The fresh scent left behind after yesterday's weekly cleaning had been replaced with the scent of spray paint, but there weren't any words written on the walls so maybe her senses were flashing back to the service center. Glancing across her open floor plan to the kitchen, the smell of pickle juice—lots of pickle juice—was easy to identify. Her refrigerator lay tipped forward onto the floor. The door had been opened prior to the catastrophe, and contents were broken and scattered across the floor.

That was the last straw.

"Son of a biscuit!" Bracing her hands on her hips, she

briefly turned toward Cain. "This is a great how do you do. I mean, what am I supposed to make of—"

"Don't worry about it. We'll take care of all this later." He half grinned "But I'd say you're going to need a new sofa for starters."

"Really?" she sarcastically sassed as she headed toward Deputy Evans standing at the entrance to her bedroom. "You look like you're waiting for me."

The deputy nodded as he stepped aside and motioned her forward. "Sorry to make you do this, Betsy, and I know it won't be easy. But I'd really appreciate your help."

Suddenly she felt alone. All alone and vulnerable. She didn't want to be alone to face whatever was waiting for her. "Is it bad, Cain?"

He moved closer. "There's not a body, if that's what you're asking. But the thugs haven't left any stones unturned when it comes to emotions."

His tone was ominous, and suddenly she felt cold. Nauseous without knowing why.

The deputy stepped back in front of the door. "That's okay, Betsy. You don't have to do this. It'll be easier if we take photos and review them back at the office."

"No," she whispered. "I'll be okay. How bad can it be?"

She stared at the floor. Swiped the palms of her hands slowly down her cheeks. Let the memories flood her mind, then shoved them aside. Through the years, a lot of things had happened in that bedroom. She'd faced them all and survived. What was one more?

Looking back over her shoulder, she held out her hand toward Cain. "You coming with me?"

"I'm right beside you, Betsy. All the way." Cain wrapped his fingers through hers and held tight as she gripped his in return.

His DEA background was so deeply instilled in him, he couldn't help but still watch for her reactions. Still keep her and Peyton's on his Persons of Interest list. Still be wary of everything Shadow had told him that first night. Plus, Cain planned to check with a handwriting expert, make sure surveillance videos from Crayton were able to alibi what was being said, and trace recent spray paint purchases.

Betsy had told him right from the beginning that she wasn't who she used to be. And neither was Crayton. That, mixed with Shadow's warnings, had put a nagging doubt in his mind. Everything that had happened the past couple of days screamed she was a target. Yet his training warned him to remember that things weren't always what they seemed. People sometimes wore unseen masks. Verify everything yourself.

He was willing to put his life and reputation on the line for her, but he wished like hell she hadn't put the doubt in his mind. This case was only going to get worse, but no matter what happened in the next few days, they'd face everything as one. Good or bad. Real or staged. All the way to the final chase, bullet or breath.

After that, only time would tell. She wasn't asking for the future. He wasn't expecting anything specific in return. Right now, keeping her safe was all that counted. That and keeping himself alive.

They followed the deputy into her bedroom where Officer Kennett was directing others on evidence documentation. Betsy nodded to them, then scanned the room, pausing at the words on the wall. The same words that had been left back at her dealership office were sprayed on her bedroom walls.

"Looks like I'll need a new mattress, too." She shook her head at the clothes from her closet, now scattered on the floor along with the contents of her dresser drawers.

Cain grunted. "I'll put that on the list."

Releasing his hand, she walked over to the ensuite and glanced in the half-open doorway. "Well, at least they didn't touch this room."

Deputy Evans cleared his throat as he stepped forward and pushed the door open with his elbow. "They left you a message on the mirror. I just need you to tell me if you recognize the writing." He cleared his throat again. "I'm sorry, Betsy, but this will really help us work on identifying the culprit."

Cain's gut told him to be quiet. Stay out of the police business. After all, the deputy was just doing his job. Many a time he'd been forced to ask a victim to do something to help in his own DEA cases. Things that solidified the evidence or clue. He'd thought nothing of it. But this was the woman he cared about, and the idea of her walking into the bathroom punched him to his core.

He lightly touched her shoulder. "Take a breath, Betsy. I'm right here."

"Is it bad?"

"It's a threat. But it's also a clue."

Her half-smile reaction stilled any nerves he'd been having. And the upward tilt of her chin as she straightened her stance showed him she was ready for anything. He wasn't so sure. People always had lines not to cross.

"Okay then…" She clenched her jaws. "The jerk wants to play games with me, he's met his match."

She stared straight ahead as she walked into her newly remodeled master bath. The one she'd paid extra to have an eight-foot double-sink vanity, eight-foot slab of hand-picked marble and the matching eight-foot mirror on the wall.

Scrawled across the mirror now was:

CLOCK IS TICKING, BETSY! Give me what I want—

I'd hate to see you end up like Phillip—
Bang!Bang!CRASH!

Betsy paled. Shivered. "Cain… I can't—"

"I've got you." He wrapped his arm around her shoulder and pulled her tight against his side. Forcing her to take a step, he got them out of the bathroom. "Deputy Evans, Betsy and I are leaving. She'll be at my house if you have any more questions."

The deputy didn't try to stop them, but followed close behind. "Betsy, do you recognize the handwriting? Does any of it make sense? Betsy! I need to know."

Cain kept hold of her, guiding them to the front door. "I said we're leaving."

Out the door. Down the steps. Crossing the yard, headed for his truck.

"Betsy!" Deputy Evans shouted from a few steps behind. "Yes? Or no?"

She raised her hand for Cain to stop. "Phillip. It looks vaguely like Phillip's handwriting."

"What do you mean?" the deputy asked.

"Believe me, I know that's not possible. We buried him in the church cemetery two years ago. You were even one of the pall bearers, Deputy Evans." Sighing, she slowly shook her head. "But there's something about the last line that bothered me."

"It's just part of the threat."

"No, it's something else. Something I can almost put my finger on," Betsy said, "and then it's gone before it's clear in my mind. But even though it looks like Phillip's handwriting, it isn't. Phillip is *dead*."

The deputy shook his head and shrugged. "Don't you worry, we'll get this all figured out. Now go home with Cain and get some rest."

Deputy Evans headed back to the house as Cain helped her into the passenger seat of his truck and clicked her seatbelt into place. As if in shock, she sat there staring straight ahead. A second later he opened a protein bar from the glove box and pushed it into her hand.

"Here, Betsy. Eat."

When she didn't budge, he tapped her on the shoulder then pointed to the bar once again. "Take a few bites for me. Okay?"

She nodded and complied as he closed the door. A few seconds later, as he buckled into his own seatbelt, she started to get a little color back in her face. And she'd eaten the entire bar.

"I can't stay at your house, Cain."

"Of course, you can. It's all torn up with the remodeling, but there's lots of room."

"That's not what I mean," she said. "Being around you makes me feel…"

"Yeah. Me, too. And we can talk about that later." For a brief moment he covered her hand with his. Then started the truck and drove toward his house. "Right now, I want you to stay because when you first agreed to let us use Peyton's as a sting setup, you said you could risk yourself but never your family. Do you remember what I said?"

"Yes." She lightly touched his arm. "You promised to keep us all safe."

"Right now, this is the best way for me to do that. Agreed?" He arrived at his house and turned off the truck, waiting for her answer before opening the driver's side door. Wasn't far between the carport and the back door, but the less time they were out in the open, the better he'd feel.

The silence in the truck was as thick as the chill rapidly overtaking the interior since he'd shut off the engine. He waited. He could wait as long as it took her to make the decision she was wrestling with in her mind.

From the pinch of Betsy's brows, she was intensely focused on something. The downturn of the corners of her lips could mean a lot of things, but from the way this day had turned out, he couldn't blame her for being down on life. Depending on her answer, his ability to protect her might get easier. Might not. Either way, he'd be there for her no matter what.

"There's someplace I want to go if you don't mind," she said, her voice barely above a whisper.

"Sure." He started the truck and pulled out of the driveway. "Anywhere in particular?"

"I want to drive around the lake." After pressing a few buttons on her phone, she laid it on the seat between them. "Just follow Siri's directions. She knows the way."

CHAPTER TWENTY

Betsy knew the route to the lake like the back of her hand. Knew what lay at the end of the drive. Knew the ever-present memories that would greet her. Maybe she'd made a mistake coming here today, but considering how the day had gone so far, this couldn't make things any worse. She needed to be here.

Siri announced they had arrived at their destination.

"Is this the place?" Cain asked.

"This is it."

"Where do you want me to park?"

She pointed to the property's parking area at the road front edge of the vacant lakefront lot. A seven-foot-high retaining wall holding solidly packed backfill of dirt and rocks sat level with the roadway. The family budget hadn't allowed for anything more than white chat on top that first summer.

In one corner of the parking pad, five sets of initials had been scratched into a small patch of hand-made cement. Even a rough drawing of a boat, thanks to Marcy and her. Right before they left for the day, her dad carried Amber over to the still setting concrete and had her dab her thumb above the boat—she'd promptly declared it the sun.

That had been a happy day. Full of laughter and food, fishing and plans. Betsy still remembered it like only yesterday.

The very first time her family—Dad, Mama, Marcy, Amber and her—had come to the lot in February of that year, she'd only been ten years old. They'd all helped make a small rock outline of exactly where they would build a cabin one day. Then on that final day of summer at the lake for that year, her parents, Sadie and Link Peyton, had spent the day laying out imaginary rooms inside the single row of rocks. Of course, the cabin had never been built. Never would be.

Over the years, as rain poured down and windstorms swept through, the rock outline gradually washed away. The only things still left from their first summer were the dock and the initials in the small patch of concrete her dad had hand-mixed with water from the lake and poured into a design she and Marcy had constructed. And of course... the memories. Always the memories.

Betsy's insides pushed against her whole being, choking off the memories. Leaving her with nothing but emptiness inside. Emptiness that magnified the promise she'd made that day. Gulping back the sob clawing to escape, she swiped her fingers across the corner of her right eye, then the left one as well.

"This is a great view," Cain said as he shifted into park and shut off the engine. "Looks like someone deliberately planned what would give the best sightline before they cleared out the trees."

She nodded, and before she could stop him, Cain jumped out of the truck. Closing the door behind him, he paced around the parking area. Like a kid who'd just discovered where the treasure might be buried, he scanned the property with his eyes, brushed his hand along the railing, pointed at the squirrels scampering from limb to limb. Then stared at the lake.

He walked back to her side of the truck and gestured for her to roll the window down. She obliged, but dang, it was cold.

"Do you know who owns this property?" he asked.

She nodded.

"Do you think they'd mind if we walk around?"

She shook her head. "They won't mind, but—"

"Good, because I know about where we are on the lake. Might even be able to figure out the mile marker if I walked down to the dock." He motioned for her to get out of the truck. "Come on. Let's go see."

Her insides shouted *stay*. Her heart and soul and future shouted *go with him*. "I'll just wait here."

In turn, he shrugged. Grinning, he pointed to his chest then walked his fingers in the direction of the lake. Reaching out toward the rail as if he were going to vault it and drop to the ground below, he suddenly stopped. His forehead wrinkled as his eyebrows pinched together, and he stooped to touch the corner of the parking pad. Evidently, he'd noticed the letters in the concrete.

He slowly stood, looped his thumbs in his jean pockets

and stared at the lake. "Care to tell me who owns this property?"

After powering up the window, she stepped out of the truck's passenger door. A few steps later, she leaned against the front side fender of his truck. "My parents bought this lot the year before my dad was shot and killed. I own it now."

Without saying a word, Cain slowly walked over, leaned back against the front grill of the truck and braced his right foot against the fender. A few seconds later he cocked his elbows back to rest on the hood. Quieter still, the two of them stood there, seemingly lost in their own thoughts as the sounds of nature lulled them into the chill of winter.

The aroma of woodsmoke from a neighbor's chimney drifted on the breeze. After time in the snow or just walking in the cold, she'd always loved a woodburning fireplace to warm up by. Her idea of a perfect winter evening was a cup of hot chocolate and a good book in front of a fire.

"Jeez, it's cold." She shivered as she shoved her hands further into her pockets. "I don't mind winter when it first comes. I'm getting tired of it now."

"Do you want to head back home?"

"No. Not yet." How could she explain why she'd come here today? Why she ever came to the vacant lakefront lot? Sometimes she left with her answer…sometimes not. Either way, she always felt more at peace. More confident. More energized.

Today, though, she wasn't even sure why she'd asked to

come. Sitting in the truck, in his backyard, she had already realized there was only one answer to whether she'd stay at his house or not. Sure, she'd asked Cain to bring her, but she knew he wouldn't let her out of his sight today. She even agreed with that reasoning, but she *never* asked for help for herself. Her top priority was to always take care of Sadie, Marcy and Amber, even when they told her to back off. Thankfully, they were out of town and safe for the moment.

Her second priority was herself, and right now, with no idea why, she was in deep trouble. But one thing she did know was that she needed to trust someone to help her, and that nagged at her deep inside.

She didn't like to depend on anyone. She made her own way in life. She owned her mistakes. Owned a whole lot of mistakes...and misjudgments, but she'd walked through them without relying on others.

Along the way there'd been a few times Sadie and Marcy had pushed their way into her trouble. Which, in the end, had landed her mama and sister in trouble of their own.

Not Amber though. Her six-year-younger sister had always been distant to her as she grew up, which was to be expected with the age difference. Betsy had hoped that since Amber was twenty-six and a college graduate now, they could become closer. More like actual sisters, instead of...what? Just what were they to each other? A few months ago, when she had offered unsolicited advice to Amber about how to live her life, she'd hit a brick wall.

Suddenly, Betsy felt frozen in place and time and emotions. Lost and alone with no one to blame but herself.

When had she quit caring about others? No! Others were the only ones she cared about.

"Well, will you look at that?" Cain yanked off his hat and gloves. "The sun has decided to show its face after all."

Stepping into a patch of sun, she turned her face upward. "Oh, that feels good. Nice and warm." She glanced at Cain. "You're right. Let's take a walk down to the dock."

"Sounds good to me."

On the way down, she pointed out where trees had been taken out that first summer. Explained how her parents, especially her dad, had wanted it to be the best view around. They didn't have money to build a house, but that hadn't stopped them all from sketching and brainstorming and dreaming about what it would one day look like.

"The tree removal and dock were our first projects that spring." She stepped onto the wooden slats of the narrow dock and immediately felt the thrill of the first time she ran all the way from the shore to the end and jumped in. "We spent almost every weekend here at the lake that summer."

"What was your favorite part?"

"Swimming and fishing."

"That sounds like what I've always liked about the lake, too."

For the next fifteen minutes or so, without any effort at all, the two of them talked about fish they'd caught and the ones that got away. Her sunburns and freckles. His ability to tan in less than a day. About the dives they'd made, the bellyflops that had hurt, and walking on rocks and acorns and gumballs to get to their shoes after swimming. It almost felt as if they'd grown up living next door to each other. Only they hadn't. In so many ways they hadn't...

CHAPTER TWENTY-ONE

Cain had plenty of memories of his own at the lake, just not the kind that made a son want to stay around. "Kind of amazing how good this dock looks after all these years."

"That's because I have it repaired every year." Betsy walked back to shore and sat on the bench next to the dock. "You probably already know that Ameren owns the Lake of the Ozarks. And they do a great job because of their regulations. From the beginning, my dad instilled in us to always follow the rules, which is exactly what he did when he built this dock. I've followed that lead every year since."

Eyeing the property, Cain was amazed by not only the view, but the mile marker, the gentle lay of the land and the easy drive from town. A rustle of fallen oak leaves in the near distance caused him to pull his gun, letting it hang down his side as if an extension of his arm.

Betsy jumped from the bench. Tensed and turning to

look in the same direction as him. Breathing faster, she inched closer against him. "What should we do?"

"Don't worry. I've got you." Without looking in her direction, he gently pushed her behind him, yet always stayed focused on the moving whisper of a sound. The sound of someone or something heavy.

Seconds later, a doe slipped from the woodline. Two more edged in and around the trees behind. He blew out a cheek-puffing sigh. Beside him, Betsy softly breathed out a sigh of relief along with a soft nervous laugh. She sat back down on the bench.

Any other circumstance, he'd have taken time to listen closer in the first place. He'd have realized it wasn't a person. But the adrenaline and intense focus of being in a possible life-and-death situation had pushed him to the worst-case scenario right off the bat.

He pocketed his gun. "What about you? When are you going to build a house out here?"

She shook her head. "Never."

"Why? You love the water."

"Too many wonderful memories can make for a painful barrier to change." Patting the seat beside her, she motioned for him to join her.

He took her invitation and sat on the other end of the bench. For a moment he considered what she'd said. He'd never thought of memories tied to love and laughter as anything but nice to have. There hadn't been many of those in his life, and he treasured the few he held on to. Yet that same happiness had somehow become a chain for Betsy.

Relaxing into the back curve of the bench, he stared

out at the sun lowering over the water. Today had been filled with good and bad. Fear for Betsy had rested heavy on his shoulders this morning. Now the day was slowly turning to warmth and friendship. He rested his forearm on the arm of the bench, his other hand comfortably braced on the seat slats between him and Betsy.

"Sorry if I triggered the sad part of memories for you," Cain said.

"No problem. It's just part of who I am." She slightly turned toward him and scrunched her knees up on the seat between them. "That end-of-summer day left me with a lot of memories. Like the last time me and my dad sat on the end of the dock, feeding the leftover worms to the fish in the lake."

"Sounds like a great way to end the day."

"More than you can imagine." Her chin trembled. "That's also when he told me I should look after Mama and my sisters if anything ever happened to him. Said he had no doubt I was the one with the strength to be in charge." She swiped her fingers beneath her eyes. "I've been looking after them ever since the day he was killed."

Cain's hand...Betsy's knees...a space the width of a penny between them. Yet trust seemed to fill that penny's space.

"I'm sorry, Betsy. That has to be a heavy load to carry."

"It's okay. I can do it forever." She pulled her knees closer. "Besides, they don't need me to watch out for them...and they let me know loud and clear sometimes. I just can't stop."

Off in the woods, a woodpecker was hard at work on a tree. From the lake, the sound of a boat motor echoed from miles away. Occasionally, the rattle and pop of pine trees gave a backdrop to the cold and wind of the season. Life went on around them as if they weren't even there.

For one of the few times in his life, Cain felt peace. "I'm sure your dad is proud of you."

Somehow, during the past hour or so, he'd let himself wonder what it would be like to settle down. To have a wife and kids waiting for him when he came home from work. To feel the heat of lying next to the same person every night for the rest of his life. The thought felt like walking in a dream. One he didn't want to end.

She straightened her legs till her feet were back on the ground. Moved a bit closer to him and glanced down at his hand before covering it with her own. "I hope he's proud. I've done the best I can. But whatever's happening now is a whole different type of danger. And I need some help."

Realizing the depth of what she'd said, he nodded. "I'm always here for you. I'm not going anywhere without you."

Her expression changed as she stood and raised the hood of her parka, pulling the zipper on her coat all the way up to her chin. "But you did leave. In fact, once this case is solved and you sell your house, you'll leave again."

"What are you talking about?"

She stared out at the end of the dock. "Can you honestly tell me you aren't going to leave Crayton?"

"I don't have any idea what I'll do when that time comes. Why is this—"

His phone rang. "Yeah."

"This is JB. Where you at?"

Cain clicked the call to speaker phone. "Betsy wanted

to come to the lake, so we're here at her lot. Where are you?"

"When I saw what was going on, I headed back to Crayton. Truman drove them to the airport. In fact, he decided to go with them to New York. He said he'd be there if anything went wrong." JB nervously laughed. "Sadie said he'd be there with his wallet if they wanted anything."

"JB, I appreciate you rushing back to Crayton. Especially because of me, and don't try to say it's only because you're the acting sheriff. I'm not that naïve." Betsy pushed past Cain and started walking to the truck. "But dang it all. *Now* I have to worry about you, too."

Cain clicked off the speaker phone. "Hey, JB—"

"What was that all about?"

"To be honest, I'm not sure." He absentmindedly pushed the remote start on his key fob. By the time she got to the truck, the heat should be warming the interior. He just hoped she wouldn't drive away with his truck.

"How's she doing?" JB asked, sincerely concerned.

"It's been a hard twenty-four hours for her. What with the lookie-loo customer being killed in the car lot last night. Now all the destruction at the dealership and her house today, I think she's about reached her limit."

JB sighed. "Makes sense. She's tough, but we all have our limits."

Cain could relate. He knew his limits. One reason he was considering leaving the DEA was because he didn't want to cross a line that took him to playing on the wrong side of the law. He'd seen that happen to agents. Usually ended bad for the agent or someone who had put their trust in the person. Wasn't a pretty sight for either one.

The day he'd reached that line, he'd turned and walked away. Even took the leave of absence his boss had offered him. Now that he'd returned to Crayton, the idea of leaving the DEA entirely seemed to be inching closer and closer with every second.

"Have you had a chance to stop by Betsy's house? Or the dealership?" Cain asked.

"Yeah, that's why I'm calling."

A few minutes later, Cain ended his call with JB. A second later an incoming text from his DEA boss caught his attention.

Hey, Cain—Just checking in to see if you've found what you're looking for yet?

Had he? How would he even know when he found it? Could be staring him in the face. Could be nothing but a mirage. Was Betsy his future? The lake? Crayton? Or was he being played by her? Set up by the person orchestrating the destruction at the dealership and her house as a way of distracting him? He hoped like hell Betsy didn't fall into that category.

Hey, boss, thanks for checking in. I'm still tied up in this consulting case with the Crayton police. Outcome iffy. May be blindside. Still looking for my place—Cain.

Starting up the hill, a gentle slope made the first three-quarters of the walk easy. It was the last section that turned into a steep incline. If anyone put a driveway in, there'd be that moment of trust as you pulled over the edge to drive down. Kind of like that one type of roller coasters that have their cars built long in front. Gives the illusion you're going to fly straight off the rail if you keep going on the same trajectory.

Illusions happened in cases, also. He'd been an agent long enough to know things weren't always what they seemed. So, he'd stay vigilant. Keep his eyes open. Hope he was just being paranoid. Trouble was—trust was easily shaded by emotion. Illusions by dreams.

With only a few more steps before he reached the parking pad, he saw Betsy get out of the passenger's side door and walk in his direction. Avoiding eye contact would probably be in each other's best interest.

"I'm sorry, Cain," she said as she stepped in front of him, deliberately blocking his way. "I was way out of line."

Reactively he raised his head to see if this was a joke of some kind. What he found was a genuinely serious look on her face. And she was close. Really, *really* close. In fact, they were actually face to face, since he was still a couple steps below where they'd be standing on even ground.

The effort it took to keep his mind, and other regions of his body focused attacked his senses. And his heart had jumped with nothing more than the sound of his name on her lips.

"That's fine. Don't worry about it," he said.

She kept staring at him as she raised her hand to keep him from going around. "No, what I said wasn't okay. And I own...I try to own my mistakes." Lowering her hand, she lifted her chin and blinked. "I hope you'll accept my apology."

Was this what life with Betsy revolved around? One second, she was strong and ready to take on the world. The next, trying to make things perfect for other people.

Suddenly a rapid flash back to her in high school, and he remembered she was always trying to help the weaker ones in class even then. Sometimes with their studies. Sometimes with being berated or embarrassed by others. On those occasions, she'd end up chastising the bully or mean girl who'd caused the problem in the first place.

"Well, do you accept?" she asked, now rapidly blinking as her forehead wrinkled in worry-lines.

Blowing out a heavy sigh, he slowly swiped his palm down his face. "Yeah, I accept your apology. Thank you."

"Good." A smile spread on her lips, and she nodded. "Can we stop to eat on the way back to town? 'Cause I'm really hungry. In fact, I'm bordering on hangry."

"Can do."

They stood still, as if this moment in time meant more than either of them had ever dared imagine. He teasingly pulled her ski hat off and her cheeks rounded as she smiled.

"Cain, I don't ever want to lose you as a friend."

"You may not believe it, Betsy, but I've always kept you in my mind during these years apart. Always thought of you as my friend, if nothing else."

He realized he had a lot to learn about the grown-up Betsy. In fact, he had a lot to learn about himself, too. Fighting to keep his mouth shut and his sarcastic comeback to himself, he closed his eyes as he braced his hand against the oak tree standing guard less than a foot away. "Any place in particular you'd like to stop for dinner?"

The soft touch of her fingers against his chest jerked him out of his thoughts. Opening his eyes, he found her right in front of him, on the same level ground as him. He pressed harder against the tree. Fought to control his body.

"I heard your thoughts loud and clear." She dropped her hand to her side but continued to stare into his eyes.

"I don't know what you mean." He looked down into the face that had filled his dreams for the past few years. The one he'd fallen asleep with many nights, especially those times there'd been an unpleasant end to a case. Or just the times, for no reason at all, he'd felt as alone as the last mountain lion of his breed. "I didn't say anything."

"Hmmmmm. Really?" She tilted her head just enough. "Is that the best you can do?"

She glanced at his lips, and he instantly removed his hand from the protection of the sentry tree. They stood close enough that the fog from their breaths mingled in the air.

A few weeks ago, he'd made the first move back at the parking lot outside Joanie's. Betsy had first fallen into his kiss, then verbally set him straight about her and him. Walked away after letting him know she was not open to them ever being a couple. That was not the vibe he was getting now. Maybe his instincts were off on what this meant, but he'd sure like to know for sure.

He gently reached over and pulled the scrunchie loose. Her hair spilled forward, surrounding her face in a perfect frame. She didn't pull away, rather, she slightly leaned forward.

"I love your hair like this. Wild...and free." Fingering back the strands of ginger red hair errantly reaching for her eyes, her mouth, he brushed the back of his hand against her cheek. "Oh, Betsy. What am I going to do with you?"

"I'm not sure." She lightly brushed the tips of her fingers across the rim of his bottom lip.

Then walked the few steps up to the parking pad before turning to watch him watching her.

Had she always moved like that? Or only for him? Only now? He couldn't remember. Didn't even matter. But damn, he liked that walk. Those boots. Her eyes. Her legs. Her voice. Everything.

Struggling to stay where he stood, he could hardly breathe.

She barely smiled as she pushed her hair back from her face. "Maybe you should kiss me. What do you think?"

Without thinking he took one step, and then another, straight toward her. Then she did that little head tilt once again. Drove him crazy. He liked that, too.

CHAPTER TWENTY-TWO

From the first time Betsy had seen Cain walking across the park next to their school, until just now as he climbed the lakefront lot's hill, her insides had always known he would be in her life.

With him gone for the past years, her belief had dimmed until a few months ago when she looked up into his face. Thought she had a concussion or was hallucinating for a moment. Then the low rumble of his voice had flicked the switch that he was pulling her out of a car wreck. That she'd broken her arm again. That Cain had come back to Crayton after all these years.

Since then, even though she'd tried to push her feelings for him away entirely, she's let the almost twenty-year-old dreams float to the surface once again. Somewhere during the past twenty-four hours of chaos, her emotions had settled into reality. She still cared for him.

"I thought you'd never ask." Strong, yet gentle, Cain brushed his fingers into her hair, his palm braced softly against her cheek.

She leaned into the feel of his hand on her skin, a cross between a new moon's crescent arc and a sexy caress of invitation. All she could do was stare at his lips, parted and reaching down for her own. In turn, she eased her hand to the back of his neck and closed her eyes. Suddenly their kiss was everything she'd ever imagined it would be.

She let herself fold into him, and he pulled her close against him, his arms hugging her to his warmth. As if floating in one of her dreams, she felt his lips move to her cheek, to her ear, to her neck when she arched in response. She couldn't get enough of him. He wanted the same. Finally, their lips found each other again...and they deepened the kiss with their tongues.

The crunch of tires on the gravel road broke them apart. Her breathlessness mingled with his heavy breaths, while his hand moved to his holster. He'd already stationed her behind him as he stepped in front. The clear reality of their situation came roaring back, hitting her with momentary fear.

She strained to stay behind him, yet out of his way to move. "What should I do?"

"Don't worry, I've got you." He crouched them lower, shifted them to the front of the truck. Hidden, but with a clear view in both directions. "I've always got you."

The flash of SUV lights turning to the left, driving for a bit before the headlights illuminated a cabin close to the lake, eased the situation.

Cain turned to her. "Well, as much as I'd like to continue where we left off, I think we should get out of here."

"Agreed."

"Just so you know though, this is..." He leaned in and gave her a quick kiss on her forehead "...to be continued."

Settling into the passenger seat, the feel of the heat on her face warmed her body on the outside. The inside warmth was for a completely different reason. She noticed he slowed at the end of the driveway where the SUV had turned. The sight of a small boy helping his dad with a bag and a woman with a toddler on her hip seemed to ease some tension from Cain's face.

A good five minutes passed with them riding in silence. Even in the darkness of late dusk, he seemed to continually be scouring the surroundings. Once they reached the main highway around the lake, he kept his eyes on the road ahead for the most part. Years of being part of a law enforcement family had trained her to stay alert when something felt off.

"JB's going to stop by my house about eight or so tonight," Cain said. "He'll bring us up to speed on any of their findings."

"Sounds good."

He tapped the top of the steering wheel. "Oh, that reminds me. He said to tell you Marcy had called about an hour ago. She'd already got word on what's going on."

"How'd she know?"

"Evidently, she and Joanie keep each other informed on Crayton happenings." He crossed his fingers. "Sounds like they're a bonded pair."

"We all three are." Betsy laughed. "I should have known there'd be no keeping this a secret."

He pulled into the parking lot of a small hometown-homemade food diner halfway to his house in Crayton. "Will this do for dinner?"

"Love their food." The moment he turned off the truck, she undid her seatbelt. "I'm starving."

Reaching out, he placed his hand on hers. "One more thing before we go inside."

"Okay." She glanced in his direction. Saw seriousness in his expression, maybe a touch of sadness in his eyes. She turned sideways to face him.

After sighing, he palmed his hand down his face, then turned to face her, too. "The woman in the photo is named Cassandra, but we all call her Cassie. She's a DEA agent. Used to work undercover. That photo is from when we were paired up as a couple on a drug dealer job."

He paused. Swallowed. Watched a group of people walking into the restaurant. She'd noticed he laid his gun in the truck's center console when they'd gotten in back at the lake. She also noticed he always moved his hand in that direction if people headed anywhere close to them.

"After a few months I got pegged as a Fed. By then, DEA had already pulled Cassie out of the job, but the bastards tracked her down. Shot her up with drugs and circulated photos to draw me in. They figured I'd come to find her. And I did. They gave me the same treatment, along with what they referred to as old-fashioned fisticuffs. Hell, it was fight club on steroids." He leaned his head against the driver's side window for a while.

Betsy noticed he'd fisted one hand on top of the console, the other around the steering wheel. Her own insides were pumping with adrenaline, with fear for him, for Cassie. She could only imagine the fear they'd been feeling.

She covered his hand with hers. "I'm sorry."

Straightening in his seat, he shook his head. "No, I'm the one who should be sorry even telling you this."

"Go on, Cain. We don't need secrets between us."

He didn't move to get out of the truck. "Finally, we heard a police siren moving closer to where they were holding us. Louder and louder. Then more sirens joined the fray, and the thugs got the hell out of there. Assuming we were done for, they left us where we lay. We heard the sirens split, as if each was following escaping members.

"Somehow Cassie and I crawled our way out of the building and into the concrete jungle of abandoned warehouses and overgrown weeds and bushes and trash. Wasn't a pretty escape, but we got it done. An hour or so later, we emerged in a residential alleyway, and a man taking his trash out called the police for us on his cell phone. Even had us stay out of sight behind his shed. Waiting there for the police to arrive was one of the longest five minutes of my life."

Betsy nodded. She'd had some of those long five minutes in her lifetime, too. "What happened to Cassie?"

"She recovered. Still works for the DEA, but she never worked undercover or active assignments again. She's a desk jockey and loves it." He paused, opened his door and jumped out of the truck, and they met in front of the hood. "Got two little boys. They call me Uncle Dude."

She laughed and lightly punched him in the bicep. "I can see that... Uncle Dude with the blue eyes."

Curling his fingers into hers, they shared a moment. He gave her a small kiss, which she gladly returned.

"I'm glad you made it out alive," she said, tightening her fingers around his as they walked to the diner entrance.

"Me, too." Opening the door, he bent in her direction. "By the way, you can have my blue eyes any time you want. But the whole Uncle Dude thing ends now. Because—

"—you're definitely not *my* Uncle Dude." She winked, and shoulder bumped him. "Now let's get some dinner. I'm hungry."

"Well, thank goodness you're not hangry."

It had been a long time since she'd felt comfortable and happy going out to dinner with a man, and for a second that was what this felt like. Dinner and a date.

As they walked in, tow-truck Randy paused on his way out of the diner. He shook Cain's hand and introduced Betsy and Cain to the woman next to him. Said she was his wife. Said he'd done two weeks in rehab. Said he was working hard to stay sober. Real hard. The wife said they'd just found out they had a baby on the way. Smiling, Randy and his wife thanked Cain for making sure he'd survived, then went on their way.

A small warmth filled Betsy's insides as they walked to the hostess counter. Then she heard him ask for the last booth in the row to the right. Saw him take in the perimeter and the occupants in a more than casual glance. Noticed his hand never left his pocket where she'd seen him put his gun after removing it from the truck console.

What for a moment had felt like a casual evening out in her mind turned into trepidation in that instant. She even found herself watching her surroundings. And when they reached the booth, she slid into the seat with her back to the door.

Her FBI dad and her uncle the sheriff had taught her long ago to let the protector of the group sit to watch the door. See who comes. See who goes. See the possible trouble before it happens. Cain was her protector tonight, and she needed to let him do his job.

He slid into his side of the booth. Grinned and chatted with the waitress, as did Betsy. They ordered their meals and sipped their water. Yet all the time, she noticed he kept glancing around the diner, even to the lighted parking lot. Even once their food was served.

Suddenly he paused eating and stared toward the front door. As if to be seen, he straightened in his seat. She didn't turn around, just sipped the tea she'd ordered.

"Officer Kennett just walked in," he said. "Looks like he's headed our way."

CHAPTER TWENTY-THREE

ain had already finished his meal, so he motioned the waitress to take the plate and bring the bill. Officer Kennett looked like a man on a mission. As he walked in their direction, he paused for a moment at the counter. Appeared like he placed a to-go order.

Finished, Kennett grabbed a chair from the few stacked in the corner then sat at the end of their booth. "Saw your truck in the parking lot. Figured I could save myself some time."

"What do you mean?" Cain asked.

The officer looked at Betsy. "The other two women in your little group have been on the phone all afternoon."

"First off, thank you for not calling me ma'am." She smiled. "Second, you're going to need to be more specific on who. I've got more than one three-musketeer group."

For some reason Cain didn't quite believe that. She had always been a very private person when it came to her family and friends. Nothing he'd seen since coming back to town led him to think any different.

"Marcy and Joanie. They got together on the phone, planned what you'd need if you were staying at Cain's house, and made a list. Since Marcy's in New York, it was Joanie who got everything together. Then she made me read off the list as she packed the tote bag I've now got in my cruiser with unofficial orders to deliver it to you." Kennett sighed in exasperation. Pinched the space between his eyebrows with his fingers. "Just so you know, I don't ever want to read that list again."

"Do you have a headache?" Betsy asked the officer, clearly concerned.

Cain was beginning to feel sorry for him, but as long as it wasn't himself involved in this evidently super important plan, he'd stay happy. And quiet.

"No. I don't have a headache. But the day's not over, yet." Kennett glanced at Cain before turning to stare at Betsy. "And just for the record...*I* don't buy that you've got another three-musketeer group *anywhere* in the world. *Ma'am.*"

Betsy burst out in spontaneous laughter. So surprising and kind of loud that a few of the diners glanced in her direction. Trying to stifle herself, she covered her mouth with one hand while she reached out with the other and covered the officer's hand.

"Oh my gosh, Kennett. That was a fantastic smart aleck comeback." She wiped a tear of laughter from the corner of her right eye. Then sucked in a breath and blew it out calmly as if getting herself back under control. "It's taken a couple of years, but *you* have become one of *us*. You've become a friend."

The officer grinned. "I'm not sure if that's good or bad."

"I've learned to just take it as good and go from there," Cain said as he stood. "I hate to break this up, but we should head on out."

Breaking the tension for a few minutes had felt good, but Betsy and he needed to get to his house before the appointment with JB at eight o'clock tonight. Cain had also picked up on the signal from Kennett, the one that was nothing more than a quick glance at the door. Odds were that they needed to talk.

"Okay." Betsy slid out of her seat as she pointed at the restroom sign above the doorway to the short hallway, then headed in that direction. "I won't be long."

"I'll go on out and get the tote bag from Kennett's cruiser," Cain said. "See you at my truck."

The two men left the diner, and after retrieving the tote from the cruiser, they walked over to Cain's truck.

He tossed the tote in the back seat. "You look tired, Kennett. Of course, it's been a long day. First, the early call to Peyton's. Then Betsy's house break-in. I imagine you've had a lot of evidence to collect."

"You don't know the half of it." Kennett leaned forward and braced his forearms on the hood of the truck. "Crayton wasn't the only place to get hit on last night."

"Where else?"

"Had five or six similar smash and spray break-in events around Missouri and Illinois. Even a couple in eastern Kansas that resulted in shots being fired. One fatality. In fact, a DEA task force has been called in to assist."

"It'll be interesting who the DEA sends since there are already undercover agents working the area."

"Would one of them be you?"

"Nope." Cain laughed. "Some months back, they suggested that since I grew up in Crayton, I'd be perfect for the dark assignment they were putting together. I said no. But I did need to come back to town and do exactly what I'm doing."

Kennett cleared his throat. "I'm not grilling you, but just *what* exactly are you doing in Crayton?"

Both men quieted at the sound of the diner's front door opening. A couple of customers exited and went toward the parking lot on the other side of the building.

Cain turned back to face the officer. "Truth is, I *am* working on the house. It needs to be sold. My dad is still up in Alaska, and he likes it there...when he remembers where he's at." Pinching the bridge of his nose, he ended with swipes to clear his eyes of moisture. "I've been able to get him into a good Alzheimer Memory Care facility up there, but it's not cheap. Selling the house will help."

Kennett swallowed and cleared his throat once again. "That's a tough one, Cain. I'm sorry.

"I am, too. He wasn't always the best dad in the world. But no one wants to see a parent in that situation."

Moving to the other side of the hood, Cain mirrored the officer's leaning stance as they spent the next few minutes hashing out clues and evidence. "Any of the other town hits have a follow-up break-in like Betsy's house today?"

"Still working on that. I do know none of the others ended up with a dead body in a dumpster. But like I said, there were at least a couple shooting incidents. Plus, Hastings and I are still following up on reports of two people getting roughed up because they were in the wrong place at the wrong time."

"Kind of like Papa Carrington?"

"Exactly." Kennett rolled his neck as if trying to work the kinks out. "In fact, I'm headed out to a few of the locations. "Sometimes seeing and talking to people in person is a lot better than reading reports and looking at photos."

Cain shivered as a passing chill raced through his body. "True. You might also try to get a timeline which might give us a clue as to whether there was one, two or more involved."

Seconds later Betsy emerged with a to-go bag and large fountain drink. She smiled and raised the items above her head as she walked toward the truck.

"By the way, we got some good footprint casts from the snow at both places. Should be able to compare them with any photos or casts the other places have taken."

She sat the officer's food order on the bench in front of the truck's parking spot, then walked the few steps over and into the two guys' conversation. Even mirrored the stance of the two men as if she were in on whatever was being discussed. "The waitress said they'd put it on your card, but I just went ahead and paid for it. My treat."

"Thank you. I do like their bacon hamburgers. And their prices."

The three of them laughed, breaking the tension of the day. It struck Cain that they had settled into a triangle on the hood. Triangles were one of the strongest bases in the world. Maybe the three of them could at least connect some dots for the past twenty-four hours. At this point, the more people, events, happenings, sightings and more that could be grouped into a circle, the better their chance of narrowing that circle.

"Now what's this about footprint casts?" she asked. "Did you find some shoe prints around Peyton's or my house?"

"Mainly at your house." Kennett scrunched his shoulders against a sudden gust of cold wind. "As I'm sure you know, the police always look for clues...footprints, fingerprints, hair...anything like that. Footprints are easier to find in mud or snow."

"And we had an inch or so of snowfall late last night," Betsy said.

"Right. Plus, that area being shaded by the pine branches, there was some snow from the storm still left, also."

A tentative quiet settled awkwardly around the three of them. Kennett stared at the hood in front of him. Betsy seemed intently concerned with her gloved hands, fidgeting to press the fingers between each other, then flattening them out to begin again.

She bit the side of her lip and made sure not to make eye contact with either of them. "So has anyone heard the latest weather for—"

"Betsy, you were really scared when you got in my truck this morning."

She nodded slowly. "Okay."

"You kept looking back at the front porch."

Again, she nodded. "Okay."

"And when we came back to your house, you mentioned someone might have been there by the porch when we left. Right?"

"Yes." Slowly she closed her eyes, then wiped the corner of her right eye. "Wouldn't have been the first time."

He picked up on her tone and attitude with that additional slightly mumbled sentence. From the looks of her reactions, this was a tough conversation, but he sensed this could be a point to put in their circle. "I asked Kennett to make sure he checked for footprints behind the pine tree at the end of your porch. Plus, to check them against any that showed up at Peyton's."

She nodded slowly. "Okay."

"Do you know whose footprint that is?" Kennett asked, pulling out his pen and small notepad.

As if a switch had been flipped, the strong, observant, clearheaded Betsy lifted her chin and straightened her shoulders. "I don't know for sure, but I've got my suspicions. But I doubt it will be of help."

"You tell us what you know. We'll work it from there," Cain said. "Just start from the very first time you thought someone was there."

Again, she bit the side of her lip. Shivered. "It's getting colder out here. Can we sit in the truck?"

A minute later she and Cain were in the front seat, while Kennett sat in the back, eating his sandwich. The heater's warmth made the tense conversation better in one respect, at least.

"The first time I ever knew someone was there, was about three months before Phillip died in the car crash. He'd said he was going out front to sit on the porch, but he still hadn't come back in by the time I finished cooking dinner, so I went out to get him." Betsy paused, then went on. "He was standing at the end of the porch, staring down behind the tree.

"Guess he didn't hear me walk up, because when I reached out to hug him, he grabbed my arm and tried to block me from seeing what he was doing. I heard rustling at the edge of the porch, but when I glanced over, the person behind the tree had pulled a branch partly in front of himself. Phillip jerked me back and that's when I heard a small pop in my wrist, felt a shooting pain up my arm."

She rubbed her forearm as her face morphed into a stare of dazed expression, like memories playing out in her mind. "Even though Phillip hadn't meant to hurt me, he had. I wore an ACE bandage for a few days. Told people I fell off the back deck and hurt my arm when I broke my fall. Finally, Marcy insisted I needed to go to the doctor, so she took me to the orthopedist."

Betsy rubbed her forearm once again. "I ended up with pins in my wrist."

Cain suddenly had his answer as to why she did that a lot when she seemed nervous. Or scared. "Did you get a look at the guy?"

"Not really." She moved her hands trying to sketch the person in the air. "He seemed to be dressed in black with a white shirt or jacket or... I don't know. There was something white. I don't know what it was. I never saw him again." She sighed. "Phillip told me to never follow him to the front porch if I saw him talking to someone behind the tree. Said he owed some guy some money and they were working everything out. Said I shouldn't worry. Didn't concern me."

Kennett jotted something on his notepad. "I'm confused. You mentioned the guy had been here a few times. But you just said you never saw him again."

Betsy nodded. "That's right. If the guy came back while Phillip was alive, I don't know, because I never again went on the front porch when my husband had gone out there. Of course, a few weeks later there was a night we were arguing, and Phillip got really mad."

"What about?" Cain asked.

She shrugged. "Said he was under a lot of stress. Me...I thought he was doing drugs again. He didn't deny it. But he asked me to trust him just a little longer. Said he'd explain everything once we were safe."

"Safe?" Cain cringed. "Did you feel scared, Betsy?"

"That night I did, so once Phillip went to bed, I called my uncle to come and get me. Grabbed a few things and waited on the front porch, but before Uncle Cal arrived, Phillip found me outside. He wasn't mad by then. Just looked determined. Swore I'd understand everything soon. He didn't even ask me to stay, instead he walked me to my uncle's car, kissed me on the forehead and said I'd be safer someplace else."

Cain exchanged glances with Kennett. What had Phillip really been involved in? He was clearly thinking of Betsy in that moment. Why was he afraid for her? He had a lot of questions that were going to require a lot of answers. The biggest question was where this was all leading.

Betsy stared at the dashboard as if remembering that

night, then slightly smiled. "As I got in the car, he said I'd be proud of him. Even looked Uncle Cal straight in the eye and told him he'd be proud, too. So, I left him standing in front of the house and went to live with Mama and Truman for a bit, then my uncle's family, then Marcy. Phillip and I would meet and talk, and before long everything seemed better."

She swiped her cheeks. "We had moved back in together the week before the company picnic. Things had been good. We enjoyed the company picnic for a while, then Phillip and Papa C disappeared for over an hour. When they came back, things seemed to have changed. My husband hovered over me like I was piece of gold, but he stayed awfully quiet. Kept glancing around. I was tired by the time it all shut down that evening. We'd ridden over with Papa C, so we had to wait till he was ready to leave, which was late. Phillip knew I was worn out from the long day, so he said I should lay down in the back seat and go to sleep."

Sucking in a deep, loud sob of emotion, her chin quivered as she told them the rest of what she remembered about that night. About the argument between Phillip and Papa C. About her husband standing up for her, ready to protect her from some unknown. About how the tires blowing out sounded just like gunshots that night.

"Phillip released his seatbelt. Tried to grab the steering wheel." She sucked in a deep breath and exhaled. "And Phillip died trying to save us."

Kennett swiped his palm down his face, then turned to stare outside. All of them sat quietly for a couple of minutes.

Cain hated putting her through this, but she seemed willing to share the story. Maybe even happy to share the story with someone besides herself. "Just one more thing, Betsy. When do you think the guy came back?"

Kennett cleared his throat and nodded from the back seat. His attention back on alert professionalism. "Even if you can't remember the exact time frame, how many times do you think he's been here? And what happened?"

She sucked in a deep breath and blew it out, then stared into the distance as if replaying scenes in her mind. Cain noticed she tapped one finger on her glove. Then repeated the process again. Two fingers. Again. Three.

"Three times for sure. Maybe four, but one could have been a squirrel." She smiled weakly. "The first time was about a year ago after the wreck. Always at the window at the far end of the living room. The one just off the front porch and behind the tree, exactly where Phillip and him had been. Never says anything. Never leaves anything"

She pulled her gloves off. Tossed her hat on the seat. And switched the heat down a couple notches. "Okay, guys, that's all I've got. And it has gotten dang hot in here."

Cain leaned across and brushed her hair back from her face. "You did great. Now just leave it all up to me and Kennett and JB and the whole, entire Crayton Police Department. Okay?"

Nodding she rested her palm on his hand. "I doubt any of that helped, but I tried."

"Don't worry about any of this right now. Just lean back and get some rest. You've had a long day." He leaned over and kissed her softly. "I've got you, Betsy. I've got you."

Kennett cleared his throat loudly. "Did you two forget I'm back here?"

She laughed lightly as Cain straightened back in the driver's seat. "This has been a long and interesting day. I think Betsy and I need some sleep," he said.

"I thought JB was coming over at eight?" Betsy questioned.

Cain shook his head. "JB texted me right before you came out of the diner. Said he didn't have any important results back yet. We'll wait to meet until eleven tomorrow."

The three of them piled out of the truck. Stretched, as if needing a break from the tension inside.

"Well, I better get on the road, see what I can find out at some of those other places." Kennett turned and started for his cruiser.

Betsy's expression turned serious as she faced Cain. "What other places?"

"I'll explain later." He took a few steps in Kennett's direction. "Watch your six, man. Call if you need anything."

"Got it. Thanks. Hope I find some clues as to what's going on here in Crayton."

"Just remember, no connection is still a clue."

"Got it." Kennett slid into his cruiser, gave a thumbs-up and buckled his seatbelt.

As he pulled out of the diner parking lot, Betsy flagged him down, walked over to the cruiser's passenger side and motioned him to lower the window. "You be careful. I don't like my friends and family being in danger. Especially because of me."

"Thanks, Betsy." Kennett nodded. "The next time

you're riled at me, I'm going to remind you of that friendship designation."

She smiled and pointed her finger in his direction, then tapped the side of the door panel a second before he drove away. Cain moved closer and looped his arm across her shoulders.

"Long story short, there were some other drug-related events that happened last night. They may all tie together." He remembered what Shadow had said about being sent to other locations in Missouri to watch who went where. So maybe it did all tie together, but for now he wouldn't hold out for any kind of an easy break in the case.

Besides, there might be an outside chance that what happened last night at Peyton's and the break-ins there and at Betsy's house early this morning were two separate cases. Coincidences happened. But not often—especially in the world of drugs. That was a business based on money and power...*and control*. Of course, there were usually a lot of strange bedfellows in that scenario.

CHAPTER TWENTY-FOUR

Pulling around to the back of his house felt like second nature to Cain. Parking under the carport felt secure. Garage would be better, but he worked with what he had. At least he'd invested in some dusk-to-dawn spotlights for the back door area. Out front, his house sat diagonal to a streetlight. He turned off the truck and glanced around the oversized double lot his house sat on.

There'd been a time when this had been his home growing up. Then his mother had left, and his dad liked the cabin at the lake better. This property had turned into rental income.

Cain had bought it a few years back when his dad needed money to move to Alaska. Now that Cain needed money to take care of his dad, he planned to sell the property. Sometimes life made not-so-funny circles. So did money. So did a person's health.

One of the first things Cain had done when he came back to town a few months ago, had been to clear out all the brush and junk and half-rotten trees that had taken over the property. Very little was left in the way of places someone could hide if they were planning to break and enter. Tonight, he was more than glad he'd done that. Tonight, that was a big plus.

Part way home, Betsy'd reclined the passenger seat a few inches and fallen asleep. These past twenty-four hours had been rough on her. Physically and emotionally. Probably felt like years since she'd flown out of California's LAX yesterday morning.

Betsy slowly stirred out of her short nap. Like a small child waking from a drive home from their grandparents' house, she fought to open her eyes. Softly grunted, then lightly sighed as she stretched. "Are we home?"

"Yeah. We're at my house." Cain grabbed his gun from the console and slid it into the holster strapped on his shoulder. "You wait here until I check inside."

Raising the passenger seat back to the upright position, she pulled on her hat and gloves. "Will do."

Feeling more than exposed as he walked to the back door, he looked for signs of fresh footprints in the snow. The only ones he saw were a jumbled, crisscross trail of rabbit tracks. Usually, the squirrels stayed further back on the lot, having made some big nests in a couple of the tall old trees. In fact, once he'd noticed the squirrels' nests, he hadn't had the heart to disturb them by taking down any limbs.

There'd never been a security system in this house, and he hadn't seen a reason to install one. But just like every job he'd been on and every place he'd ever lived, even as a teenager at the lake cabin, he had used his own carefully devised security system. Like placement of lint and paper, and clothes tossed in movement paths. And one he especially liked—a smooth broom sweep of carpet to show new footprints if there were any.

Stepping inside his kitchen, he quickly did a perimeter check and recon from room to room. Satisfied everything was safe, he motioned Betsy to go inside as he walked to the truck and grabbed her tote bag.

He followed her back into the kitchen and locked up behind them, then swept his arm in a circle of the room. "There's all kinds of food and drink, so you make yourself at home while you're here. May not be exactly what you're used to, but you won't starve."

"Don't worry about me. I can make a meal out of anything." She followed him as he started down the hall. "Once I unpack my tote, all I need is place to take a bath and sleep."

"Here you go." He tossed the tote onto the chair by his bed.

She glanced around, then tilted her head as she focused her look on his eyes and crossed her arms over her chest. "Uh...this is *your* bedroom. Where do I sleep?"

He raised his hands in self-defense. Evidently, he needed to explain reasons for his actions before they happened. "*You* will sleep here. *I* will sleep in the living room. And tomorrow we'll figure this whole arrangement out."

"Why can't I just sleep in one of the other bedrooms?"

"Go on. Look." Knowing the other two bedrooms were filled with everything from doors to lumber to almost anything else he needed to get this house back in shape to sell, he nodded toward the closed doors in the hall.

"Okay. I will." She headed toward the closest door. "I've known how to make my bed since I was four years old. And I must say I'm— Oh. My. Gosh!"

Quickly, he stripped the sheets from his bed and grabbed a clean set of sheets from the chest of drawers. He was just shaking out the fitted one when she walked back in and stood on the other side of the bed.

He raised his eyebrows and grinned. "Which of those bedrooms should I put your pillow in?"

"You think you're so funny." She grabbed the other side of the sheet and together they made the bed. "It's cold outside, so I understand why you keep the remodeling materials stored in there. But I do have a question. Why did you keep those doors up, but didn't do the same for your own room?"

"Ump! Good question. I'll let you know when I come up with that answer." He tossed the pillow in her direction. "Now, if you'll finish the pillow-in-pillowcase saga, I'll get the doors put up in here."

She'd barely finished the pillows while he had already hung the door between the hall and bedroom and was installing the handle and lock. "You don't have to do that."

"Won't take but a second. Then I'll do the bathroom door. You go ahead and unpack your tote. See what all your sister and Joanie sent you. In fact"—he opened one of the drawers in the chest and then pointed to the nightstand on the left side of the bed—"there's some empty spaces there for you to put things."

"Thanks. Do you mind if I set a few things in the bath? Hang a few things in the closet?"

A slight twinge ricocheted from his brain to his chest.

His gut clenched. He'd heard those questions from a few other women in his lifetime, and for a second his body had automatically reacted like it always had. *Say no. Shut down the relationship. Move on.*

But this was different. This was a job. Nothing more than a protective situation. Helping the police. Investigating a crime. Keeping someone safe. He'd done this before. Might last a week. Maybe two. Nothing more. Just a job. He was just helping an old friend. An old friend who—

Who was he kidding? This was Betsy. This was his future. His life. His home. His freedom. *This* was his choice. Would her choice be the same as his? Would she see the future and take a chance...just like him?

For now, though, he smiled as he walked to the closet and swiped his few clothes hanging there down to one end. "Sure. Whatever you want."

Reaching into the closet she grabbed a few empty hangers from next to his clothes. "You travel light. But that looks like a nice suit."

He fingered the material. "Yeah. The first suit I ever owned was the one my dad bought for me to wear to my mom's funeral. Now that he's not doing so well, I figured I should buy one for whenever his time comes."

"That's nice, Cain. Real nice."

"When my mom's cancer got worse, she had fewer and fewer good days. One of the last times she and I had a coherent conversation, she told me she figured my dad and I would butt heads someday. Made me promise to always stay in touch with him when I grew up. Said I'd understand when I got older and had seen more of life."

Cain tried to pull the rickety closet doors closed, but one wheel came off the track. "Damn it, I need to fix the closet, too."

"Don't worry. We'll get it done." She touched his arm. "You've been a little busy watching out for a lot of people, too."

"Now, most times I visit my dad, he doesn't recognize me." Cain sighed. "Funny thing though, even on those days, he always tells me to make sure his son Cain has food in the house and money for school lunch. Guess Mom was right, I'm still seeing life in new ways all the time."

Swiping his palm down his face, he went across the hall and came back with the door for the ensuite bathroom. He hated getting caught in memory conversations. "I'll get this door up, but they've given me the wrong knob and lock. I'll stop by the hardware store tomorrow."

While he worked on hanging the door, she started unpacking her tote. After putting a couple of things away, she suddenly stopped. Rezipped her bag. "I'll finish this later."

"Problem?"

She kicked off her boots and sat on the bed as she leaned back against the headboard. "Let's just say Marcy and Joanie have some interesting ideas about what I might need while I'm at your house."

"Interesting? Care to elaborate?"

"These for one thing." She blushed as she held up a few condom packets.

He felt it best not to comment, but noticed she shoved them into the drawer on her bedside table. Good to know. Doubtful they'd be needed.

Turning back toward him, Betsy's expression looked serious. "I would like to finish telling you what I started earlier today when we were down by the dock."

"Sounds good. You talk. I'll listen as I work." He'd keep working on the door that he already had done, but that way she wouldn't feel like she was in the spotlight with her story.

Tugging off her socks, she wiggled her toes then bent her knees and scrunched them tight, against her chest. Hugged them even closer. "My parents, Marcy and I had had a wonderful last day of summer at the lake. A few weeks before, Dad had had us all put one item in our so-called memory box. Said we'd bury it right before we finished the parking area the next year."

Her dad sounded like a man who loved his family and life. Cain had known others like him, others who'd lost their lives just doing their jobs. Some day he might, too. He'd made sure to enjoy and love life whenever possible, but he suddenly realized that having a wife and children to enjoy life with him had seldom, if ever, crossed his mind. Felt good to at least consider the idea.

Betsy cleared her throat. "By the time Mama, Marcy, Amber and me came down to the lake the next year, Papa C had had the parking pad completed with a poured concrete surface and surrounded by a sturdy metal railing on three sides. My parents had planned to do that, but there hadn't been money or time the year before. Papa C had simply said he'd wanted to do something in appreciation for all my dad had done for the community."

They sat there quietly for a while. Each in their own thoughts. Content to just be. To be together for a moment.

"Did you all ever bury the box any place?"

"No. Mama has it stored away in the safe room at her and Truman's house. I've often thought about opening that box and seeing how my treasured purple pen with a fuzzy road runner on the end has fared after all these years. But I haven't." Betsy smiled. "There was even a photo of me sitting on the dock fishing." She grinned larger. "And a plastic purple worm lure with a grungy dried-up worm still on the hook." She teasingly stop-signed him with her hand. "And before you ask. *Yes*, I always added a live worm onto *all* my lures."

Listening to her tell her story gave Cain the opportunity to connect with her on a whole different level. One that invited him into the family's world. He might not appear to be paying close attention, but he felt everything she was saying. Storing it away in his own memories. They'd always belong to him even if Betsy didn't.

"What about the initials I saw earlier today?" he asked.

Suddenly she giggled and waved her index finger in the air as if writing. "My dad had brought a couple bags of quick-setting concrete, mixed it with water from the lake and poured it in the hole me and Marcy dug. Once my daddy smoothed it out, we each etched our initials in it, all in a row."

Cain did a quick open-close-open on the door, then leaned back against the chest of drawers on the side wall. "Smart man. Sounds like he really cared about making things special for his family."

She nodded. "Once we finished up the concrete writing, we washed off our hands in the water at the edge of the lake. The weather was already cooling into fall temperatures, so swimming was out of the question. Then we all took a walk in the woods. Marcy and I kept stumbling over the roots and acorns. Lots and lots of acorns. Skinned my knees. Scraped the palms of my hands. I was the biggest klutz around."

He felt the rounding of his cheeks as he burst into laughter. "Well, I can outdo that. When I was seven, I broke my leg falling off my bike."

"I can do better than that." Squinting, she stared at the palm of her right hand then smiled as she pointed to a tiny scar on the pad of her palm beneath her thumb. "There... right there is proof of the *horrendous* injury I suffered when I fell over a downed tree that day. Landed on one of the snapped-off branches on the ground."

"While Mama and Marcy gathered up the food and drink from the picnic table," Betsy continued, "Daddy and I loaded fishing stuff. Then, we all piled in the truck and headed home to Jefferson City." Closing her eyes, she softly took in a deep breath and slowly blew it out.

"Sounds like it was a great day."

"One of the best days of my life."

She glanced into his eyes, and he saw that her own were glistening with tears. A couple spilled over onto her cheeks. So much for shoving his emotions aside, because they seemed to be tangling in with her own. Without thinking, he moved over beside the bed and wiped the wetness from beneath her eyes. Even scrubbed the heel of his hand against his own left eye. "Must have got some dust in my eyes as I hung the door."

She let go of her knees and reached her hand out to him. Interlacing his fingers with hers, he sat down next to her on the bed, offering the support of his arm as she leaned against him.

"Little did I know that would be the last time we were all together there at the lake," she said. "Three months later, he was killed walking down the steps of the FBI building in Jefferson City."

CHAPTER TWENTY-FIVE

Betsy woke with a start, but quickly oriented herself, remembering that she was in Cain's bed. Better than that, she realized they were spooned together with his arm draped across her middle. Her legs gently tucked between his. She smiled. Snuggled closer. The warmth of his skin against hers was everything she'd ever dreamed it would be. And last night had been—

"How are you this morning?" he asked in a husky whisper of tenderness. Kissing the sensitive spots across the back of her neck, he brushed his hand down the side of her hip and angled his body closer.

Turning slightly, she looked into his eyes and knew she'd found her soul mate years ago. Last night she'd finally felt his energy and passion. "I'm perfect. Simply perfect. How about you?"

As she turned toward him, she felt the heat in his lips on hers. Slowly, he eased his hand up her body, his fingers teasing as they found their way across her skin, and she arched into his touch. Loving every movement, every sensation, every moment, she fell into his hold, clutched the muscles of his back as they came together.

"How do I feel?" he said as he eased over her. "Like a man finally coming home."

Letting herself glide free of the past, she thought only of the future...and more specifically, the next few moments. And those moments turned into minutes...and minutes.

An hour later they both stood, showered and dressed, in the kitchen, staring at a slow-gurgling coffeepot. Cain answered texts on his phone, while Betsy made a couple of phone calls. Cups full, texts momentarily answered and calls finally finished, they leaned back against the counter and stared out at the snow in the backyard.

"What are your plans for today?" he asked.

"I just made an appointment to meet Crestfall's Insurance at the dealership. We figure it will be just as easy for him to see the damage as we fill out the report." Betsy sipped in the strong warmth of dark roast coffee. "He'll get the police reports as he needs them. How about you?"

"First, I need to meet with JB at the police station soon. But I don't want you to be out and about by yourself today." Cain quickly sent a text message. "What time is your appointment?"

"Mr. Crestfall said he'd be there about one. I plan to stop by the hospital and check on Papa Carrington this morning." She finished her coffee and rinsed the cup. "Don't worry about me, I'll be fine."

Cain's phone binged. "That was JB. He's sending Officer Hastings to keep a distant surveillance on you. And yes, I know you're not happy, but just give me this over-protectiveness for a couple more days. Okay?"

She'd learned a long time ago to be careful picking her battles, because sometimes it was just her trying to be in control. In this case, surveillance might be a wise decision. "Okay. Just this one time."

Smiling, he pushed her hair back behind her ear. "I know that was hard for you."

More than he would ever know. She valued her independence. Her mother had instilled that in all three of her daughters as they grew up. And with every decision they'd had to face...and make...along the way, her mother had always stood behind their choices and fought for their right to be who they were. Of course, a few times, once they got home Sadie had explained a better way of achieving the same wanted outcome in a more tactful manner. Marcy had learned that well. Herself, not so much. And Amber made her own way, somewhere between hardheaded perseverance, polite tact, obvious in-your-face sass, and an unnerving eye for reading people and clues.

"Hey, can you drop me by Peyton's this morning?" Betsy asked. "I need to pick up one of the SUV loaners we use at the dealership since my car got trashed at my house yesterday."

"Sure thing. You ready to go?"

She nodded, then brushed his cheek with a passing kiss. "By the way, on the way over, I'll give you some of the details about the day of the wreck that killed Phillip. Since you're involved in this case which somehow links to him and me, something tells me you need to know all of this."

"That would help. In fact, take all the time you want.

I'll swing by the donut shop and pick up a couple of coffees and donuts for us at the drive-through."

Twenty minutes later, Cain dropped her at Peyton's "Thanks for sharing the specifics on that day, Betsy," he said, grasping her hand as she squeezed tighter.

She swallowed the emotions fighting to overwhelm her. "Yes. In fact, I feel like some of the weight lifted a little more. Felt good to take about it."

"Just so you know, I'm gonna check on a couple of things you mentioned."

"May not be possible. Since the crash investigation was done through the local police department where the wreck happened, my uncle wasn't involved, even though he was the sheriff here. He said that without proof he had nothing to go on to call for further investigation. The case closed as an accident. Me, I still think of it as a cold case."

"What do you mean, a cold case?" Cain's tone deepened. His brow furrowed as his expression hardened with a penetrating stare of his suddenly very, very steel-grey eyes.

She loosened her hand from his and pulled on her gloves. "No one believed me about the gunshot sounds. Not even when they agreed the freak event of two tires blowing out on the *same* side at almost the *same* time was hard to believe. Papa C wouldn't even corroborate my account of him and Phillip arguing. Not even when I told them what Phillip had said."

She clenched her teeth in disgust. "Papa C said I must have been dreaming. Suggested I'd had too much to drink." Jerking her head in Cain's direction. "I'd had *one beer* the entire day. I know what I saw. I know what Phillip said. I know what I heard." She sighed as she slid out of the truck. "And no one believed me. No one."

Walking to Cain's side of the truck, she took time to slow her heartbeat and release her anger. He was out of the truck and standing by the bed as if he'd always been there for her. Leaning into his open arms brought her some peace.

"I'm sorry you had to relive that," Cain whispered against the top of her head. "I won't forget what you described. And thank you for trusting me, Betsy. Thank you."

They pulled apart and she searched in the side pocket of her purse for the loaner key she always carried. The SUV beeped as the doors unlocked, and she got inside and rolled the window down.

He kissed her lips then stepped back. "I'll do my best to be at the dealership when Crestfall's Insurance arrives for their walk-through. Will you two go to your house to file that report afterward?"

"No. For my personal insurance, I use the agent my mother always used. Crestfall's is the insurance agency Papa Carrington had always used for the dealership, so it's always been easier to keep that one in place. There's never been a major claim that I know of, so the rates are good. Or *were* good, anyway. I'm sure they'll increase after this type of major claim." She waved as she raised her window and drove away.

Forty minutes later she arrived at the hospital in Jefferson City and walked straight to Papa Carrington's room. Through the years, she'd spent too many hours in this hospital. Sometimes visiting patients, but after the car wreck that killed Phillip, she'd been a patient here herself, first in ICU for a couple days before transferring to a room and then home. Longest days of her life...but she'd at least survived the rollover.

Yesterday, talking with Cain and Kennett had somehow seemed to make things clearer about the day of the wreck. Papa Carrington, Phillip and she had spent the day at one of the dealership's big customer appreciation picnics. By the time everyone had left and the vendors had closed, it was dark and close to ten o'clock. Papa Carrington had insisted on driving that day, so she and Phillip had had to wait on him to drive them home. Tired, she'd curled up in the back seat and snapped on her seatbelt, leaving Phillip to ride shotgun in the front. Dog-tired hadn't come close to how she'd felt after the day of festivities, and she'd rapidly dozed off, only to be woken up by her husband and Papa C arguing.

The last thing she remembered before the crash was hearing Phillip shout that he'd be damned if he let them drag her into the middle of everything. Said he'd bring the whole group down before she became a pawn in their plans. Papa C had reached across and backhanded Phillip, who had shoved him in return. A second later a loud gunshot had reverberated from outside the driver's side of the car. The car had jerked. Swerved. Papa C had yelled as he lost control of the car.

She'd fought to right herself in the back seat. Watched Phillip release his own seatbelt and move across the front seat's middle console, reaching to regain control of the steering wheel for his dad. Another shot had jerked the car again. The passenger side veered off the road, sideswiped a tree and tilted into a double roll. Phillip had slammed against the windshield as it crumpled inward. Screaming, she'd tried to reach for him.

After that she remembered nothing but silence and darkness. A couple days later she'd woken up in this same hospital. Her life had changed in those few fast and chaotic moments. Phillip had died instantly in the crash.

Everybody had told her she'd only imagined the gunshot. That a tire blowout could sound the same. Could cause the same car reaction.

The doctors. Police. Papa Carrington. Even Mama. They all pooh-poohed her statement, noting she not only had broken bones, she had a concussion. To this day, she still held the belief that she'd heard a gunshot. No, she'd heard two gunshots.

Sometimes she still woke up in the middle of the night hearing what Phillip had said. How he had stood up for her. Defended her against—what? That she didn't know. And she'd never know.

She was content to remember the words and conviction in the way he had said them. That was one of the few times she could remember feeling her husband truly loved her. Phillip hadn't been perfect, but he'd got himself together. Was trying for himself and for her. In that moment, Phillip had been perfect.

That was just one of many reasons she hated hospitals and avoided them when possible. Some days she still blamed Papa C for the wreck, but accidents happened in life. Today she was here to see how he was doing. To let him know he still had someone to care for him, since his son and wife had passed on before. Phillip would have wanted her to see after his dad even though they had seldom agreed on anything.

After stepping off the elevator she followed the door numbers to his room. She softly knocked in case he was sleeping, then slowly opened the door to his room.

Someone from behind the door jerked it open and out of her hand. She stumbled forward as the door scraped out of reach, and a man reached out and roughly grabbed her arm to stop her from falling.

"Betsy, what are you doing here?" Papa Carrington asked from his bed.

Momentarily surprised at the spacious room, she quickly realized it was a private room. Of course, he'd always insisted on having the very best. Especially when it came to cars and boats, houses and vacations.

"Yeah. What do you want?" the bearded man from behind the door angrily asked, seeming to hide in the shadow of the open door.

For a split second she felt threatened, but then she saw Earl Millerton sitting on the chair beside the bed. A third man, almost a carbon copy of Papa C, yet greyer, lounged back on the two-person sofa in front of the window. He slightly raised his fingers as if calming the man behind the door.

"I came to see how you were doing, Papa C." She moved to stand on the other side of the bed, then rested her hand on the bedrail. He looked pretty good for all the injuries the floor nurse had talked about when she'd called yesterday afternoon to check on him. "Sorry I couldn't stop by sooner. Besides the destruction at the dealership, the thugs trashed my house, too."

He glanced at the grey-haired man on the sofa, but the man simply picked up the magazine on the side table and thumbed through it, then paused as if reading.

In turn, Papa C stared at the man behind the door, then patted her hand. "Oh my, that must have been traumatizing. No one had told me about that. Are you okay?"

"Yes, I'm fine. Thankfully I wasn't there when it happened. But how are you? The police said it appears you were hit from behind as you walked into the service center." Glancing at the bandage on the back of his skull, she shivered, knowing how painful that must be. "Are you going to be okay?"

"You know me, I'm always a survivor." He glanced around the room again. Swept his hand in the direction of the two men. "These are friends of mine who made a special trip from out of state just to see how I'm doing." Then as an afterthought he nodded in her direction. "This is Betsy Peyton. My daughter-in-law."

The man behind the door stared at her as if he were photographing her in his mind. She hadn't got a clear look at him, but something felt oddly familiar. Yet there was something just different enough that she couldn't make the connection.

Laying the magazine aside, the man on the sofa stood and offered his hand. "It's nice to meet you, Ms. Peyton. I've heard great things about you. Carrington's always raving about your business capabilities. I should stop by one day and see about a ordering a fleet of cars for my business."

She shook his hand and looked into his eyes. The hand

and the look were both cold as ice. "Call and make an appointment. I'll be happy to work on getting you the best deals on what you need. What line of business are you in?"

He stepped toward the door. "A little of this. A little of that. You might say I'm extensively diversified." Heading toward the door, he glanced at Papa C. "Well, we better be heading out. Was good to see you doing so well. You can never be too careful when you get knocked around. Let me know when you're released, and we'll continue our chat."

Papa C nodded.

The man behind the door opened it and waited until the sofa guy walked out. Then he glanced at Earl. "We'll talk soon."

"Whatever you say," he meekly replied, looking uncomfortable as he rocked back and forth in his seat.

A moment later, the two men were gone. She noticed that neither of their names were ever mentioned. She had never seen them around town before.

"That was nice of your friends to stop by," she said.

Papa C didn't answer but motioned her to pull a chair over by the bed. "So what's new at the dealership? Do the police have any clues? Anybody giving you a hard time?"

"Nothing major until this break-in. Well, nothing except the murder of the lookie-loo customer in the parking lot the night before all this happened." Feeling lightheaded, she exhaled slowly, with a slight tremble, as a vision of the body in the trash receptacle flashed through her mind once again. "I'm sure you heard about that. Right?"

He nodded. "I heard."

The room became quiet as if waiting for more

information. From who, she wasn't sure. "How are you feeling, Earl?" she asked.

"Good. I'm doing good." Her former service manager fidgeted and avoided her eyes.

"We all miss you at Peyton's, but I'm putting everything in place for when you feel like coming back." she said, smiling. "In the meantime, you'll be happy to know things have worked out good once I promoted someone to be temporary service manager."

"Who?" Papa Carrington asked.

"Derek Johnson. You know, the man Earl had hired a few months ago. He'd been working in the maintenance area for a while, and now he's turned out to always be on top of everything as the service manager."

"Did you know about this, Millerton?" Papa C asked, agitation clear in his tone and his blatant stare.

"Yeah. He came highly recommended."

"By who?"

"The people at the...uh, the poker game." Earl shot Papa C a direct narrowed eye look and held.

"I don't think I like—"

"You weren't available, so I needed to do what I thought was in everyone's best interest." Earl stood and walked to the window. Stared outside. "And Betsy offered me a desk job promotion when I'm back on my feet. So, I'll still be there to keep an eye on everything in the service center."

"Is there a problem?" Betsy asked, turning toward Papa C.

"No. No problem. It's just that the people at the *poker game* aren't always the best ones to rely on." Clearing his throat, her father-in-law reached out for her hand. "You be careful out there. Always check your references."

She felt the concern in his demeanor. "Don't worry, I do. In fact, this time, Earl had done a background check before he hired Derek, so I had all the info I needed."

The room quieted once again, so she took that as a sign to leave. She'd come to show concern and now it was time to go. The vibe felt off, but with everything that had happened in the past couple of days, she was probably just imagining the feel.

Glancing at her watch she pretended to be shocked at the time. "Oh my gosh. I'm about to be late to my meeting with the insurance agent. Mr. Crestfall's coming by the dealership to help me file the claim."

"If you wait a couple days, I can do that once I'm released from the hospital," Papa C said. "That's a lot of extra work on your shoulders."

"Don't worry about Peyton's. You just need to focus on your health right now." She leaned over and gave him a slight hug. "Besides, Cain said he'd stop by to help me if I had any questions."

"I don't know if I'd trust him." Papa C narrowed his eyes and set his jaw as he pushed up on one elbow and pointed his finger at her. "Some things are better left to those in charge."

A threat? Had he just threatened her? No, he'd meant it as intimidation. The tone had been the one he'd always used to bully people. Evidently this time he felt it would make her change her mind on filing the claim herself.

She'd seen Phillip bullied by his dad. Sometimes he'd even stood up against him. She'd been bullied by a lot of people in her life, too. The lessons had stuck as she learned to stand up for herself.

"You seem to forget, *I am* the one in charge." She smiled her sweetest smile as she opened the door to leave. "Cain *will be* my advisor. I trust him with my business. I trust him with my life."

Carrington slid back on his pillow. Tried to stare her down. Lifted his phone as if to call some unknown entity. "You might want to reconsider what you just said."

Now that was an all-out threat.

"You don't scare me, Papa C. Never have. Never will." Stepping out the door, she glanced back once again. No smile in her expression this time. "You don't scare me in the least."

CHAPTER TWENTY-SIX

Standing amid the yesterday's destruction in the service center, Betsy felt the same chaos in her life that she'd felt the day, years ago, when her uncle had stood at their front door to tell them her dad had been killed. Throughout her life, anytime she'd faced change or catastrophe, her own reaction had always been the same. Sadness. Disbelief. Anger. Then perseverance. Always perseverance to move forward.

For just this reason, Betsy had deliberately arrived at the dealership thirty minutes before the appointment with Mr. Crestfall was scheduled. She hadn't entered the main building which housed her office. That she couldn't face yet. Instead, she'd gone to the service center building.

Her instinct was to reach out and begin cleaning up the mess, but she knew the insurance adjuster would need to see everything just as it had been left. Of course, there were also remnants of the yellow crime scene tape still draped around the interior of the building. Around the entire Peyton's Dealership lot, also. She'd leave that until the police gave her permission to remove it.

With nothing she could really do at this point, she wished she hadn't arrived early. Depending on the time of the year, the service center was always noisy with conversation and music and machine noises—fans whirling, a/c whooshing or heat humming. Today there was utter silence.

She sighed. The building's empty loneliness was almost overwhelming. The past couple of days had been filled with activity, but Cain had been by her side all the way. And after all her doubts about his possible involvement in drug dealing, she'd come to realize that half of her doubts had been due to her past paranoia. The other half were because she'd always had a hard time trusting people

Paranoia might take a lifetime to master, but she was working on it. Relying on Cain had become part of her subconscious. They still might just be friends when this was all said and done, but she'd learned to trust her gut where he was concerned. Now, at this moment, she missed his support and confidence and protection.

Not that she felt afraid; the back door would squeak when someone entered. People were always trying to get her to WD-40 the hinges. But she never had, never would. Non-important doors worked smooth as silk. The one outside her office door in the main building, that one also had a sound that she thought of as her own built-in security alert.

Her phone rang with Marcy's ringtone.

"Hey sister of mine, are you having a good time in New York?" Betsy said as she answered the FaceTime call, making sure to keep it tightly focused on her face. Seeing the destruction of the repair shop in the background would only upset them. Of course, seeing her sister's face felt comforting.

"We're just getting ready to head out on the tour bus," Sadie said as she leaned into the frame. "I wanted to check on you before we go. Truman is staying in touch with JB and Cain, but I wanted to see you for myself. How are you holding up?"

Betsy smiled. Her mama was always a rock to the outside world and a strong shoulder to her girls. Yet, she almost had a sixth sense when it came to feeling others' need.

"I'm okay. Right now, I'm at the dealership waiting for the Mr. Crestfall," Betsy said.

"I thought you used Roosevelt Insurance Agency."

"Yes, that's who insures my home. But Papa Carrington had always used Crestfall's Insurance, and it's still through that agency. There's a discount for being a long-time customer."

The back door squeaked, and she spun around.

Cain stepped inside and a weight lifted from her. Since when had just the sight of him made her feel as if everything would be okay?

Quickly, she motioned him over with the hand holding the phone. Without thinking, she'd given Marcy and Sadie a view of the entire shop. Might have been a fast swoop, but she immediately heard her mama suck in a loud breath and yell for Truman.

"What all actually happened in there?" Straight and to the point, Marcy grabbed the phone and walked. "Show me, Betsy. Pan the room right now and show me how bad this is."

"No. I can't."

"Yes, you can, sister of mine. And I mean right now!"

Cain walked up and put his arm across Betsy's shoulder, and she leaned for a moment before straightening once again. This was going to be another long day.

Marcy cleared her throat. "Who else is there?"

"Hi, Marcy." He leaned into the view. "It's me

"It's Cain Connery. I'm staying at his house since mine is trashed." Betsy sighed. "But I'm sure JB already told you that part because you and Joanie sent me a tote bag. And before I forget, thank you. Thank you both very much. Even for the extra goodies you included."

"No problem. We had fun putting it together. Now it's all up to you," Marcy replied in a teasing manner.

Cain's glimmer of a smile along with a slightly raised eyebrow caught Betsy's attention. Sooner or later he'd probably see all those goodies in one way or another. Even she felt the corners of her own mouth turn up a bit, and for a moment she felt a lot warmer than she had a second ago.

"Now show me the damage to the repair shop," Marcy said, lowering her voice.

She knew Marcy wouldn't give up on this, so she might as well give her a glimpse at least. "Fine! But don't let Mama see."

Marcy nodded as she seemed to walk across the room on her end of the conversation. Slowly, Betsy panned the room with her phone. She tried to avoid the crime scene tape and the chalk outline of where Papa Carrington had been found before the EMTs took him to the hospital. "There. You satisfied?"

"I'm going to give that husband of mine a piece of my mind the next time I talk to him," Marcy huffed in agitation. "JB said there wasn't much to see. Not much he could say."

The door squeaked once again, and Cain moved in front of her as his hand eased in the direction of his shoulder holster concealed by his leather jacket.

"Hey, Mr. Crestfall just arrived. I'll talk to you later, sister of mine." Betsy ended the call, then turned to Cain. "Do you mind staying for this?"

"Whatever you want. I'm here to help anyway I can." He glanced in the direction of Mr. Crestfall and a couple of other people walking beside him. "You've got this, Betsy. You've got this."

Mr. Crestfall had arrived right on time. The man and woman with him quickly introduced themselves as adjusters. Of course, the insurance agency was well known in Crayton, but the two adjusters had probably been dispatched by the policy company's main office.

"It's good to see you," Betsy said. "As you can see, this is a mess. You tell me, where do we start with filing the claim?"

"I was able to get a lot from the police report, but there's still paperwork we'll need to fill out. Photographs. Forms. First though, do I have permission for myself and the adjusters to take photos and catalog the specifics of the damage?" Mr. Crestfall asked.

"Sure. Whatever you need to do." She pulled out a few sheets of paper from her briefcase. "In fact, I've already printed out the building specs plus the MRO...I mean the Maintenance, Repair and Overhaul inventory list. I can email you those files, also."

The insurance agent reviewed the paperwork, then handed it over to one of the adjusters. "Be sure to get documentation in photos, also."

The woman nodded and started working down the list. The man stood nearby as if waiting for further instructions.

Betsy's brow wrinkled. "What do we do about the customers' vehicles that were damaged? I don't know how to document those for insurance coverage."

Mr. Crestfall motioned to the other adjuster. "Can you take photos of the damage and get the VINs, the vehicle information numbers? We'll have to work from that for now."

Cain offered to show the adjuster the layout of the vehicles and shop. "Of course, they trashed the computers, too."

She pulled an iPad out of her case and handed it to him, then turned to Mr. Crestfall. "As you may remember, I had Cain Connery's name added to our employee coverage a few weeks ago. He's in town on some personal business, and also working with the police as a consultant. I hired him part-time for extra help this winter. I completely trust him with my business records."

CHAPTER TWENTY-SEVEN

Cain made sure to stay within earshot of the conversation going on between Mr. Crestfall and Betsy. Considering the insightful meeting with JB this morning, and everything that had happened yesterday, nothing about this case was normal. Robberies normally could be categorized, but first of all, this hadn't been a robbery. Second, his gut told him this was more than just an outside job, so he'd keep watching for signs of an inside connection.

Who, how and why were still the top questions on his list.

"Is Mr. Millerton still your service center manager," the insurance agent asked.

Professional to the core, she looked Mr. Crestfall in the eye with every answer she gave. "He's still on disability. I've promoted Derek Johnson to that position. Should I call him in to help, also?"

The insurance agent glanced around the building. "Why don't we see how far we get today? We also need to examine the showroom and administrative offices, right?"

"Yes. I have a whole different set of MOR paperwork on that."

"Good. Will Papa Carrington be joining us today?"

"No, he's still in the hospital. In fact, I just stopped by to see him this morning." She looked in Cain's direction. "Mr. Millerton was there visiting. And a couple of other men I didn't know."

The insurance agent made a note, then checked a text that had just binged. "Did you get the idea he would be able to join us tomorrow?"

Betsy straightened and shot a stone-cold serious stare in Mr. Crestfall's direction. "Are you insinuating you'd rather speak with Papa C than me? Because I'm the controlling shareholder in this business. Or is it because I'm a woman?"

"No. No, not at all." Mr. Crestfall fidgeted. Stuttered with his answer. Sucked in a shoulder-raising breath, then blew out loudly before he glanced at Cain. "It's just..."

Cain turned away from the adjuster he'd been assisting and moved a bit closer to Betsy's conversation. Being sure to take the iPad with him. "It's just what?" he asked.

Mr. Crestfall faced Betsy head on. His expression a mix of respect and compassion and a little bit of I'm-caught-in-the-middle nerves.

"You know me. You know I would *never* demean you, or any other woman," the insurance agent said. "The thing is that, besides the two adjusters with me today, the regional office is sending a couple of senior adjusters to look at this case. They plan to meet with you and the police. And they've requested a conversation with Papa Carrington, also."

"Why?" she asked.

Cain wanted to ask the same question, only in a totally different way. One that involved a whole different set of legal and law enforcement questions than what Betsy would ask. But he'd wait.

Mr. Crestfall motioned toward the back door, then whistled to the two adjusters working in the service center. "You all keep working on this. When you're finished here, head over to the offices and showroom."

Turning back to Betsy and Cain, the insurance agent glanced back and forth between them once, twice, three times. Finally, he lifted his arm in the direction of the squeaky door. "How about the three of us take a walk outside? Get a little fresh air before we start in your office."

Cain had been involved in a lot of walk-and-talk conversations in his career. Most times it gave everyone a chance to relax. Hopefully that's what this was about. Betsy needed something good happening after the past few days.

For a few minutes the three of them walked casually around the perimeter of the Peyton's lot. A break in the clouds gave them a chance to enjoy the warmth of the winter sun for a moment. And for once in the past twenty-four hours, the wind had died down to an occasional breeze. Any other time, this would have been a perfect time to take Betsy's hand. Right now, this was still about business, so he followed the insurance agent and Betsy's lead.

Gradually Mr. Crestfall slowed. "You asked why the main office wants to speak with Papa Carrington?"

Betsy nodded as they stepped inside the showroom. The police had already scanned for fingerprints, clothing fibers, hair, and other clues in both buildings. "Yes. I get the feeling there's something I don't know. What would that be?"

Motioning everyone to the customer waiting area, she grabbed bottled water for each of them from the free vending machine she'd had installed. This area was one of the few sections of the building that had been overlooked, deliberately or not, by the intruders.

Mr. Crestfall settled at one of the mostly clean tables and opened his briefcase. "My guess is that it has to do with the three large claims previously filed by the dealership."

She frowned. "Sure, we've had a few claims through the years. Nothing out of line, though. Nothing major, that I can recall."

"Two of these would have been before your ownership happened. In fact, they both occurred within a year of each other, over twenty years ago."

Cain cleared his throat. "So that would have been back when the place was called Carrington & Son New and Used Cars?"

"Yes." The insurance agent sorted through some papers he'd laid on the table, then opened his laptop and started typing. "My agency has handled all the dealership's insurance business since it originally opened. The claims have stayed with the ongoing policy."

Cain moved away from the wall and stepped closer.

"Betsy, I remember you said you kept the same policy because of the cheaper premiums. Right?"

"Yes, I was advised to keep the same policy," she said, starting to pace.

"Who told you to do that?"

"Papa Carrington." She pointed at Mr. Crestfall. "He said he'd checked everything out with you before he transferred ninety-five percent of the business to me. Said you told him that would be the cheapest way to go for insurance."

The insurance agent checked something on his computer. Took a moment to read whatever had come up on his screen. "Yes, Mr. Carrington and I met about a month before Phillip and your wedding. Papa C gave me an overview of how he planned to give you majority ownership of the business. I compiled some options to consider on the insurance needs and premiums. In fact, a couple of the plans would have been a cheaper premium than what Papa C ended up choosing."

"Then why did you recommend staying with the same policy?"

"I didn't." Mr. Crestfall adamantly shook his head. "As a matter of fact, I showed him all the paperwork that would need new signatures. He said he'd need to talk to his partners and get back to me the next day. I even printed a packet out for him to take home for consideration. I assumed he'd be talking with you also."

Questions were being answered, but the answers were only leading to other questions.

"I need some coffee," Betsy said as she moved to the

individual coffee maker in the customer service waiting area. "How about you two?"

Thankful for a moment to let the tension in the room ease, Cain made a strong black coffee for himself. As did Mr. Crestfall. Making herself a second cup of coffee, she poured both into her coffee tumbler. Added a few creamers and a couple sugar packets. She looked tired.

Mr. Crestfall's phone rang, and he told the adjusters, who were just finishing up in the service center, to leave for the day once they were done in that building. Said they'd finish in the showroom and administrative offices tomorrow morning.

"Okay, back to the questions," Betsy said. "I assume the partners were Phillip and"—she shrugged—"Who? Did Shorestone keep a partial ownership?"

"Oh no, when Mr. Shorestone left to run for office, he sold out entirely. Mr. Carrington was never overly forthcoming about his new investors." The insurance agent shut down his computer and closed the lid. "The few times I tried to get an answer, he said the group was a private partnership between a few people who wished to remain anonymous. Made it appear they were people familiar with Crayton, who wanted nothing more than to give back to the community. My guess is he pays them an agreed amount out of his share of the business."

She shot Cain a look. Raised her eyebrows. "Going back to the new policy conversation, when did Papa C call back with his answer?"

Cain was proud of her. She was staying on top of everything being discussed and not flinching a bit at what was being thrown at her. He was also impressed by the way

Mr. Crestfall was handling this conversation. As far as he could tell, the insurance agent was being forthcoming and honest.

"*Bright and early* the next morning. And I mean he woke me from a sound sleep at four thirty a.m." Mr. Crestfall quirked the side of his mouth. "You know, I receive a lot of calls at all times of the night. But that's the only time I can recall someone calling that early when it wasn't a matter of life and death. Or some kind of catastrophic loss. I remember, he sounded like the whole world depended on me knowing ASAP."

Betsy looked thoughtful. "I know what you mean. Sometimes Papa C can be on edge for no reason. Especially when a big decision is needed."

Mr. Crestfall shoved his laptop into his briefcase. "Well, in this case, his answer was no. Leave everything the way it was, except add your name as controlling owner at ninety-five percent, and he was reduced to five percent ownership. He also added Phillip as an employee which was the first time his son had been officially added as anything in the business. Papa C changed the business name on the policy to Peyton's. Plus, added you and Phillip to the business partner life insurance."

Cain had a gut reaction. One that said *ask the next question*, but Betsy didn't ask. Probably didn't know what that question would automatically be in a criminal case.

"I'm sure Betsy would like to make sure the correct people are on the business partner life insurance," Cain said in a nonchalant way. "Maybe you could send her a list."

"Sure. I'll send you an email." Mr. Crestfall entered a voice note in his phone to do that. "But I can tell you right now, it's just a few people. Betsy, Papa Carrington, Earl Millerton, Steven Millerton and Cain Connery."

"Cain? Why?" she asked.

"Papa C called the day after you put Mr. Connery on the regular company liability insurance. Said to put a two-million-dollar business life policy on him." Mr. Crestfall looked up another note on his phone. "Said you had approved it personally, Betsy."

She jumped to her feet, shivering with rage. "How could I approve adding someone to a list I know nothing about?"

The back of Cain's neck tensed. Icy cold chills raced across his shoulders. *Target* flashed through his mind. Whose cage had he rattled? How? When?

He pointed back and forth between the insurance agent and Betsy. "Take my name off that damn policy. *Right now!*"

CHAPTER TWENTY-EIGHT

Cain pulled his phone from his jacket. Something wasn't right. He didn't know what yet, but he planned to find out starting now. First, he needed to get Betsy home where he stood a better chance of protecting her. In his opinion, nobody's name on the current business partner life insurance list was safe.

"Mr. Crestfall, we all got to talking so much," Cain said. "You didn't answer her question about the two big settlements twenty-some-odd years ago."

"Oh my gosh, I'm sorry, Betsy. That just completely slipped my mind." The insurance agent popped his palm against his forehead. "Anyhow, the first one was when Mr. Dash was killed in the robbery at the original car lot."

"He was one of the original partners, right?" Cain clarified.

"Yes. From the second the three original investors signed their partnership agreement, there was a business partner life insurance policy plan dropped into effect. Three partners. Three policies. When Mr. Dash was killed, that policy was paid out per the policy arrangements. All two million dollars."

Betsy paled as her mouth dropped open. "Two million dollars. That can't be. Joanie and her mother barely had money to put food on the table."

"It wasn't paid to the family," Mr. Crestfall said. "It was paid to the owner of the policy—Carrington & Son automotive business."

Seeming paler than before, Betsy stared at a picture on the wall, one of mountains with a lake in front. Cain stepped up beside her and guided her to a chair. Grabbing her purse, she rummaged inside till she found a small zip-bag of jellybeans and hard candy. As she chewed a few of them, he grabbed a bottle of Gatorade from the mini fridge in her office.

"Of course, when I said two events, that didn't include the most recent policy payout," the insurance agent continued. "As you are aware, when your husband Phillip died, his two-million-dollar business partner life insurance disbursement was paid directly to you—excuse me, I mean Peyton's—in the form of a check."

"What? *What* are you talking about? I *never* received a check from your company for Phillip's death." Her tone and words were strong and clear. "*Never.*"

Mr. Crestfall flipped through the records on his phone. Stared at what he was evidently searching for. "Ah, now I remember. I personally brought the check here to your office, but Papa C said you were still at home recuperating from the accident. Said you weren't accepting anyone but family as visitors at that time. He offered to take the check to you so it could get in the bank as soon as possible."

Betsy began pacing. "I'm telling you, I never received a check."

Slowly guiding his screen info upward on the phone, he stopped and turned the phone toward her. "Here's a photo of the check and endorsement for the check's bank deposit. This is all here in our company files."

Taking his phone, she stared at the front and back of the check. Showed it to Cain as she turned to the side and leaned close to his ear. "That's *not* my signature. What should I do now?"

His brain compartmentalized each issue that needed further investigation. The problem was that things were piling up rapidly. But since Betsy trusted him enough to ask him for advice, he'd try to get as much info as possible from Mr. Crestfall without out and out lodging a complaint now.

Cain took the insurance agent's phone from Betsy. Enlarged the endorsement bank codes long enough to snap a photo with his own phone before handing it back. "Mr. Crestfall, Betsy's not recalling this check. Could you send her a copy of the front and back. And can you or the main office send her copies of any and all paperwork, notes, etc. pertaining to this payment?"

"Certainly." With only a few clicks he emailed Betsy the check copies on his screen. "As soon as I'm back in my office, I'll have everything else sent as requested."

"Thank you. I'm not feeling well, Mr. Crestfall," Betsy said. "Could we finish this conversation tomorrow?"

"Certainly. Take care of yourself. Call any time. I'll make space on my schedule." Mr. Crestfall nodded and stepped outside, pulling the door closed behind him.

She watched the man leave, then turned back to the mountains in the picture. Cain readied to call JB. Suddenly she raced past him. Yanked open the back door and chased after the insurance agent. Cain chased after her.

"Wait!" Betsy shouted, catching up to the insurance agent as he tossed his briefcase into the back seat of his van. "What was the second big settlement from over twenty years ago?"

Mr. Crestfall glanced in Cain's direction, then turned to face her. "I figured you already knew, Betsy."

"Knew what?" she asked. "How would I know what the other settlement was about? I was only ten, going on eleven years old at that time."

The insurance agent swallowed big and blew out a heavy sigh. "The other two million dollar pay out to Carrington & Son was after the death of your dad."

Cain stepped up next to Betsy as she paled, then started to tremble. All he could do at this point was be there for her no matter where this conversation led. Investigating would come later.

She steadied her hand against the nearest car. "*My dad*?"

"Yes. Mr. Peyton was insured as a business partner with Carrington & Son New and Used Car. He'd been added to the policy just a couple months before he was tragically killed there at the FBI office in Jefferson City," Mr. Crestfall said.

"That can't be right. My dad *never* worked for the dealership. *Never!*" Then as if this was more than she could take, tears trickled from her eyes. More and more. Fuller and faster until her cheeks were wet. Her chin quivered as tried to speak. "My mama and us, we never saw a penny of that insurance disbursement."

Calmly, Cain motioned the insurance agent to leave, then followed up with a gesture indicating he wanted to talk to him later. Mr. Crestfall nodded in return, then started his car and drove away.

For the next few minutes, he held Betsy, and she let him. A lifetime of emotions seemed to be spilling forth from her. He figured he was one of the very few people who had ever seen her cry. Especially with such raw to the bone emotions fueling the crash. Especially when she'd been holding everything deep inside since she was eleven years old.

All the while he held her, his mind scrambled to think of all the assorted implications this information could have. Others who might have been on that insurance list at one time or another in the last twenty years. Right now, though, his only concern was Betsy and her family.

Finally composed, she eased back, and he gave her space.

A stab of pain jagged through his body from his gut to his heart to his brain. Right now, he needed to ignore his heart and think only with his brain. His gut feeling was always his brain's trigger. Just knowing his name was on the business insurance list had put his flash point on alert.

The last few minutes had been what cases were made on. Where hints of clues tumbled forth from nowhere. He needed to catch up on Crayton and its people. The entire region might fall into whatever this was...maybe even more. Priority, make some phone calls. Review what he already knew. What he didn't know. He didn't like his premonition. This had been a hell of a long couple of days. His gut told him this was only the beginning.

Walking far enough away to be out of earshot with Betsy, he called Truman in New York. No answer, so he left a voice message to call him back ASAP.

The moment he disconnected, his phone rang with an incoming call. "Yeah. That was fast."

"I don't know who you're expecting, but this is Joanie." Her voice was tense, and she seemed to be talking faster than usual. "I've got a jalapeño pizza for you. Where should I deliver this ASAP special double-boxed order? *ASAP* was his exact word."

His shoulders tightened. For the second time in less than an hour, the back of his neck chilled. Corner of his eye twitched. "Joanie, are you where you can talk without being heard?"

"Give me a second."

He heard the closing of a door and a lock being thrown on her end.

"What do you need?" she asked.

He started to follow Betsy into the building, then he stopped and glanced around the car lot instead. Nothing to see but the usual cars and trucks and SUVs. Still, he lowered his head and covered his mouth with his hand. He'd learned a long time ago how easily someone could zero in with a pair of binoculars to read a person's lips. And just in case the building hadn't been swept for listening devices, he walked over to an SUV in the second row and leaned as if checking the insides.

"Lift the top box and see if there's a note beneath it." He'd always trusted Joanie and had no reason not to at this moment. In fact, she'd be in the top ten people he could trust in Crayton if he was making a list.

"Yes, there's a note, just like you said. And I know for a fact it came from the guy with the white hat. I saw him fix the box myself," she said.

"Good. Now read me the note." Funny how quick he had fallen into his undercover routine. Guess some things would never change. "Oh, and this is all confidential."

"Of course," she replied in a snarky tone, then sighed. "Everything to do with you or JB or the sheriff...in fact, any of the local law enforcement, is always confidential."

Suddenly the back door of the building opened, and Betsy stepped back outside and closed the door behind her. Glanced around the lot as if looking for him.

"Hey, Betsy. I'll be right there," he shouted over to her.

She nodded then jerked on the back door as if making sure it was locked. "I'll walk on down to the service building and lock up down there, too."

"Sounds good. I'll meet you there." He turned back to his phone conversation. "Okay Joanie, what does the note say?"

"Arrest me ASAP—middle of town—front of a lot of people. Make it believable! White hat between 5:30 p.m. Armed. Won't draw." She lightly cleared her throat. "That's all there is except in all caps he wrote HBL with a double-slash mark underneath."

HBL—hell broke loose—Cain's flash point went off. "Joanie, take that pizza and note to the police station. Give it *only* to JB, Kennett or the sheriff."

"On my way. Bye."

Texting JB as he ran across the car lot toward the service

center, Cain told him to read the note when Joanie arrived. *I'm on my way to the station, also. Bringing Betsy.*

He shoved his phone in his pocket as he saw her do a doorknob jerk on the door to the service center. "Get in my truck ASAP," he shouted. "We're headed to the police station."

CHAPTER TWENTY-NINE

The past hour had flown by in record time at the police station. Cain, JB, Kennett and Sheriff Davis had devised the plan for arresting Shadow. Kennett did the takedown along with JB, Deputy Evans, and Officer Hastings as backup. Quick and fast and even, with a few punches thrown in for good measure. It was about making everything look real and getting Shadow out of the deep undercover assignment alive and in one piece.

Like clockwork, a live stream of the arrest had popped up online, with others posting their own videos right up until the handcuffed Shadow had been walked into the Crayton police station. Even the Jefferson City news station picked up on the happenings and promised their listeners they'd keep them posted for anything further.

Inside the police station, Shadow had been booked and tossed into a cell, awaiting pickup by the DEA's St. Louis office. By this time tomorrow, Shadow might be on a long-deserved vacation or headed for a new assignment. First,

Cain and the others needed to hear Shadow's briefing before he left the area.

Everyone involved in the fake arrest gathered in the sheriff's office, as well as Betsy. Cain wasn't letting her out of his sight until he knew what was going on that had Shadow running to escape from his case.

Kennett kicked back on the sofa while he nursed his swollen jaw with an ice bag. But he'd still been able to down a couple slices of the jalapeño pizza.

Biting the inside of her cheek, Betsy motioned she was headed to the restroom. She'd been nothing but quiet so far. So quiet, her uncle and JB had pulled Cain aside to ask if she was okay. He'd nodded and told them it had been another long day for her, and that Mr. Crestfall had shared some information which needed further investigation.

"Hey, you better have my white hat," Shadow said as he stepped inside the office and pointed at Cain. "Or they're going to owe me a another new one."

Cain reached behind the desk, then tossed the Stetson to him. "Never fear, I've got it. You know, I could have retired a long time ago if I didn't have to keep buying you new hats so often."

The agent centered the hat on his head before reaching for the box of jalapeño pizza. "Looks like I've got competition on my favorite pizza."

Kennett stood, closed the door behind the agent, then held out his hand. "That would be me. I don't think we've officially met. I'm Officer Kennett."

"I'm Shadow," he said as he offered his handshake in return. "Thanks for getting me off the street with as little damage as possible. Sorry about your jaw."

Tossing the ice bag toward the agent, Kennett grinned. "What, this little bump? Nothing at all. How's your cheek?"

"Stings like hell." Shadow caught the bag and held it against the side of his face for an instant before laying it aside.

"The important thing is, you're out of the line of fire from the assignment," Cain said as he also shook his sometimes partner's hand. "Let me officially introduce you to the others. This is Acting Sheriff JB Bradley, Deputy Evans and Officer Hastings. You already met Sheriff Davis in his office earlier. Basically, he's still supposed to be in St. Louis for rehab and physical therapy from when he was shot a couple months back. But what with everything going on with his niece Betsy, he got back in town late last night. We've convinced him to head home for some sleep, but we can get him on speaker phone if needed."

After shaking hands all around, Shadow picked up a piece of the pizza and leaned against the wall. "This everybody in on arresting me? Everyone who knows about me?"

Cain nodded. "Everyone except Betsy and Joanie."

"Good. The fewer the better. Once the St. Louis DEA picks me up, it'll be as if I never existed in Crayton or this whole assignment." He bit into the pizza. "That is, unless this all comes to trial. Which at least some of it will, sooner or later."

"What makes you say that?" JB asked.

"For the past few years, I've picked up on a lot of criminal history, dating all the way back to—"

The office door opened and Betsy stepped back inside.

Took one look at Shadow. Paled. Screamed. Grabbed one of the pizza boxes and slammed it broadside against Shadow's shoulder and head. His white hat flew off as he deflected a second hit from Betsy. Then another...and another.

"Betsy!" Cain rushed forward. Enveloping her with a gentle bear hug, he pinned her swinging arms to her sides. "It's okay, Betsy. This is Shadow. The DEA agent I told you about. He's—"

"No! He's not who you think he is." She shook off Cain's hold, then moved directly in front of the agent. "He's Phillip's drug supplier. The one I saw him talking to on the front porch that night. And I'm sure that, ever since Phillip died in the wreck, he's the same man who stands outside my window sometimes."

Cain pulled her behind him as he took center stage, confronting his sometime partner. "That right, Shadow?"

JB and Kennett tensed, stood and rested their hands on their guns. Officer Hastings and the deputy took up secondary positions. Deliberately or not, all of them kept pushing Betsy back and to the side.

Shadow raised his hands, palms facing out, between Cain and himself. Pumped them in a slow yet urgent manner. "Hold it. Hold it right there. Everybody needs to slow down for a second."

Clenching his fist, Cain held on to his composure by the width of a thin thread. "I asked you a question."

"Back it on down, Cain." Acting Sheriff JB placed his

hand on his friend's shoulder and pulled him back toward the desk. "Give him a chance to explain. Shadow, what have you got to say for yourself?"

The agent nodded, then slowly picked up his white hat from the floor and set it on the edge of the desk. "Betsy's partially right. I was talking to Phillip the night she saw us on the front porch. He and I met there several times. It was the safest place we could come up with under the circumstances."

Betsy pushed through the law enforcement personnel, moving slowly to the front of the group. Cain had regained his professional demeanor, but at no time did he make eye contact with her. He just continued to keep his eyes on the agent.

"What do you mean safe?" Betsy asked. "Safe from what?"

"Phillip had contacted the DEA a little over a year before you saw us." Shadow turned to face her directly. "He provided information on some criminal activity happening at the dealership in Crayton. When the Agency checked out the details, they found there might be more going on than he thought."

"At my dealership? Peyton's?" Betsy felt like she might throw up.

"Yes, ma'am."

She straightened with indignation. "That's not possible. I run an honest business. Always have. Always will. DEA or not, I don't take kindly to your insinuation." She crossed her arms over her chest. "And that includes whatever Phillip told you. He really wasn't even involved in the dealership. Never spent more than a couple hours a week at the place."

Shadow glanced at Cain and JB.

Clearing his throat, JB got everyone's attention. "Recently, I've been involved in Shadow's assignment. So has Kennett. And I filled Cain in early this morning. It's important that all of you hear what this DEA agent has to say."

For the next few minutes Shadow proceeded to explain the assignment parameters. Originally the DEA had sent him to gradually ingratiate himself into the regional drug ring. Which he'd done. Which was why he'd needed to be arrested today and gotten out of harm's way. Because that group was fighting amongst itself, and splintering factions were scattering to other locations in North America.

But during his time in Crayton, Shadow had also learned of another crime family trying to take hold of the area. One that had been in business for almost a century. Dealing and stealing, loan sharking and blackmail, anything and everything had been fair game through the decades. It wasn't just local either, the group had radiated from northern Illinois to Iowa, Missouri, western Kentucky, and even eastern Kansas.

As if a switch had been flipped, Kennett sat down. His expression cried alert. Slow and precise, he leaned forward, rested his elbows on the tops of his knees. "Did you say Illinois?"

"Yes." Shadow stared directly at him. "If you want, we can have a confidential conversation about that later."

"I'd like that." Kennett nodded and rested back in his

seat. His expression suddenly harder to read, ranging between stress, anger and misery.

Shadow turned back to the group to continue. The DEA and FBI had decided to keep him in place so he could keep an eye on the other group from his position in the original drug cartel. The FBI had someone already in place tracking the group from Illinois. "That would be the man killed at Peyton's."

"The man I called the lookie-loo?" Betsy asked.

"Yes. He was a good man. A good agent." Shadow shook his head. "But there was a leak somewhere and that got him killed."

The room was quiet for a bit, as if giving respect to the agent who had lost his life. After a minute or so, everyone seemed to come back to the situation at hand.

"I'm sorry for that loss, but that still doesn't explain why you were meeting with Phillip," Betsy said.

"You're right. We all knew going in that the case would be a slow build. One that might take years. Cover a lot of ground, physically and research wise." Shadow turned to face Betsy. "The break came when Phillip agreed to work with the DEA, FBI and myself."

Betsy looked as if someone had just punched her in the gut. Her mouth dropped open, her breathing became jerky. "My Phillip worked with you?"

"Yes, ma'am. I trusted Phillip from our first meeting. Even more so when he verified some points only on my radar. From that point on, things progressed fast and expansive. We needed a place to meet that would be safe for both of us. Your all's house seemed like the logical spot."

Blinking away tears from her eyes, she cleared her

throat as her chin quivered. "You behind the pine tree. Phillip on the front porch."

"I want you to know that Phillip quickly became one of the most trustworthy informants I'd ever had on any job," Shadow said. "Our system worked fine for a while. Then things started getting dicier. Wasn't long till my side of the assignment seemed to be changing. I got the feeling there was a new bull trying to move in and take charge with the group I'd first infiltrated. Also, got word here and there that they were planning another expansion in the Midwest."

Trying to stay with the story being told, Betsy had to admit there were times she couldn't keep all the ins and outs straight, but she listened. Listened close to everything that the agent had divulged about his assignment. Knowing Phillip had been helping with the drug case brought her a sense of pride that he'd taken his rehab seriously.

Still, part of her was not a bit happy with the fact JB had kept her out of the loop once he'd been added to the DEA info path. Or with Cain for not filling her in when he got the whole report from JB. She understood why—still didn't make her happy.

"I warned Phillip to be careful, but he just kept digging and digging on his side of the assignment." Shadow removed his hat and placed it on the desk. His brow pinched together as he raked his fingers through his hair. "Phillip was so close to finding the final piece of the puzzle regarding the Illinois group. He'd almost figured out how his dad had had such a sudden success in the auto business."

The agent shook his head. "He was so determined to do what was right and take down the controlling element. Even if it meant taking down his dad, the dealership, and possibly even more of their estranged family."

Betsy felt lightheaded. Those words she'd understood. "Wait! What did you just say about the dealership? What did Phillip and you find out?"

"Nothing specific, but we were close. Real close," Shadow said. "In fact, Phillip planned to confront someone at that picnic. I told him not to, but he was determined. He always talked about buying some land so you two could build a bigger house and start a family. But first, he wanted whatever hold there was over his dad to be put to rest. Said he didn't want a child of his to ever be threatened or blackmailed because of their past."

Shadow braced his legs a foot apart, his body swaying forward and back, forward and back, forward and back as his expression shadowed remorse and strength. "I've often wondered if the wreck had anything to do with that final piece. And I'll never know if he talked to anyone at that picnic or not. Once he was killed in the wreck, the trail went cold. Cold and quiet as ice."

Suddenly all her business pride flew out the window as Shadow, Cain, JB, Officer Hastings and Kennett laid out everything they knew—not only from the past few days since the events at Peyton's had happened, but evidence that dated back five, ten, even twenty years.

Gradually, they pieced together the possible premises they'd started with and tried to see where the information she and Cain had gathered from the insurance agent earlier today fit into the mix. Especially the business partner life insurance policies that had been paid out through the years. And the people on the current list.

The intercom buzzed with news that the DEA and FBI had arrived to take Shadow out of the assignment, out of the line of fire for being a plant. Word had also come in that the regional cartel had gone into silent mode and scattered to the far winds.

"You all wrap this up. We need to get Shadow on the road to a little peace of mind for a while," JB said as he motioned to the others and shook the agent's hand. "Thanks for everything. You've made a big dent in the local drug case."

"I think there's more going on in Crayton than drugs," Cain said, holding out his hand. "A whole lot more. Some of it may tie into the drug operation, but I've got a bad feeling the worst reveal is still to come. Sorry if I was out of line before."

Accepting the apology, Shadow took his hand. "No problem. I knew this would be tricky, trying to get everything out in the open without being on the wrong end of your punch."

"I don't mean to be out of line, but I do have one more question." Betsy stepped in front of the agent. "Once Phillip was killed in the wreck, why have you been standing outside my living room window every so often?"

Shadow braced his hands on his hips. "One thing Phillip made me promise was that if something went wrong and he didn't make it, I'd keep an eye on you. Especially when I had any inkling you might be in danger. So, been there a few times. Even volunteered when the local drug boss asked for someone to watch your house one night. I still don't know what was going down, but I wasn't about to trust your safety to anyone else." He straightened a bit and swallowed. "You see, I try hard to *always* keep my promises."

Betsy couldn't explain why, but without a second thought she reached out and hugged him. "Thank you for helping Phillip. And me. Thank you for everything you've done."

"Don't think too bad of Phillip," Shadow whispered in her ear as he returned her hug. "He loved you more than you'll ever know. And even though he wasn't perfect, none of us are. We're all just human, trying to do the best we can."

Dropping his quick hug, he stepped back. "By the way, until Cain came on the scene, I'd stay around the general area of the dealership most Friday nights until I could make sure you'd left work. Had some mighty good home-cooking at that little hole-in-the-wall diner on the corner across the street." Concern inched into his expression. Shadow looked her right in the eye. "I figure you've got your own protector in town now."

The two men shared a brothers-in-arms hug as the others scattered to arrange the so-called prisoner transfer with the federal agents. Betsy knew when she wasn't in control or even needed, so she tried to stay out of the way. She had no doubt this conversation and planning and strategizing would continue tomorrow.

All she could do was accept the fact she wasn't as insightful or observant or street smart as she'd thought. From now on she'd do whatever the police and Cain needed her to do. Nausea suddenly hit her broadside. If there was a ringer working at the dealership, then who had she mistakenly trusted? Who would be the one to shatter her memories? She'd do whatever the police asked.

This was her reputation. Her town. Her village. The place that over twenty years ago had accepted her mama, her sisters and herself as part of their family. Now Crayton had an infestation that needed to be stopped. She'd help every way she could.

"Looks like I owe you another new hat," Cain said as he picked up the white hat from the desk, streaks of pizza sauce and toppings staining the brim, and handed it to his friend.

"Nah, what's a little jalapeño between friends? Not like it's a bullet hole." Shadow centered the hat on his head and headed to the door. "You watch your six, Cain. There's a ringer in this fiasco. Maybe more than one."

Cain quick-nodded his head. "It only takes one.

As Shadow left the building under the protection of other DEA agents, Betsy's phone beeped that a text had arrived.

Hey, Sweetie, we're on our way home. Thought you might need us. Just outside Jefferson City. See you soon. Love, Mama.

Another beep. Another text.

"Sister of mine, you better stop telling me everything's okay. See you soon! Love ya—Marcy

And another one.

"I'm gonna expect the truth when I get there...you hear? - heart emoji- Amber

"My mama and sisters have cut short their trip and are headed this way. All because of me." Betsy swiped her fingers across her cheeks. "They shouldn't have done that. I can take care of me."

Cain wrapped his arm across her shoulders and pulled her in for a hug. "Betsy, Betsy, Betsy. You have got to let people care about you. And take care of you sometimes."

"That's not how I'm built. *I always* watch out for *them.*"

"Well, I think it's time you had an upgrade on your system." He grinned and answered his ringing phone. "Yeah, Truman. I hear everyone's headed this way. Good! We can use all the help we can get."

CHAPTER THIRTY

Breakfast with her mama and sisters had been exactly what Betsy needed. She hadn't realized how much she'd missed having Sadie and Marcy around during the past few days.The fact Amber had made the trip to Crayton to give her support touched Betsy more than the others could ever understand.

It had taken a lot of convincing to get Cain and JB to agree to this outing. Late last night they'd grumped about the idea. But early this morning she'd persuaded Cain that he couldn't spend all his time being her protector. That wouldn't work for more reasons than she could imagine. She had a life to live and a business to run, and he had to solve this case. He'd finally agreed but had insisted on being part of the periphery of the group.

The women had taken a seat in the furthest booth to the back of Joanie's Café. He'd taken a seat on one of the swivel stools at the front counter. Truman had followed his lead the moment he'd walked in with her mama and sisters. Her stepfather might have semi-retired from the FBI, but he still did consulting and would never lose those protective instincts. She'd even seen JB drive by the diner more than a few times. They *were* a family—*her* family.

She wasn't fooling herself as far as Cain was concerned. After waking up early this morning wrapped in the warmth of his body next to hers, her anxiety of the past few days had calmed. Knowing he was there for her seemed like everything she needed to be happy. They'd lain in bed talking about nothing yet everything for a good long time. Then his phone had beeped with an incoming text alert from the real estate agent he'd been using to look for acreage where he could build his security business. He'd broadened his search to include all along Interstate 44 from St. Louis to Springfield, MO.

The call this morning had opened the possibilities of two separate large locations available. One parcel between Mark Twain National Forest and Fort Leonard Wood. The other one set a little south of Interstate 44 between Springfield, Missouri and Fort Leonard Wood. The agent said both were prime locations and reasonably priced, so he needed to see them as soon as possible.

She'd listened to his plans and his excitement at the prospect of owning his own business. But when he asked her to go look at the land with him, her reaction had been *no*. He asked her for her opinion on his plans; she tensed and mumbled something about how she really couldn't say. He asked what she planned to do once this case was over, and she pretended not to hear him.

After a minute of no response, Cain had gone to shower. She'd gone to make coffee. The happy carefree moment they'd awoken to had suddenly disappeared.

Before they left the house, he loaded his motorcycle into the back of his pickup. Tossed his winter riding overalls, gloves, boots and face mask in the rear seat along with his helmet. Her instincts told her he was preparing to move on after this brouhaha was all settled.

Glancing in his direction at the counter, she met his eyes watching her. He winked. She smiled. In that moment, she realized how much she wanted him to stay. Wanted him to be part of their own little family. Wanted him to keep discovering all the ways to please her while they cuddled in that big king-sized bed every night for the rest of their lives.

"Well, will you look at that? Betsy's blushing." Marcy glanced over her shoulder toward the front counter, then slightly laughed as she turned back to the table. "Looks like you and Cain have been doing more than evading the bad guys."

Amber pointed to the security mirror positioned in the corner a few steps from their booth. "All I know is...I've been keeping an eye on the front of the café. And that hunk of a man called Cain has been looking at Betsy as if she's a tall glass of water."

Betsy lightly kicked her sisters beneath the table. "Don't start with that, sisters of mine."

"Ouch!" Sadie kicked her back. "That was my foot, not Amber's."

"Sorry," Betsy said as she rubbed her shin, then quickly tapped Amber's foot.

"Wish I had someone who looked at me like that. Guess he's taken, though." Amber teasingly popped her fingers on Betsy's hand. "The men I meet are either already taken, aren't really worth my time, or they turn out to be wonderful friend material."

"Don't give up." Betsy lovingly patted Amber's hand. "You'll find someone."

"Well, I'll never give up looking, that's for sure. Doesn't mean my happily-ever-after will arrive. And—"

"Maybe you should move to Crayton," Sadie said as she placed her napkin on the table and stood. "You never know what might be waiting for you in this little town."

"Like who?" Marcy asked as she slid from the booth.

Betsy could think of a few. One in particular. "I think Sadie's onto something. A change of scenery might be just the thing you need."

Amber stood and stepped to the side. "You forget I've got a thriving..." She raised her finger for a pause. "Make that a *somewhat* thriving private investigator business in St. Louis."

Betsy took up the rear and the women laughed and teased all the way out the front door. Cain and Truman followed, and JB just happened to pull to the curb right then. That was after he'd made a good ten circles of the block while they'd had breakfast.

"Looks like everyone had a good time," Truman said. "What's next?"

"Mr. Crestfall emailed that the adjusters got an early start this morning and have already inspected the showroom and main offices. He gave me the okay to start my cleanup, so I'm going straight to the dealership and start cleaning." Betsy said, her look and her tone daring Cain to disagree.

Crossing his arms, he narrowed his eyes and frowned. Truman followed suit.

Amber looped her arm across Betsy's shoulder. "If you want some help, I'll go along."

"Me, too." Marcy smiled sweetly at her husband.

JB's jaw tensed. "I don't think that's a good idea."

"Well, I do. So there you go." Marcy stepped to the other side of Betsy and looped arms with her.

"Sounds like a plan." Betsy felt an overwhelming joy that they had banded around her. "What about you, Mama? You coming with us?"

"No. I love you all dearly, but I'm going to pass on this" She tugged on her gloves. "After all our talking last night out at the house, I didn't get to sleep till two in the morning. I'm tired now. Think I'll—"

"See? Sadie knows this is a bad idea." Cain lowered his arms and stepped forward as JB and Truman followed his lead and nodded agreement.

Betsy had to agree that time had flown by last night as the entire family discussed everything from the dead body at Peyton's to the vandalism at the dealership and Betsy's house. From Cain and Betsy's meeting with Mr. Crestfall to the two-million-dollar insurance payouts—including the fact Sadie had not received any of that money and had no idea why her husband would have been named on the policy in the first place. From their brief trip to New York to where Betsy was staying and why. At least, the why-version they gave her mama and sisters, which she doubted any of them believed for even a minute.

She'd noticed that nothing was said about Shadow, or Phillip, or the body in the dumpster being an undercover agent. No doubt, Cain and JB probably considered that confidential information. Although she suspected they had shared that specifically with Truman when it had taken all three of them to unload the SUV last night—had taken them almost an hour, and most of that time outside.

Pulling her hat on with an extra tug, Sadie cleared her throat. "That's not what I said. In fact, I think it's a grand idea. I'm just a little tired from my New York trip, so I'm going home to take a nap." She hugged and kissed each of her daughters. "You girls lock the doors over at Peyton's. Make sure your phones are on. And have fun."

She held on to Truman's arm as they walked toward their SUV. Suddenly she stopped and looked back at the group. "Betsy, don't take chances. Watch your back and stay safe. And Cain, I hold you responsible for making sure she is."

As Truman and Sadie got into his armored SUV and drove away, Kennett pulled his police cruiser into their vacant spot. He motioned JB and Cain to join him as he walked in their direction.

After a brief conversation with the men, Cain made a phone call. When he had finished, he walked over to her. "You stay safe today. Don't take chances. I'll be back later."

"Where are you going?" Betsy asked.

"The real estate agent texted that another agent had called to show the property south of Interstate 44 later today, that's one I told you about this morning. Sounds like another buyer who'd been watching for land. Tells me they're ready to buy, also." For a moment, his tone and demeanor seemed all business. "So, seeing that I don't have to be in a meeting at the police station until three, I'm going to make a quick run over and take a look at the land."

"Oh, I didn't realize you were going to look so soon."

"I hadn't planned to, either, but I've missed other chances at acreage listings when they got snatched up before I could make an offer. And this one...this one sounds perfect, Betsy." He grinned and his expression looked as if he'd just won the lottery. "I talked to JB and he'll have patrols drive by Peyton's while you and your sisters are there. You okay with that?"

"Okay? Sure. It's just that..."

He pushed her hair back behind her ear and kissed her on the forehead. "I asked you to go. You said no. In fact, you ignored me after that. Thought you might be getting tired of having me around so much."

"No... Yeah... I mean..." she stammered. What was happening? "Maybe—"

"Don't worry about it. Figured I should at least take a look."

"Sure! That makes sense. It's just that..." Betsy couldn't blame him for going. She'd been the one to shut him down this morning. "Never mind. I'm just a little scattered today."

"Don't worry, I'll be back before two. We can go shoot a game of pool at Joanie's after my police meeting." He pulled her close and kissed the top of her head, then tilted his head till his lips touched her ear. "Might even let you buy me dinner after I win."

She lightly punched his bicep, then cocked her hip to the side. "You mean after I wipe you off the table without a shot?"

"You wish. Hey, seriously, if you need me just call," he shouted as he walked away. "If you need anything ASAP then call JB or Kennett. If I don't make it back tonight, you go stay at your parents' house. Got it?"

"Got it." Something seemed off to Betsy. Something in his tone, his words, his sudden need to move forward on his business property Then again, he'd been up front with her from the beginning. Suddenly, she realized that she had half expected him to give up his plans for her sake. Instead of thinking of them as we, she'd put that part out of her mind and held on to her here-and-now daily plans that never varied. "Drive careful, Cain."

"Yeah. I will." His expression softened for a second, then he gave her a quick thumbs-up and walked away. Not more conversation. Not another wink. Not a deeper kiss. Just a friendly thumbs-up and he was gone.

Betsy felt that was her cue to leave, so she grabbed Amber's hand as Marcy hugged JB one more time and then caught up with her sisters and joined hands. Amber and Betsy glanced back at the men, now animated and intently discussing something with a third man.

"Who's the policeman that joined JB and Cain?" Amber asked.

"Kennett. Officer Kennett," Marcy said. "Why?"

"Oh, no reason." Amber glanced back again.

Betsy smiled. So far this was the best day she'd had since she got back from Anaheim. She guided her sisters to her car.

By the time she snapped her seatbelt in place, she saw Cain do a U-turn in the middle of the street, then pull up close behind JB as he followed Kennett down the street.

"Wonder what that's about?" Marcy asked from the passenger seat.

"Don't know, but they sure had serious looks on their faces." Betsy flipped on the heat, but it didn't even have time to get warm before they pulled into Peyton's car lot.

She parked right next to the back door of the showroom and office building. Most everyone knew that was her parking spot no matter what she was driving. If it was vacant, she wasn't there. A few steps later they were safe inside with the door locked behind them.

Reaching to set the security alarm, she noticed the pad had been smashed, and when she walked to the other entrances to the building she found they were also smashed. She hadn't noticed that yesterday, but she'd only set the alarm from outside when she and Cain left. Without another thought, she called her security company and told them the pads needed to be replaced ASAP.

The alarm company said they'd do a rush order and start work on it overnight or early tomorrow morning. The peace of mind she felt was palpable. One thing she knew for sure, there'd be no more forgetting to set the security alarm when she came into the office early. Any sense of safety she'd felt in the past had been completely shattered at this point.

For almost two hours, Marcy and Amber helped Betsy get a handle on cleaning and sorting in her office and the conference room. With the help of the insurance company, she'd already arranged for a crime-scene cleanup company to start their in-depth cleaning of the entire dealership. No doubt, there would be a plethora of construction contractors, dealership phone calls and equipment reps to deal with in the next few days and weeks. She'd like to start with at least her office and conference room clean and organized.

Standing in the doorway leading between the two rooms, Amber and Betsy glanced around the somewhat organized spaces, then high-fived each other. There might still be stains on the floor and holes in the walls, but those were nothing but a minor inconvenience. Thankfully, someone had come in Sunday evening and covered the broken windows in plywood.

New windows would be one of the first things on her list for installation. She hated not being able to see outside. Sunshine always made her feel better...even when it barely glowed from behind clouds.

Marcy grabbed a piece of ice from the fridge and wrapped it in a paper towel. She rubbed it across her forehead, then sat down on the leather sofa in the conference room and held the ice against the small of her neck. Then suddenly she jumped up and ran into the private bathroom and locked the door.

Betsy raised her eyebrows at Amber and shrugged. Less than a minute later, Marcy opened the door and took one step out, looking like a pale waif in some stage play.

"You want to tell us what's going on?" Betsy asked.

Amber looked to the floor and raised her hand. "Do I get a star if I guess right?"

Marcy rubbed the cold paper towel across her face once again, then rapidly headed back to the bathroom. Betsy followed close behind while Amber held the door tight as Marcy grabbed the handle, trying to shut them out once again.

"Nope. Not this time," Amber said.

"Oooooooh! You two are going to be..." Marcy huffed an exasperated sigh, then leaned over the toilet.

Betsy doused a fresh paper towel in cold water and held it to the back of Marcy's neck. All of them had basically eaten the same thing for breakfast, but she and Amber weren't sick. That meant...

"What's going on, sister of mine?" Betsy asked in a teasingly insinuating tone as she brushed her sister's hair back.

"My guess is that our sister is pregnant." Amber winked as she handed Betsy another cold paper towel to use. "My assistant was just like this for the first month."

Marcy lifted her head, then stood and washed her face, tossing in a few handfuls of cold water to gargle with. Finally, she sighed softly and smiled as if she felt better. "Now, give the woman a star. Yes! I'm pregnant."

"Yay!" Amber grinned as she looped her arm over Betsy's shoulder. "We're going to be aunts."

"The best aunts ever." Betsy pulled Marcy into their group hug. "I'm going to teach her—"

"Or him," Amber interjected.

"—everything there is to know about fishing and worms and crickets. Then we'll talk about shiny cars and shooting pool."

She caught a glimpse of them in the vanity mirror. *They* were sisters. Sisters to the core. Sisters forever. The warmth of family and belonging eased into her mind. She was happy. Truly happy. And from the glow in Marcy's expression, she was ecstatic at the prospect of being a mother.

"Does Mama know?" Betsy asked.

"No. JB and I only found out for sure the day before we left for our New York trip." Marcy grabbed her purse. "We planned to tell all of you at once in the middle of Times Square."

Amber smiled. "That would have been a great memory to have."

"Sorry about messing that up, but"—Betsy held out her arms and pulled her sisters in for one more hug before releasing her hold—"I think our finding out in the middle of the dealership bathroom will make quite a story for the future, too."

"Especially since I won a star for guessing right." Amber winked and pointed at Marcy picking up her purse. "Going someplace?"

"Yes. If Betsy will let me take her SUV, I'm going to Pete's Soda Fountain and Deli to grab us three large root beers to celebrate."

"And a double large order of French fries, with lots of ketchup packets."

After agreement all around, Marcy slipped on her coat, hat and gloves, then headed to the door at the end of the short hallway just outside the office.

Holding the door open, Betsy gave her sister a quick hug. "I am really happy for you and JB."

"We are, too." Marcy hugged her in return, holding on for a few second longer. "I hope you find what I've found. Do you think Cain will stay in town?"

"Your guess is as good as mine. I hope so, but I'm always realistic. Guess only time will tell." Betsy shrugged as she stepped back. She was even less certain after the way he'd left earlier today.

CHAPTER THIRTY-ONE

Betsy suddenly felt more alone than she had for the past few weeks. Somehow, she'd gotten used to having Cain around. Liked the way they'd settled into a nightly routine of love making. How they'd talk about this and that, over and over, sharing emotions and dreams and plans. No, truth be told, she hadn't shared her dreams and plans, but Cain had. She hadn't even given him that much of her, only her passion and emotions.

If he came back tonight, she needed to rectify her part of their relationship. That was, if they still had a relationship. Or had she imagined everything?

She wrapped Marcy in another hug, then pointed in the soda fountain's direction. "Now go grab those drinks and hurry back before Amber and I have planned your entire baby shower."

Marcy beeped the SUV open.

"Hey, since the security system is broken, I'll lock the door from inside. Press the buzzer when you get back."

Her sister shot her a thumbs-up as she slid in and drove away.

Betsy shut the door and flipped the lock. Without missing a beat, Amber and Betsy went back to organizing some of the clutter that had been made by whoever was targeting her and the dealership. The destruction was bad enough, but the unanswered *why* question was tied with the *who*. Even with the information Shadow had shared yesterday there were still way more questions than answers.

She walked into the front display room and was greeted with only the occasional stripe of winter sunshine oozing through between the four-by-twelve plywood sheets covering the shattered windows. "Amber, you're a good PI. Do you have any theories about what's going on, with all that's happened here in Crayton the past few days?"

Her sister walked over to one of the shiny red new cars, hot off the line. "Not really. If I lived closer, I'd have a network of contacts. But from St. Louis to here is not only a lot of time and miles, it's a totally different feel."

"Just thought I'd ask."

"One thing I will say is, you need to be careful. I've handled a lot of cases. There's petty vandalism. And there's big city crime. Something about this doesn't feel small town. Feels professional. Planned. Direct. That's all I can give you."

Betsy sighed. "That at least helps me know I'm not just imagining the danger."

"You're not. And I'm sure Cain and JB and Uncle Cal and Truman would tell you the same thing." Slowly, Amber ran her fingers down the ugly scratch on the door panel. "Will they be able to fix this?"

"I hope so. You'd be amazed at what they can do with paint nowadays." She led the way back to her office. "Marcy should be back soon. Maybe we can get her to let us go with her over to Truman and Sadie's place. I'd love to be there when they tell Mama about the baby."

"Agreed." Amber sat in one of the customer chairs in front of the desk. "Mama will be beside herself with excitement over a grandchild."

Betsy's phone beeped with an incoming text, but as she reached to check the message, a noise near the back door caught their attention. The doorknob jiggled.

Betsy quickly laid her phone down and held up one hand to stop the conversation. She placed her finger over her lips with the other. Amber silently mouthed *Marcy?* Betsy shook her head. Uneasy, she moved cautiously to her chair and opened her bottom drawer, slid open the fake bottom panel concealing her gun.

Empty. The gun had been there yesterday when she checked prior to the insurance agent arriving. Now the secret compartment was completely empty. Not even the holster or extra bullets had been left.

The back door deadbolt clicked, which meant someone with a key was coming inside.

She glanced at Amber. "Gun?"

"It's in my lock box at the house." Shaking her head, she took a step closer. "And I forgot to charge my phone last night."

The ding of the back door opening ratcheted Betsy's fearful apprehension up a few notches. A mingle of muffled men's voices made trepidation soar. Each of the women reached for their phone.

Betsy motioned Amber to hide in the attached office storage room. "Don't come out unless I call you by your full name."

"Got it." Amber grabbed the stapler and three-hole punch from the top of the file cabinet, then disappeared into the room, pulling the door closed behind her.

"Who's there?" Betsy loudly asked as she shoved a small table and stacks of boxes in front of the storage room door to camouflage the idea of anyone being in there. "I heard you come inside. Tell me who's there or I call the police."

"It's me, Papa Carrington. Didn't mean to scare you. Didn't see your car parked by the back door. Figured no one was here."

He stepped into the office wearing a coat over what looked like his hospital gown and a pair of orderly pants. Dragging the brown house shoes he was wearing along the floor, he shuffled weakly toward the chair.

Inconspicuously, Betsy shoved her phone in her pocket before racing around the desk to steady him as he bent to sit. A heavy half-groan, half-sigh seemed to explode out of his mouth.

"What are you doing out of the hospital?" Betsy asked as she noticed a large bump with the beginning of a bruise on his forehead. She touched it lightly then saw a slight trickle of blood from a cut along his eyebrow. "Did you fall? Are you hurt?"

"I'm sorry, Betsy. Truly sorry, but there's nothing I can do now." He laid one hand on hers and gripped her wrist with the other. "I can't protect you any longer."

She jerked to free herself, but old man Papa C was suddenly up and out of the chair. Strong and spry as ever, he tightened his grip. At the same time, the younger guy from the hospital room yesterday rushed in the door.

"Stop struggling." Gun drawn, eyes narrowed on hers, and smirking, the thug motioned her to step back. "Move. Now! *Don't make me tell you again, lady.*"

She stepped back.

Suddenly, she remembered where she'd seen him before yesterday—Peyton's service center. The night Earl supposedly fell on the floor. That night Papa C said he'd clean him up. Said he'd stay to help fix the *customer's* truck. The so-called customer—the bearded thug standing in front of her now—had been clean shaven that night, but it was him.

She'd never forget the way he'd stared at her. He had the same threatening look today except now he had a beard. Changed his overall look. A beard. What was it about the beard? The beard...

"Oh my gosh. You're Phillip's drug dealer." The one she'd seen the night she'd followed her husband to a drug buy.

The thug lifted the corner of his mouth in a menacing smile. "Interesting. You know more than we thought."

"Well, isn't this nice." In walked the older, grey-haired gentleman from the hospital yesterday. The one who had said very little yet gave off the vibe of being in control of everything happening in Papa C's room. "Looks like everything's already fallen into place."

Betsy turned her attention toward him and his black wool overcoat and black leather gloves. His creased trousers and shiny black shoes seemed to top off who he felt he was in whatever this involved. To her, he looked like a big-city crime boss personified.

"Can someone tell me what's going on?" She glanced back and forth between Papa C and the thug. Narrowed her gaze to the older gentleman. "Who are you? Why did you drag Papa C out of the hospital? Can't you see he's not well?"

"Some people might say I'm the brains behind the operation. You can just call me Mr. Partner. And my assistant"—he pointed at the thug standing by his side—"you can call him James. As for Papa C, he came along willingly. Isn't that right, little brother?" The man smirked behind his sinister tone. "Sooner or later, he always does the right thing for the family. Always."

For a split second, Papa C loosened his hold, and Betsy jerked her hand free. He grabbed at her, but she backed away and to the side, trying to put the desk between the men and herself. She felt better knowing Amber was secure in the storage room, which had been designed with no windows to double as somewhere to shelter in place during a tornado.

Suddenly she tensed. *Marcy...* Marcy would be back soon. Then what? Betsy's phone rang and she reached to grab it from her pocket.

"James!" Partner shouted as he pointed at her.

The thug grabbed her wrist. She twisted to pull away. If she could just push the answer button, someone would hear what was happening. The man tighten his hold and jerked her back, doing his own twist on her arm. She cried out in pain.

"Don't answer that call, Betsy. That's not a request.

That's an order!" Papa C's loud and angry tone was one she'd never heard him use with her before. "And stop moving around, too. Right now. Understood?"

She stopped fighting. Stopped moving. The glaring expression on his face gave her pause. She'd only seen that one other time—when Phillip had argued with his father. That had been the day before the wreck. She hadn't thought of that since she'd woken up in the hospital. Broken and battered and alone.

Her phone rang two more times before clicking to voicemail. Blowing out a sigh of defeat, she cradled her aching wrist and waited. "Understood. I'm not going anywhere."

"Let her be." Partner moved closer, staring straight into her eyes. "But you're wrong on one thing. *You will* be going with us when we leave the building."

"Why?" Papa C asked.

"She's our ticket out of town and any other situation that arises."

"I don't think that's necessary."

Partner stepped closer to his brother. "I don't care what you think. Thought you learned your lesson years ago when you tried to turn on the family. Remember how that ended?"

Papa C looked thoughtful, almost sad, then nodded. "I remember."

Betsy intently listened to the conversation. She wanted to be sure of every clue they were giving. There was no doubt but that somewhere in the future she'd be called on the stand to testify against one or all of these men.

"Don't you ever forget that I'm the one in charge

here." Partner unbuttoned his overcoat and turned in his brother's direction, waving his hand toward the office door. "Now, where's your office, brother dear? This safe you say you've got hidden better be there."

Betsy felt his ominous meaning before the words even hit her brain. The vibe in the room was changing. Right now, the future seemed to hinge on something in a safe she had no idea even existed in this building.

"I know where I keep my money. I'm not a complete incompetent." Papa C straightened.

"Well, you're only half right on that. Seeing that you left a whole lot of it at the casinos and can't even remember which one." Partner looked in her direction, motioned her to follow Papa C as James walked behind her. "You going to do whatever we tell you to do? No questions asked?"

She had to save Amber. Had to get these men out of the office before Marcy returned. Had to hold on to the idea that Cain and JB and the others would find all of them in time. She could do what these criminals asked until that moment.

"Yes. Whatever you want." She followed his orders. Now was not the moment to show any animosity. At least, none she couldn't back up.

The three of them followed Papa C to his office. Once inside, Partner took off his overcoat and handed it to Betsy. Authoritatively, he pointed for her to put it on the coat rack, then pointed to the chair in front of the desk. She sat quickly and quietly. The game had begun, and she needed to cooperate. Sooner or later, someone would find her. No matter where they took her, someone would find her.

Partner laughed as he watched Papa C tip three books

on the bookcase behind his desk, then pull a statue forward. Instantly the bookcase clicked open to reveal a safe hidden behind it. "Didn't know you were this clever, brother."

"We'll need to stop by the house for the other safe's contents, too." Papa C laid a stack of papers and money and flash drives on his desk. Tossed his briefcase to Betsy. "Fill it up."

With no complaint, she did as told.

"You seem to have calmed the beast here. She may be a lot of help to us." Partner watched Betsy, then smiled as she closed the briefcase. "She's smart. Compliant. Probably learned that from her dad. Makes me think I may have missed a chance with that FBI agent years ago."

Betsy leaned back in the chair and waited for the next command. He seemed to know a lot about her family. About her background. Seemed to enjoy taunting her with conversation.

Partner motioned for her to hold his coat up for him, then slid into it like the most important man in the world. After tugging on his leather gloves, he stared at Betsy once again until she finally stared right back.

He laughed. "Yeah, I should have tried negotiating with your dad. Too bad I had him killed instead."

CHAPTER THIRTY-TWO

Cain had spent the last hour driving to Nature's Crossing, and as he closed in on the location, he still couldn't stop puzzling together everything that had happened in the Crayton case. They were close, but missing parts were still out there. Hopefully, some out-of-sight clues might unexpectedly fall into their hands. Finding others would require some outside-the-box thinking. Right now, though, when, where and who kept evading him.

He needed to free his mind. Let it wander. That's one reason he'd brought his motorcycle along. This time of year, he tended to feel cooped up by the cold and ice and snow. His riding coveralls hadn't been cheap, but they were worth it when he chanced a road trip on the cycle in this weather.

Although today, the sun had made an appearance. Felt like a false spring day. Especially since the forecast was for more freezing rain and snow.

He'd fill up his thermos at Red's Corner Market where

he was supposed to meet Wheat McIntosh. He was a state trooper with the Missouri Highway Patrol, and also the owner of the acreage for sale. Some kind of inheritance he was splitting into a few one-fifty- to two-hundred-acre plots.

Which brought him to the other reason he'd wrangled the motorcycle into the truck bed. Of course, he'd done that so many times, it all fell into place like clockwork because his truck bed had been specially fitted for an on-off ramp, wheel chock and tie-down straps and hooks. Since he didn't have a Gator yet, riding the land on the cycle would give him at least a partial view of the pros and cons.

Cain had been looking for land like this for years. He'd shared with Betsy how much this would mean to him, to his planned business, to the family he hoped to raise one day. She'd listened, even seemed to understand. Yet the way she'd responded this morning when he asked her to come along to view the property, he'd evidently misread what he thought they had been building in their relationship. Evidently, his dreams and hers had split. Or maybe his plans had never been her vision and she'd only pretended.

Come to think about it, she never talked about the future. She was all about the past. Taking care of top priorities ASAP. Making sure she could take care of Sadie, Marcy and Amber. And she'd also included Truman, JB, Joanie, and her uncle, along with his family, under her umbrella of responsibility.

Life hadn't been kind to her at times, but it hadn't always been kind to him either. He'd learned a long time ago that all you can do is learn from the past and move forward. Embrace the hopes and dreams and plans with open arms, because the past would beat you to the ground and stomp on you if you didn't learn to fight back.

"Damn it, Betsy. What are you doing?" He slammed his palm against the side of the steering wheel. "I'm right here for you. Why can't you see that? Why? Don't you know I need you just as much as you need me?"

The Nature's Crossing Welcome sign greeted him, and the flashing stop light signaled he was at the four-way junction. And there it was—Red's Corner Market. Cain checked how long the trip had taken and calculated when he would need to leave by to make the meeting with Earl Millerton and his attorney back at the Crayton Police headquarters. A little longer than he'd anticipated, but he'd slowed down at times to avoid damaging the cycle. He'd have to amp it up on the way back.

Stretching as he walked to the small grocery's front door, he smiled at the porcupine boot and shoe mud scraper next to the doormat. Pausing only a moment, he stepped inside the door and was greeted by an alert bell and a large sleeping dog near the end of the counter. He liked the town already.

"Cain. Cain Connery." The greeting came from the opposite direction, where a man stepped towards him.

His hand automatically jerked toward his side a second before he paused. Grinned and held out his hand for a brothers-in-arms shake to the CIA agent he'd worked alongside on a couple of cases a few years back. "Mark. Mark Garmund. I didn't know this is where you lived now."

Mark returned the gesture, and the two men slapped each other on the shoulder. "Good to see you, man. When

Wheat said you were coming to look at his property, I knew I had to be here. That was before he got called out for an emergency. He asked Red and me to make you feel at home. Show you around."

"Red? I don't think I know him," Cain said.

Mark stepped around the dog.and nodded towards the man coming out of the curtained doorway behind the front counter. "Cain, this is Patrick 'Red' Horton. CIA for a whole lot of years before he retired and moved to Nature's Crossing."

Cain grinned, again. He knew the man, knew his reputation anyway, knew his courage in battle. He took the offered handshake. "It's a pleasure to finally meet the man behind the newspaper photos."

All three of them laughed at the memory of the case involving wrong photos in Washington, D.C., years ago. Red filled mugs for the three of them while they lingered over stories of previous assignments, pausing just long enough to tend to customers that came and went. Something inside Cain slowly eased.

He liked the men standing in front of him. Liked how their wives had already taken Betsy in without even meeting her. Liked what he'd seen of Nature's Crossing so far. If the land lived up to his expectations, he'd finally found his place. Found what he'd been looking for. His boss at the DEA would be happy for him.

Would Betsy? If only she'd come with him today. If only—

"Whenever you're ready I'll take you out to Wheat's three plots that are for sale," Mark said. "I see you brought your motorcycle, but I've got the keys to Wheat's Gator and can drive us around in that."

Suddenly a double beep sounded just outside the front door. A few seconds later Mark held the front door open and kissed the woman entering.

"This is my wife, Ashley. And this is Cain, the man I told you was coming to look at property in the area."

She held out her hand. "Hello, it's nice to meet you. You'll love this little town."

A cold wind blew in from the curtained doorway behind the counter, then a shorter lady with pinkish-blonde hair raced through and kissed Red on the cheek.

"And this is the love of my life who puts up with all my shenanigans, Janie." Patrick beamed with the happiness of a man who'd found his dream. "This is Cain Connery."

"Hi and bye, Ashley and I are headed to Surryfield, the closest thing to big city shopping in the area. And we're already getting a late start. Welcome to town, tell your wife or significant other to give us a call." The two women rushed out the door. "We'll take her with us the next time."

"I'm working on that." Cain couldn't believe the friendliness of the people here. "Tell me Mark, Red. How did you give up your life with the CIA and move to this small town and end up with two women who clearly adore you?"

"Luck!" Patrick smiled.

"Luck, and in my case, a dance." Mark nodded. "What about you, Cain? I heard about all the trouble over in Crayton. Heard you'd taken a leave of absence from the DEA to consult with the Crayton police. Even heard a rumor there was something going on between you and a lady named Betsy."

Cain shook his head at himself. What was he doing here? How could he have left Betsy, even for a few hours, while she was still in danger? She *wasn't* a chain around him like his dad used to say about his mom. Betsy was the woman he loved. The one he'd give his life for. The one he wanted and needed with every ounce of his being.

He swiped his palm across his hair. "You know, sometimes I'm just a flat-out fool. I went off and left her there in Crayton today just so I could see this land. Just because we'd had a spat...and it wasn't even that, it was just a disagreement."

Red walked up beside him. "We've all been there, man. We've all been fools and worse. Takes a little time to realize the give and take in love is two-sided. It's not easy, but it's worth it."

"Do you love Betsy?" Mark cut right to the chase.

"Yes. I think—*I know*—I love her." Cain swallowed the emotion he heard in his voice, felt in his whole body. "And I don't want to see the property for the first time without her by my side."

"Then get on out of here. Tell her how you feel and go from there. We'll explain everything to Wheat. He'll understand."

Cain shook both their hands and headed out the door, then turned back. He rolled ten hundred dollar bills out of his pocket and handed them to Mark. "Tell Wheat this is a deposit on one of the parcels."

"What if she says no?" Red asked.

"I still want one of the parcels"—he stepped outside as

the men followed him to his truck—"but sooner or later, I'm banking on her saying yes. *Sooner would be a hell of a lot better.*"

He texted Betsy that he was starting home, then started his truck and headed down the road. Back to Crayton. Back to Betsy. When he was well over halfway back, JB called and said Mr. Howard, Earl's attorney, had called, asking for the meeting to be moved up an hour.

"Why?" Cain asked as he pulled into a gas station to fill his gas tank.

"Said his client was nervous. Felt like someone was watching him. Earl said he knows for sure there's a price on his and his son Steven's life."

"That means he knows about their two names being on the business life insurance policy that Mr. Crestfall told Betsy and me about." Cain finished and jumped back in the truck. "Means he knows more than we thought."

JB grunted. "That's my thought, too."

"I'll be there in less than thirty minutes."

Their call ended and Cain called Betsy. She didn't answer. Instead, he was left leaving a message on her voicemail:

"Betsy, I'm on my way back and we need to talk about our individual plans and dreams, because...well, I didn't plan to say this on voicemail, but damn it, Betsy—I love you! See you soon. Call me."

CHAPTER THIRTY-THREE

Thirty minutes later, Cain arrived back in Crayton with no idea what he was about to learn. All he'd known was that while JB and he had been busy watching Sadie and her girls have breakfast at Joanie's Café this morning, local attorney Mr. Howard had contacted the sheriff's office. He had a client needing to meet with the police ASAP. The client had important information to be shared. Possibly matters of life and death.

Currently on his way back to St. Louis for additional surgery, Sheriff Davis quickly referred everything to JB as acting sheriff. JB had called in Deputy Evans, Officer Kennett, and Officer Hastings. And since the attorney insinuated it might have relevance to the drug case and other recent criminal activity, he also invited the FBI agent assigned to continue working the unfolding case Shadow had been on.

At that point, the only other thing Cain knew was that the attorney, Mr. Howard, had also suggested—*requested*—Truman and he be part of the meeting.

Then there'd been Mr. Howard's phone call asking for the meeting to be moved up. Now they were all in the police department's private conference room with not only law enforcement and everyone Mr. Howard had requested, but also a police stenographer. On the attorney's side was Earl Millerton, his wife, Wanda, and their son Steven, plus the paralegal from Mr. Howard's law firm. Their other children were with their grandparents in an attorney-arranged safe house outside of Crayton for the moment.

And still Betsy hadn't returned his call. Or even acknowledged his text.

After all the particulars were handled to the satisfaction of JB and Mr. Howard, the paralegal passed out a statement of facts that had been signed and dated by Earl Millerton.

Cain realized several of the questions that had been running through his mind were being answered. Not all of them, but enough to solidify that he was headed in the right direction with his suspicions. The main facts he was getting from Millerton's answers to the questions they threw at him was that the man was scared and truthful.

Millerton had worked for the dealership for over twenty years. He'd worked his way up from part-time mechanic about a year after the car lot opened to being service manager for the past ten years. The first time he met Papa C's brother was at a small picnic at the local park that the three owners had arranged for the staff and their families. The brother just happened to be down from Illinois to visit and came to the park, also.

"It was friendly enough," Millerton said. "Everybody calling each other by their first names. Laughing and joking. That was before Mr. Dash was killed in the robbery. Before Papa C got so nervous. Then got rich enough to expand the car lot to an all-out dealership. Sometimes I even got the impression Papa C was afraid of something... or someone. Especially right after his brother would pay a visit."

Mr. Howard asked for a pause for his client. People took a short break to stretch their legs or grab a coffee, then moved back to their seats. "Does anyone have further questions about the items listed on our statement?"

"Not at this time," JB said. "We appreciate all the information and know this hasn't been easy."

"Is there anything else you'd like to say, Mr. Millerton?" the attorney asked.

Wanda held her husband's hand for a moment. She weakly smiled and nodded. He straightened closer to the conference room table. Clasped his hands firmly in front of him, took a deep breath and exhaled.

"Yes, yes there is. I need to tell you this for the good of my family." He sipped some water and swallowed it. "About a year or so after that picnic, Papa C finally confided in me that his brother was a dangerous man. Could cause a lot of financial damage if he wanted to. A lot of physical, too. Said I should be careful around him, but not to worry. Said he was working with a guy that would get it all straightened out. Said everything would be alright for all of us."

Millerton raked his fingers through his thinning hair. "A few days later word came over the television that FBI Agent Peyton had been killed coming out of the Jefferson City FBI Office. Most of the town knew the Peyton family from their times at the lake and local family members, so we were naturally all concerned for Sadie and her girls. But Papa C took it even harder. Stayed home for the next week. He had bruises on his cheek when he came back to work. I always wondered if he fell and hurt himself.

"Papa C never mentioned working with anybody who could help us again. In fact, he changed drastically. Told me his brother was his new partner in the business and that I should do whatever he said. Warned me there'd be some changes happening and I should do what I thought best for me. For my family. He couldn't watch out for everybody. Shouted at me that I should get my things in order. One wrong step and I could end up like Mr. Dash. Or Agent Peyton."

Cain and Kennett glanced at each other as JB leaned in to confer with Mr. Howard and Truman. Mrs. Millerton wiped tears from her eyes.

Unconsciously tapping his fingers against the table, Millerton finally reached for his water and gulped it down. Set it abruptly on the table with a thud. "I know my name is on a list that is worth a lot of money to someone. I've been threatened and blackmailed for years by this group and Papa C. But I knew I had to put an end to this now. Six months ago, they showed me a copy of an insurance policy with Steven's name."

"*What?*" His son shoved to his feet, then slowly sat back down as his mother reached out and took his hand.

Kennett opened his laptop, keying in his search over and over. Then he turned the screen to face the rest of the people in the room. "Is this the man? Is this Papa C's brother?"

"*That's him!* The next time he came to the dealership he and his muscle forcefully told me I would do what he said, when he said. And the first order was to call him *Mr. Partner.*"

Swiping to another screen, Kennett continued with other photos. After a lot of *nope* answers, Millerton leaned forward and pointed at the man on screen. "That's one of his muscle. Been here many times. Running drugs and I don't know what else. In fact, he may have been the one to slip something in my coffee the day I flipped out. I know for sure he'd been there at the service center earlier in the day."

Steven cleared his throat and slightly raised his hand. "I don't know if this helps, but that guy was there the day that lookie-loo ended up dead, also."

"How do you know?" JB asked.

"The new service manager, Derek Johnson, had me come in to do some cleaning after school that day. Said he had an important meeting and since Ms. Peyton was due back the next morning, he needed things straightened up. Told me to just pull the exit door closed behind me when I left." Steven glanced toward his dad. "That was the guy Derek took into the lunch area and...well, I'm pretty sure I heard him lock the door behind them." He looked back to JB. "I got my work done, clocked out about four, and got the heck out of there."

"Thanks, Steven. We appreciate your help," JB said.

Standing to stretch, Cain leaned over and patted Millerton on their back. "I thank you for all the info. You have no idea how much this helps. I only have one more question."

"Okay. What do you need to know?"

"After the car wreck that killed Phillip, were you involved in taking the car to the salvage lot?" Cain asked.

"Nope, I was never involved in that wreck or the report. In fact, I heard there was a mix-up on tow trucks. The Missouri Highway Patrol straightened that out, though. But I know where the car is now." Millerton nodded as he shared a direct and perceptive look with Cain. "It's stored in a shed at the far back end of Papa C's property."

That's all the info Cain needed. One of his top priorities would be to get a search warrant to look at the remains of the wreck. He'd bet good money there were bullets still lodged in the tires. Betsy needed an answer to what kept worrying her about the night of the accident. And if the bullets were there, then he needed answers on why Papa C had denied her rendition of what she'd heard.

Not long after, the Millerton family and Mr. Howard left. The rest of them had stayed put in the police conference room. Truman had moved to the far end of the room, dictating notes on his phone and making calls— turning his back and speaking quietly. He might be retired from the FBI, but he still had some connections none of the others had. As always, he was keeping them close to his vest.

Bit by bit Cain, Kennett, Evans and Hastings were making their own lists for what had just happened. Soon enough, JB rolled one of the eight-by-four dry erase boards over to the end of the table. Evans and Hastings pulled another one into the room, while Kennett started his own Post-it notes arrangement on the white board attached to the wall. Cain kept working at his own list, with only the occasional note stacked to the side of his yellow legal pad. They all had their routines. Later they'd compare thoughts.

The meeting had been informative, including a lot of innuendo and links that tied some of his suspicions together. He was grateful. He was angry. He was ready to take this case forward a whole lot of steps. At the same time, part of that investigation would be decided by the Crayton Police Department.

JB's phone rang and he accidentally pushed the speakerphone button as he answered. "Hey, Marcy, what are you—"

"Help me, JB. Help." Her voice was barely a whisper, but the intensity said everything loud and clear.

"Where are you?"

"I'm hiding among the cars at the dealership. I just came back from Pete's Soda Fountain after picking up root beer for the three of us. Something's wrong here. There's a black SUV parked at the back door, and a black Gladiator I've never seen before, with the top removed. And there's a strange man walking around dressed in all-over camo... carrying a long rifle, with a ski mask over his face."

Everyone in the room was on their feet in a flash. After everything they'd learned in the meeting with Earl Millerton, this was a rocket launch to the next level.

"We're on the way." JB checked his gun and motioned the others in the room to circle up and move out. "Stay where you are. Understand, Marcy?

"Hurry. Please hurry. I thought I heard—"

Pop! Pop-pop-pop!

Everyone in the office stopped. Listened. The phone

seemed to take on a life of its own. One that blared through the air like a crack of lightning, over and over and over.

JB headed toward the door as Cain and Truman followed close behind. Kennett notified the SWAT team and grabbed his own SWAT gear. Office protocol fell into place as Officer Hastings grabbed the two-way and alerted other officers on duty to be ready to assist.

"Do you hear that?" Marcy's voice broke with fear and worry. "Do you?"

"Yes, I hear." JB walked faster. His expression rigid with the look of a person focused on the job at hand.

"Wait a minute. The back door's opening," Marcy whispered. "There's a guy in a bomber-style camo jacket...holding on to Betsy as they come out. She's fighting back and—" Marcy sucked in a shocked breath. "He...he just knocked her to the ground. A grey-haired man in a black overcoat and...and Papa C keep shouting at her. Pointing back at the office doorway. The masked guy in head-to-toe camo is walking toward the back door."

Marcy's voice quivered as she snuffled quietly. "Betsy's shaking her head. Pleading. She's trying to stand back up. Pumping her hands as if trying to calm people down. The guy in the overcoat just said something to the man in the mask and motioned him to the driver's seat in the SUV."

"Stay quiet, Marcy!" JB shouted. "Climb under a car and stay absolutely quiet."

"I will. I will." She grunted. "Papa C is in the SUV's passenger seat. The guy who drug Betsy out the door has shoved her in the passenger seat of the Gladiator. Looks like—"

"Get under the car. Now!" JB commanded in a tone he'd normally never use with his wife.

"I'm trying." She grunted. Grunted again and again. "I'm under a maroon van. All I can see from here is them driving away."

"We're on the way. Stay where you are even when I get there. Have you seen Amber?"

"No."

JB notified Kennett of the possible hostage situation, then glanced in Cain's direction, raised his eyebrows in question. Cain nodded in return. He'd gotten that loud and clear. Amber was missing. Marcy was hidden. Betsy had been taken. They were all on the same mission, mindset and messaging. Yet, at the same time, they each had a specific goal.

"Let's go." JB shoved open the side door leading out of the police station. All the years of training were working like clockwork.

Cain had felt the moment JB had gone on lawman alert. Followed by the moment fear for his wife had catapulted the whole scenario in the office. Cain had had the same reactions himself. Betsy might not be his wife, but she was the person he'd promised to protect...the one he planned to marry someday. Hell, Betsy was everything to him.

Somehow, she'd become more important to him than life itself. There were no questions to ask regarding police protocols or backup or anything else. JB and the others would handle all those specifics. For him, only one thing mattered. He bolted out the front door, headed for his truck.

Truman ran right behind him, making a phone call. "Sadie, no time for questions. Safe room. *Now!* I'm on the way."

As Cain jumped into his truck, ready to pull out, Truman pulled his Range Rover up beside him and rolled down his window.

"I'm headed home to Sadie." Truman said. "You and JB are the front line now. You got this?"

"I've got this!" Cain had never said anything he'd been more sure of in his life. "Tell Sadie she can count on me. I *will* bring Betsy home."

As Truman turned toward his house, Cain floored his truck, fishtailing through the few patches of slushy snow melting in today's unseasonably warm and sunny weather. JB flew past, lights flashing on the speeding police car as they made a silent approach. No more shots had been heard, but they were still approaching as if they were under attack. The couple minutes needed to reach Peyton's seemed a lifetime

Enroute, over the police band radio, and once on-sight, Cain listened to JB shouting commands without hesitation —ordering lockdown of schools and the surrounding area, sending SWAT into both buildings, police at every entrance and a perimeter established for the public, requesting backup from surrounding communities and the state. Patrolman Hastings was assigned to find Marcy under the maroon van. The rest of them followed police procedures once the SWAT teams entered the buildings.

Cain had stayed directly on Kennett and his SWAT team, following his lead as he tracked from room to room. The man had seen plenty of action in SWAT team tactics back in Illinois. And from what Cain was seeing, he hadn't dropped a step in procedure, leadership and courage.

A sudden banging echoed from Betsy's office. Kennett and Cain quickly narrowed in on the source of the loud and forceful thuds coming from inside the office. The door to the storage room was blocked by furniture and a couple of boxes, but the noise was coming from inside.

"Crayton Police. Put down the weapon and step back," Kennett shouted as he kept his own weapon trained toward the sound on the other side of the wall. He clicked his communication button and alerted JB of their location.

Cain banged his fist against the wall, then shoved the table aside. "Who's there?"

"Amber!" she shouted as she kept banging at the drywall. "The door's jammed."

"Anyone else?"

"No." She started banging against the wall once again. Suddenly, the end of a three-hole punch jabbed through.

Kennett grabbed the end of the improvised escape tool and held on. "I've got you. Hang on. I've got you, Amber."

JB joined Kennett and Cain as they shoved boxes and anything else blocking the door out of the way. But the lock had malfunctioned, and the door was stuck.

"Door ram!" Kennett shouted to his SWAT team backup. "Step away from the door, Amber. Now!"

As if already waiting for the order, one of the SWAT members handed him the Enforcer. With a single blow to the door, Kennett had it open. He was met by a trembling, panting Amber, trying to get out through the open doorway as she handed him a stapler along with the three-hole punch.

"Where's Betsy?" she asked, pushing to get past all of them and to a bottled water sitting on the edge of the desk. She opened it and poured the water over her head.

"One of them took her." Cain stepped aside to give her room. "Are you okay?"

Motioning that she needed a moment to regroup, she pushed her now wet hair back from her face. "I don't do well in confined spaces."

He felt the tightening of his chest. Didn't want to stand and listen. Didn't want to make a plan. Didn't want to report to someone else. But JB was in charge, and he'd follow his lead. Deputy Evans had already called for drones, choppers and contiguous counties backup.

Kennett called an all-clear on the SWAT team while JB radioed the policeman who was with Marcy, said she could come inside now. Even before the police had entered the dealership, Deputy Evans had been working with a team of officers, contacting the highway patrol and even news stations for coverage. Using the descriptions Marcy had given them earlier, they had been able to get some APBs out. She'd even been able to film enough on her cell phone to get a partial license plate on the black SUV.

"Now, tell us exactly what happened inside, Amber," JB said as she straightened up, ready to talk now that the panic had passed.

She relayed everything that had occurred. Even down to minute details at times. Her background in private investigation served her well. "Once Betsy motioned me into the storage room, I made it a point to be quiet and still. The interior isn't finished so there's only the one layer of drywall. Made it easy for me to hear what was going on.

That's when I heard someone say to call them Mr. Partner, and he referred to someone else as James."

Kennett handed Amber another bottle of water, then pulled up photos from their meeting with Earl Millerton. She once again pour some over her head and chugged down the rest, as she nodded yes to each of the photos. . "At one point it sounded like they were heading down the hall to the back door. Betsy kept yelling that she was not going to Papa C's with them. Then they faded out of my hearing."

Cain's insides exploded with pride. His Betsy was doing good. Thinking on her feet. Leaving him clues to find her. That's all he needed—the trail. 'Cause he *would* find her, even if it took the rest of his life. "Anything else?"

"Then all of a sudden, I could dimly hear them again. There's a vent in the storage room that must be connected to the heating system that runs throughout the building. That's when things seemed to get a little jumbled. I can't remember exactly what it was, but something Betsy said made me think they had told her there'd been a contract on our dad years ago. Does that make sense?"

"From what the police found out during the past hour, it makes a lot of the pieces fall into place." Cain couldn't believe so much had been happening in and around Crayton all these years.

Thanks to Amber and Marcy, they at least had a start. Papa C, Mr. Partner, James—the man from the photo Kennett had shown Millerton earlier—and one other thug involved in this abduction had already fled the scene. Fled with Betsy riding alone in the Gladiator being driven by James—at least, that's what they could assume from calls coming in to the station of possible sightings. The other three men were in the black SUV.

The back door opened and Marcy ran into JB's arms and held on as if her life depended on feeling him close. The second person Marcy hugged was Amber. And within seconds Truman walked into the room with Sadie close behind him. She bundled her daughters tight against her, tears running down her cheeks.

Slowly she lifted her head to make eye contact with Cain. "Where's Betsy?"

"We're working on that. JB's got a lot of incoming information, and Amber just provided us with more," Cain said. "I'm sure Truman has already filled you in on what Earl Millerton told us this afternoon."

She nodded, then pulled Amber and Marcy close again. "Truman, can you take me and my girls home to our house? We need to get out of the way and let the police do their job."

Truman followed the women toward the door, then turned toward Cain and JB. "Call if there's anything I can do. Or anything you need. *Anything*."

"I'll send a policeman over for surveillance at your place, also," JB said as he headed over to tell Marcy goodbye.

Truman shook his head. "No need. I've already called in a couple of retired FBI agents to give some backup at the property. You all stay focused on Betsy. And while you're at it—take down whatever the hell Papa C and this group have been doing to my family...and to Crayton."

Cain understood what Truman said, but he had one,

and only one, priority right now. Find Betsy. And nobody better get in his way. *Nobody.*

JB answered his ringing phone and immediately headed toward the door, motioning others to follow. "Spotters saw the SUV headed toward Papa C's property outside of town. A black Gladiator followed. Caller said there appeared to be a woman in the passenger seat with her wrist zip-tied to the overhead rail. We'll head—"

"Hold up a sec," Deputy Evans shouted. "911 just took a call that the SUV and Gladiator have split up at the three-way junction. SUV headed toward Papa C's. Gladiator turned the opposite direction. Busted through a fence and tore out cross-country."

"The Gladiator's my chase! Nobody better get in my way." Cain was out the door, in his truck and gone before anyone could tell him no. For the second time today, his gut battled his brain. "*Nobody!*"

CHAPTER THIRTY-FOUR

Betsy's body ached from slamming back and forth against the side door of the Gladiator. For the past five minutes, the ride had been ragged and rough. One gravel road and then another, winding across the back of the back of the hilly backcountry acreage.

Thankfully, James had left one of her hands free when he'd strapped her other wrist to the crossbar. Being able to brace herself had helped, but her other wrist had been mercilessly jerked as they drove. This guy didn't know the first thing about driving in open terrain. Cared even less that he might break her wrist. She'd finally been able to pull the seatbelt over and snap herself in.

"Lady, don't play dumb with me. You know where the two million dollars is hidden," James said. "Just give me that and I'll let you go."

"I think you've got the wrong person."

"You're Betsy Peyton, formerly Carrington, formerly Peyton, right?"

"Yes." She needed something to make this more personal. "You know my name. What's yours?"

She'd been in tricky situations before. Years ago she'd started carrying mace, sometimes even her gun. Today, she had nothing. Just her words and her brain.

"As Mr. Partner said, you can call me James. Now where's the damn money?"

"I don't know anything about any two million dollars." She weakened her voice, let it tremble as if she were scared to death, which was only partly an act. "Tell me why you think I have it. Maybe that'll help me remember what you're talking about."

A crazed look overtook the man's eyes as he squinted against the blinding sunlight angled right into their faces at this time of day. He held one hand in front of his face as if to protect his eyes from the glaring sun. "Don't mess with me, lady. And don't think for one second, I believe Papa C when he says he lost the money gambling. He's smarter than that."

"Did that Mr. Partner actually have my dad killed?" Breathing had suddenly become heavy for her.

"He sure did." James snapped his fingers. "The boss makes decisions on a second's notice when it comes to his business or his life.

"Why? Why would he kill my dad?" Her insides were raging. Her brain was screaming. Her emotions plowed into her soul. And there wasn't anything she could do but keep asking questions.

James grabbed hold of her loose wrist and jerked her toward him. "Because Papa C tried to turn on Mr.

Partner's business. Tried to turn on the family, so to speak. The boss found out Papa C had become an informant for the FBI. Had been talking to Agent Link Peyton."

"My dad?" Betsy swallowed hard.

"Yeah. Partner exploded." James snapped his fingers once again. "You see, your dad had a good reputation for crime solving. Even worse, your dad was honest. Honest to the core. Everybody in the whole region knew Link Peyton couldn't be bought. So, Mr. Partner decided he'd just have him killed. Paid someone to shoot him there in Jefferson City—in public, and in broad daylight—to send a message."

She couldn't breathe. Tears poured down her cheeks. The land stretching out before her blurred into panic. James shoved her back across the seat and released his hold on her wrist.

"You mean you...you..." For the life of her, she couldn't get the words out.

All she could think of was Cain. Cain and her. Cain and life. Life they might never have at this rate. She needed to get past the shock of what James had just told her. Needed to strategize. What would her dad have told her to do? What would Cain tell her?

Stay alive. Do whatever you have to do to survive. But bottom line. *Stay. Alive!*

"I heard you were that DEA dude Cain Connery's woman." The killer reached over and touched her hair, then wrapped a handful around his fist, pulling her head in his direction. "That right?"

She stared straight in front of her.

He yanked. "I asked if you were Cain's woman?"

Unsure of what to say, she shook her head.

"Don't lie to me. I saw you two together." The man shoved her aside, putting his hand back on the steering wheel. "You know, most men would be willing to trade anything to get their woman back. Of course, Cain's known to be another one of those good-reputation agents. Honest to the core."

What should she do? Say? *Lie*. Lie like her life depended on it. "We used to be together. But we had an argument."

James reached over and touched her hair again. "That works, too. I'll just keep you and the millions all for myself."

She flinched. "I swear I don't know where it's at."

A few rabbits skittered across the open ground. James jerked the Gladiator to the right. The truck tilted slightly off the ground on two wheels. *"That's a problem, lady*. In fact, why do I even need you? Why should I even keep you alive? You see, all I want is *money*. Without the two million, the boss man won't pay me my million for the hit on Phillip and the million he still owes me from before over twenty years ago. So *I'd suggest* you think a little harder and come up with the money?"

"What do you mean the hit on Phillip?" she asked.

"Nothing. You're hearing things, lady. I didn't say anything about Phillip."

She knew what she'd heard. Exactly what all did this guy do for Mr. Partner? What all had he done? And how did Papa C figure into all this? Had Papa C been involved in Phillip's death? James had also said two million dollars. Where had the other million come from?"

"You said the other million you're still owed" Betsy couldn't stand not knowing. "Are you the one who killed my dad?"

"No!" He looked away from the horizon and glanced in her direction. "But I killed the man who'd pulled the trigger." He laughed. "I'm the one who cleans up afterwards and I get a million for that, also."

"Did you—"

"Shut up. You ask too many questions. Where's the money?"

Realizing there were no morals or scruples running through him, she considered all her options. Cain was the one that kept coming forward in her mind. If this didn't work, then she'd just be putting Cain in danger. Even if it did work, she'd put Cain in danger. But, for some reason, that seemed like the right thing to do. Like what Cain would tell her to do. *Without the danger, there'd be no way to stay alive.*

"I gave it to Cain." Her voice loud and strong, Betsy lied. "We plan to move out west and buy a ranch."

"I knew you were lying earlier. You're Cain's woman. It makes sense that you gave it to him." James stopped the Gladiator and jumped out. "That's even better."

He yanked the passenger door open, released her seatbelt, pulled a knife from beneath the seat and sliced the zip tie on her wrist free from the crossbar. He yanked her out so fast, she fell hard on the packed dirt. Lashing out with her legs and feet and free hand, she plowed her foot into James's knee. He buckled but caught himself and yanked her arm. She aimed for his crotch with her second kick but missed when he rolled away.

He came back with a vengeance and shoved his gun in her face. "You try that again, I'll shoot you where you lay." His upper lip curled into a fierce sneer as he shoved her back. "Don't think for a second I was joking when I left you that message on the mirror."

CHAPTER THIRTY-FIVE

Flashing police lights caught Cain's attention as he barreled out of Crayton heading toward Papa C's house and surrounding acreage ten or fifteen minutes away. He slowed as the police cars neared, letting JB and Evans pass him to take the lead. Kennett pulled in behind him with a few others following him, but Cain knew the cars he saw weren't the only ones heading to the same location. Law enforcement from surrounding areas had to be closing in, also.

At the three-way junction seven miles out of town on the two-lane road, JB and Evans turned right toward Papa C's house a mile down. No doubt the cars behind him would follow them.

Cain turned left on a dime. Kennett followed his lead. The others didn't. Guess Kennett had orders. Of course, he got the impression that Kennett occasionally made his own decisions.

Broken fence rails and fresh tire tracks across the ditch caught his attention. On the other side of the road sat an older truck, half on, half off the pavement as if it had been run off the road.

Without another thought, he pulled to the shoulder on his side of the road and jumped from his truck. "Betsy! Betsy!"

Limping out of the field, tow man Randy stopped, bent over and braced his hands on the top of his thighs. Blood trickled from beneath his left hand. "I've been shot."

Kennett ran over and held the man up as he put in a call for medical assistance.

"What happened?" Cain asked.

"I heard the vehicle pursuit on my police scanner. When I passed the black Gladiator, I whipped my truck around to follow." Randy moaned. "Looked like Ms. Peyton kept hitting the driver until he lost control and plowed through the fence. Got stuck."

Randy yelled in pain as Cain tried to stop the bleeding. "Saw the guy get out and try to push the Gladiator out of the hole."

"What'd he have on? Look like?" Cain always asked the questions even if he thought he already had the answers.

"Camo bomber jacket. Dark beard. Mean eyes. I'm telling you, me and Ms. Peyton, we did everything we could to stop him. He's got her wrist strapped to the overhead crossbar, so she's pretty well trapped." Randy blew out a breath laced with pain and relief and exhaustion as Kennett and Cain lowered him to the ground. "I tried to save her. Got in a couple of good blows. That's when he shot me."

Officer Hastings pulled up behind Kennett's police

cruiser. Paramedics arrived within the minute and took over tending Randy.

Rage steamed toward Cain's brain as Randy's words settled in. His body heated with the power of adrenalin working overtime. He'd spent the past couple of days figuring out his future, and now someone thought they'd take that away. They'd take his Betsy. He'd be dead in the dirt before that happened.

His phone rang with an Unknown Caller ID. He answered it on the speaker phone as Kennett moved closer.

"Cain Connery?" The man on the phone had a deep voice. Muffled tone. Unfamiliar.

"Yeah. Who is this?"

"Shut up and listen if you want your woman back."

Cain clicked into agent mode. Play along. Listen. Decipher the background noise. Track the clue. There had to be a clue. "I'm listening."

The man laughed. "I figured you would. We're going to do a little swap. Mine for yours."

"What have you got in mind?"

"Tell me where the two million dollars is hidden, and I'll let Betsy go."

That was a lie, but the more time Cain kept him on the phone, the more apt he was to get something out of the conversation. Like a clue to where this supposed two million came from. Might as well poke the bear. Make the man on the phone mad. Make him lose his confidence. Concentration. Courage.

"I like to know who I'm making a deal with. So what's your name?"

The man laughed again.

"Oh, that's right, you're *James*. Mr. Partner's errand guy. Saw an online photo of you holding his coat, *James*. Looked to me like you were stuck with no way to move up." Cain paused for effect. "Now what is it you really want, *James*."

"Shut the hell up, Connery. I know your game."

Cain heard the slightest change in his tone and cadence. "Smart. You're a smart man, James. Maybe we can strike a deal after all. I might be able to use you in my group, James. What do you think? Work for Mr. Partner? Work for me—*James*?"

"Are you stupid, Connery? I work for me! Me, you understand?" The man grunted into almost a growl. "Like I said before. Give me the money. I give you Betsy."

The background on the other end was quiet. Too quiet. Outside? Inside? Cain couldn't tell. "Let me talk to Betsy."

"No. I'll call you later with details for the exchange."

Cain gave a sarcastic laugh. "Now who's being stupid? You and I both know you're gonna have to let me talk to her before I agree to the exchange."

The man on the phone huffed. "Wait a minute."

Kennett leaned in closer. Moved his fingers that the man was walking. Formed the silent word "gravel." Cain nodded in agreement.

"Lady, if you kick me again, I'll bind your legs. Nod if you've got that." The man was quiet. "Good. Now tell Cain you're okay."

Silence.

"Don't shake your head at me, lady. I said tell him you're okay." A single gunshot echoed through the phone.

From the south, the shot reverberated across the land. Kennett and Cain both looked in the same direction. Across the pasture. Way across. A hawk's screech sounded in the distance on the other end. A flock of birds rose as one, while a group of ducks took flight and circled in a V-formation. All from the same direction. To the south. Near the lake.

"Betsy, say something." Cain shouted. "Anything."

"Water through the trees. Ducks squawking. Speck of dam far, far away." Betsy rattled out words. Calm, but fast. "We're north or west shore maybe near—"

What sounded like a hard smack to skin flashed through the phone. "Shut the hell up."Betsy grunted. Loud. A whimper. Still she kept talking as fast as she could. "Papa C's brother hired a hit man to kill my dad. May have caused Phillip's—"

Another smack. Harder. She screamed. The phone call went dead.

Cain fisted his hand, choking back the words that threatened his control. She'd given them clues as to where they were. The words about her dad and Phillip had stung. But her scream had stabbed him in the gut. Somebody was gonna pay for that.

"Help me get my motorcycle off," Cain yelled as he ran to his truck. "With it, I can go straight to the location where we heard the shot, saw the birds take off."

Running to his truck, he jumped into the bed as Hastings followed his lead on the opposite side of the cycle. Together they unhooked the straps and loosened the chock. Kennett yanked the ramp off the back of the truck just in time for Cain to walk the cycle down. "Did you pick up on the bit about water and distant dam?"

Kennett nodded down the road. "I'll circle toward the same area on the paved roadways. Hastings, you got this here?"

"Yep. As soon as more backup arrives, I'll run some of the gravel backroads I know."

"Keep in touch," Kennett said. "Cain, which route you taking?"

Cain's motorcycle roared to life as he raised the kickstand and pointed straight to the spot where the fence rail had already been broken. "Right through there."

"Be careful, man. Don't take chances. Don't do anything stupid. We'll get her back."

Cain snarled. "That SOB laid his hands on her. He's mine. All mine!"

"I'll radio everyone else the directions we're all headed." Kennett jumped in his cruiser.

"Hastings, my keys are in the truck ignition. Use it if you need to," Cain shouted as he revved the cycle engine.

He shifted the cycle into gear, circled for a short run down the road, then jumped the ditch and raced through the hole in the fence. The engine roared as if it was being ridden by someone who knew how and when to push. Whined with the power from a fast start.

With every grab of the gears, the cycle shot forward. Speed increasing by the second as the tires grabbed the ground. Each gear shift brought more speed and danger to the rider. Airborne as often as not, the motorcycle shot forward.

He gripped the handlebars. Mentally confirming he

had his gun. Then the backup. That's all he had to fight with, everything except muscles and rage. Confident in the outcome, he had to calm the rage. Calm it enough to make no mistakes on the ride or the takedown. Betsy's life hinged on that. So did his.

BETSY HAD RISKED EVERYTHING. Would her clues be enough? Had Cain understood?

James shoved her back in the passenger seat, strapped her wrist again then raced around to the driver's side. She struggled to get her seatbelt buckled and felt the click just as he barreled down the road, not even taking time to buckle in.

He angled off the gravel road, increased the Gladiator's speed and steered across the open field in the opposite direction of the lake. Betsy knew why. If he could throw Cain off the trail there would be a better chance of using her as a negotiating tool again. Where did that leave her? He knew Cain would come for her. That's what he wanted. After that, she'd only be extra baggage.

"Nooooo!" She grabbed the steering wheel with her one free hand and yanked with all her might.

James shoved her away. The Gladiator slammed deep into a hole. Jolted rough with the speed. The wheel jerked back and forth in his hand. She reached out again, stretching as far as she could. She grabbed the lower T-bar of the steering wheel. Looped her elbow around it and jerked the wheel from his grasp. Hanging on, she pulled with every muscle she had.

The Gladiator jerked to the left, clipped a downed tree, and shot a gulley. James flew from the vehicle as the driver's side tires bounced off a small boulder lodged in the field. The Gladiator shot upward, and her head jerked as it flipped in the air.

She heard herself scream. Felt the pain as the strap twisted and scraped her wrist. She was going to die. Out here—in the open—gasping for breath she couldn't breathe—she was going to die. She closed her eyes to block out the rocks and trees and sky that tumbled in her vision as the open truck rolled over and over and over. At some point, the airbags inflated. Held her close. Close enough? The shaking in her brain couldn't tell.

Finally, the Gladiator came to rest on its side. Rocked for a moment. Steadied. Dazed, she felt a warm trickle of blood at the side of her head.

⚬⚬⚬

CAIN RAN the motorcycle full out across the open land. So far, he'd navigated the gullies and boulders and underbrush, but the everyday ruts that dotted the acreage were pounding him and the tires on his cycle

Suddenly, something up ahead caught Cain's eye. Looked like a big chunk of metal flying through the air. The Gladiator? Cain shot the speed upward.

The first thing he saw as he neared was the vehicle resting on its side. Then he saw Betsy as she stood up and waved her arm in a circle as if to get his attention. Pointed out in the field with one hand and held up one finger on the other. That's when he saw the strap around her wrist.

Bullets whizzed through the air. Some missed. Some scraped across the metal of the motorcycle.

Since she couldn't get out of the Gladiator, he needed to draw the line of fire away from her before a stray bullet hit the truck's gas tank. Betsy scrunched down as far as she could as he steered his cycle to a crop of trees. From there it didn't take long to track down James, hiding behind a small boulder, rising every so often to take a shot.

Gunfire erupted again. Grazed the side of his coveralls. Time to stop the give-and-take of the situation. Eating up the ground, Cain widened his circle around the man. This was going nowhere. Sure, he could take him out with one shot, but he needed the guy alive. Alive to answer questions. Alive to give up names.

Head on. That was the only way to end this. Head on.

Cain whipped the motorcycle around and lined up with the boulder. His aim was to graze the rock. Force the man to panic and run. Cain floored the cycle, shot forward. By weaving erratically, he threw the man's aim off. Fighting to keep the motorcycle upright and moving closer, he wouldn't pull his gun till it was his time to do some shooting.

James took off running toward the Gladiator. Toward Betsy. Cain could not let him get there. Could not let him take her hostage again right in front of his eyes. With the front bumper on the cycle, Cain took aim on the man. Closed the ground between them. He spun a one-eighty at the right moment to take out James with the rear tire. Cain slid with the fall of the motorcycle, hoping like crazy he'd calculated the right speed to survive before he ended up the victim in the situation.

James struggled to his feet and dashed back toward the boulder. Halfway there, Cain physically ran him down. Pinned him to the ground. Bracing his forearm across the man's chest, Cain aimed his gun into the air and fired to pull in his backup.

Leaning within an inch of the man's face, Cain had reached his limit. "*You*. Have. Crossed my line, mister! One wrong move is all I need. Just one." Cain chambered a round as he loosened his arm from across the man's chest.

Evidently, the man on the ground figured he had one last opportunity and threw a punch toward Cain's chin. Cain purposely tossed his gun out of reach as he dodged the fist. He powered a one-two punch into the man's ribs, then landed a return fast and hard uppercut to his chin. The man's head jerked back and hit the ground.

This time James stayed on the ground. "Go to hell, Connery. Go to hell."

Cain bent over the man. "Already been there."

Half of Cain wanted to end this with James, here and now. The other half said Cain was a better man than that. Behind him, Cain heard the police cruiser's sirens. Saw his own truck close behind with Officer Hastings at the wheel. More sirens. More SUVs. More voices shouting directions. He knew those voices.

Crayton Police had landed. Betsy was safe. That was good enough for now. Officer Kennett rushed from his cruiser to cuff the man and stand him up.

"Read him his rights." Sucking in air, Cain swiped the back of his hand across his forehead. "Twice if you need to."

He glanced in the direction of the Gladiator and saw

that JB had already cut Betsy loose and helped her climb out.

Running toward him, the closer she got, the better she looked, even if she did have a giant knot on her forehead and a trickle of blood. She rubbed her wrist, but at least it didn't appear to be broken, just a lot of scrapes down the side of her arm. His biggest concern was with the already blackening bruise on her cheekbone. Overall, she looked to be in one piece. He could live with that.

He wrapped his arms around her, holding on to her as if there were no tomorrow. "Are you okay?" Cain whispered, burying his face in her hair.

She nodded, her cheek rubbing against his as she clutched him to her. "I thought you'd left forever."

"No, honey. I went to find myself." Taking her face in his palms, he rubbed his thumb across her lower lip. Kissed her gently. "I will never leave you. Never."

The next kiss was deeper. Stronger. And said everything they needed to say to each other right now.

JB walked up and slapped him on the shoulder. "You did good, Cain. By the way, Betsy, we've already arrested your service manager, Derek Johnson, and an older associate of Mr. Partner."

"Hey. How about a deal?" James shouted. "Get me an attorney. Maybe we can negotiate an arrangement on Mr. Partner's other dealings. Maybe you'd like to know about Illinois...Texas...Kansas...even who shot Mr. Dash over twenty years ago."

"Get him in a cruiser." JB pointed at Officers Kennett and Hastings. "Then book him in the Crayton jail. And call the FBI, we may need their help."

Cain felt as if everything were falling into place. Just what he always hoped for with a case wrap-up.

"What about Mr. Partner and Papa C?" Betsy asked.

"Evidently there'd already been an escape plan in play. Partner and Papa C boarded a helicopter already waiting for them in the field behind his barn. It took off before we could get there. Law enforcement in Illinois is keeping track of it. They'll let us know where it lands." JB cleared his throat. "As far as Papa C goes, we found him on the ground about a half mile away. Someone on the chopper had pushed him out and kept on flying. He was in bad shape when the paramedics loaded him in the ambulance."

Deputy Evans pulled out the notepad from his shirt pocket. "Got word a few minutes ago that Papa C had a heart attack and died enroute to the hospital. The last thing he said to the medic was 'Tell Betsy to look under the concrete.'"

"Anybody got any idea what that means?" JB asked, glancing between Betsy and Cain.

Cain grinned as he pointed to Betsy. "The parking pad at your lake lot, or—"

"Somewhere on the Peyton Automotive property," she said. "We're going to need a metal detector. A whole lot of them."

"You need ground-penetrating radar that'll see what's under that concrete." Cain pulled out his phone. "If it shows what I'm thinking, you're gonna need a jackhammers and backhoe."

An hour later, James was locked up in Crayton Jail, the Gladiator towed to police impound, and there was news that a four-seater helicopter crashed in Illinois.

Everyone involved in the arrests had wrapped up their parts and driven away. As quick as the chase and capture happened, it all closed out even faster. Kennett and Hastings had even reloaded Cain's motorcycle in the back of his truck before they left on their way back to Crayton.

Betsy had made a Facetime call to Sadie, Marcy and Amber. Meanwhile, Cain phoned the Memory Center in Alaska, just to hear his dad's voice. For a couple of minutes, his dad knew who he was talking to and actually called him his son—Cain.

Already back in Crayton, JB phoned to say he'd stationed a cruiser at Betsy's lake lot until arrangements could be put in place for excavation. Plus, one at Peyton's until all the security systems and cameras were working again.

After checking the motorcycle straps one last time, Cain leaned back against the side of his truck and pulled Betsy into his hold. "Do you know how much I love you?"

"A lot?"

"Even more than that, honey. Even more than that."

"I love you, too."

Cain figured now was a good time to take the step. "I've got some land I want you to look at with me." He paused and sucked in a tentative breath. "*But* only if you want to... I mean ...I don't want to look at it without you by my side...but I'll understand if—"

"Hush, Cain." Betsy placed her fingers against his lips. "I'd love to see the land. Might just want to raise a family there. But what about your DEA job?"

Pulling the scrunchie from her hair, he glanced at his

phone. "No problem. I officially resigned two hours and eighteen minutes ago."

Thank you for reading
CHASED BY MEMORIES

PRE-ORDER NOW
Book 3 — SEARCH FOR ANSWERS
Join Amber Peyton and Brian Kennett
as they band together to solve questions from their past.
Without the answers, their heart-and-souls
will never be free.
ORDER NOW

WANT MORE WHILE YOU WAIT?
Turn the page for a Sneak Peek at
SLATER'S REVENGE,
Book 1 of my Shades of Leverage series.

Books 1 and 2 Now Available
Book 3 coming 2027

ORDER NOW

CHAPTER ONE

"Are we about done here?" OPAQUE Agent Josh Slater shot to his feet, knocking his chair over backward. Loud and to the point, the chair hit the floor with a resounding thud. He'd had enough of this beat-around-the-bush, quasi-interrogation for one day.

The past two hours of debriefing had made him wonder what the hell he'd done wrong on his last assignment. There'd been nothing out of the ordinary, just a simple tourist kidnapping case. Go in, rescue the hostage, get home. Everything had gone as planned. In fact, except for the knife-in-his-back fiasco, he could have done it blindfolded.

Sure as hell hadn't come close to the hard-liner assignments Operation Protector Agent Quantum Elite (OPAQUE) was known to fight against Coercion Ten. Those jobs were adrenaline-pumping, hazardous-to-your-health rides all the way to the final bullet. That was one of the reasons he'd joined OPAQUE. The other reason was still at large.

Agent Mitch Granger shuffled papers around. "I've got only a few—"

"No. You've asked me the same damn questions one too many times." Josh loosely rolled his fingers in and out of a fist. The two of them might be friends most days, but right now Mitch was an obstacle. "If I didn't know you better, I'd think you doubted my credibility." Josh fisted his hand tight. "That would be a mistake."

"Calm down, okay?" Rising to his feet, Mitch braced his hands on the table between the two of them. "I'm just following the boss's orders."

"Which are?"

"To keep you in this room."

"You and what army?" Josh knew he hadn't done anything to get fired, reprimanded, or a thousand other unpleasant procedures. Yet, everything about this scenario screamed trouble.

"Listen, Slater, I'm not in the mood for any of your macho-dude attitude." Mitch's eyes narrowed. "Now, stay in the damn room."

They both stood six-foot-one. Both worked out at least once a day. Both could settle an argument with their fists, gun, or knife. Hard to know which one would come out the winner if they ever pushed each other past the edge of restraint. So far, they both knew better than to cross that line.

Josh leaned across the table, invading Mitch's space.

"Just why the hell do I need to stay in this room?"

"Why not?" Drake Lawrence's words cut through the tension as he approached the table.

Josh winced. He'd missed the opening of the door as his boss, the director of OPAQUE, had walked in. Drake had come from a law enforcement background, and he still moved with the quiet stealth of an agent on the prowl. A technique Josh had mastered for his own use.

His boss quirked the side of his mouth with the cockiness that came from one-upping someone. "That is, unless you've got a hot date."

Josh straightened, figuring Drake's hot date question didn't need an answer. "How've you been, sir?"

"Never better." The boss casually stepped farther into the room, seeming to fill every inch with his six feet, still-in-shape, pushing-fifty frame.

Faster than a kid released for recess, Mitch grabbed his paperwork and fled the room.

"Good to have you back, Josh. I missed your in-my-face attitude gracing the hallways." Drake reached out for a brothers-in-arm forearm grasp. "By the way, the hostage's family sent word to thank you for bringing their father home alive."

Josh clasped the offered arm. "Just doing my job."

A scowl grabbed Drake's expression. "I meant to be down sooner. Got tied up with our decoders. They intercepted a message from Coercion Ten last night."

"Good intel?"

"Yeah, I got the message."

Josh zeroed in on his boss's use of the word *I* instead of *OPAQUE*. But the most telling sign that something was off was the harsh snarl—angry, personal, and real. What the hell had Josh walked back into?

"Something wrong, sir?" Josh asked.

"They've added a new column. Titled it Leverage."

"I guess intimidating a target by threatening to harm someone near to them could be called leverage." Josh shrugged. "Cut the bull, Drake. What's going on?"

"Nothing next to your name in the Leverage column. Next to mine is one name." His boss straightened back to his tough-as-nails stance. "My niece—Mackenzie Baudin."

Josh's chest tightened as if his belt had been notched three sizes too small. Macki! The only woman he'd never shook from his system.

ORDER NOW

ACKNOWLEDGMENTS

Thank you once again to my family! With humor, suggestions and an understanding heart, you all support me through each and every book I write. From websites and banners, to story ideas and pen names, to suggested genres and characters, I love knowing you all are proud of my books. That means a lot to me!

Now on to this story, Chased by Memories. Let me begin by saying I'm not sure if this book would have ever been completed without my four-days-a-week writing accountability group—Lisa Wells, Barbara Bettis, and Linda Gilman. We are not a critique group—we are an accountability group. And their laughter, friendship, and perseverance are great ways to start my morning. Thanks for dragging me out of my procrastination!

Here's to all who have stepped in to mentor, coach, guide and motivate me in my traditional and indie writing career. Plus, I couldn't do this without the people on my indie writing team—Bev Katz Rosenbaum (BKR Editing,) Monique Conrod copy editor, Jennifer Jakes (The Killion Group), Cathy Yardley (Rock Your Writing), Calli Influencer Marketing, and Kari March Designs for my book cover.

As always, I'm grateful for all the readers who invest in my books with their time and money. If you happen to have a moment, reviews are always appreciated. Plus, if you enjoy my books, please share that with your friends.

I've gotta go now. Gotta put my fingers on the keys and do some writing. Gotta get another book out for you to read!

Claudia Shelton

ALSO BY CLAUDIA SHELTON

ROMANTIC SUSPENSE

The Agent's Legacy Series

Risk of a Lifetime

Chased by Memories

Search for Answers

Shades of Leverage Series

Slater's Revenge

Dangerous Lies

CONTEMPORARY ROMANCE

Nature's Crossing Series

A Week at Most

Time to Grow

PCS Hometown: Awesome

Cocoa for Two

ABOUT THE AUTHOR

Claudia Shelton is a bestselling author of suspense thrillers, romantic suspense, and contemporary romance, with an occasional holiday book. Her series include The Agent's Legacy, Nature's Crossing, Shades of Leverage and PCS Hometown: Awesome. Her books are available in e-book, paperback and audiobooks, with hardcovers and translations in the works. On a personal note, Claudia is a nature and music lover, a traveler and water person, with life goals of making moments to remember. Her main priority is spending time with family, friends and her two sweet, conniving rescue dogs, Daisy and Abby.

Website & Newsletter: - http://claudiasheltonauthor.com/

THANK YOU IN ADVANCE FOR
LEAVING A REVIEW ON THE BOOKSELLER'S
SITE